Mystery at Farfield Castle

BOOKS BY CLARE CHASE

EVE MALLOW MYSTERY SERIES

Mystery on Hidden Lane

Mystery at Apple Tree Cottage

Mystery at Seagrave Hall

Mystery at the Old Mill

Mystery at the Abbey Hotel

Mystery at the Church

Mystery at Magpie Lodge

Mystery at Lovelace Manor

Mystery at Southwood School

TARA THORPE MYSTERY SERIES

Murder on the Marshes

Death on the River

Death Comes to Call

Murder in the Fens

Mystery at Farfield Castle

CLARE CHASE

bookouture

Published by Bookouture in 2023

An imprint of Storyfire Ltd.
Carmelite House
50 Victoria Embankment
London EC4Y 0DZ

www.bookouture.com

ISBN: 978-1-80314-939-4
eBook ISBN: 978-1-80314-938-7

This book is a work of fiction. Names, characters, businesses, organizations, places and events other than those clearly in the public domain, are either the product of the author's imagination or are used fictitiously. Any resemblance to actual persons, living or dead, events or locales is entirely coincidental.

For Kendy – sending love from Cambridge

PROLOGUE
FARFIELD CASTLE

Kitty Marchant strode through the trees on land that had once belonged to her grandparents. All that history... and hurt.

The noise of the party receded as she moved further from the castle. Dusk deepened. The sun had set and the light was almost gone but the air was still warm. The scent of the earth and the smell of the laurels brought back childhood so sharply. That precious feeling of safety. She remembered hide and seek with her brother, Nate, followed by orange squash, poured from the old crystal jug with the tiny chip in it. Handed over by her grandfather, with a bow, as though he were a waiter. Her grandmother watching, smiling.

So many vivid images. The vast stretch of lawn where people were currently drinking champagne had been her and Nate's preserve. They'd practised archery there, held birthday parties, danced and dreamed.

And yet she'd left it all behind, joining her father when he rejected his mum and dad and everything that went with them. Beautiful Farfield Castle could have been his. Siding with him had ripped her from her grandparents and now they were lost to her forever.

It was weird how much had happened since she'd returned. The heart-to-heart with Nate had been hardest to take. He'd spoken gently, but told her at last what he really thought. That when she'd stuck with her father, seeing herself as stoical and brave, she'd been manipulated. That even now, when their dad behaved badly, she was conditioned to hold out an olive branch, each and every time.

She thought back to Granny and Gramps. How generous they'd been with their wealth, inviting all comers to share it. Taking people under their wings, helping them when they struggled. Nate was right. Her dad had been jealous, pure and simple. He'd walked away to punish them after years of resentment. That huge, final row had been an excuse. She remembered the pleasure in her father's eyes as he'd watched Granny and Gramps's life fall apart. And she'd stood next to him.

She thought of the way she was involving him in her plans and felt her legs wobble. As if there was a sheer drop, right in front of her, that she'd only just noticed. It was a horrible feeling. Not only was Nate right, she realised she'd known it for years. It had simply been easier to close her mind.

It wasn't her dad who'd caused this current crisis, though. It was a mess of a different kind. She wouldn't be weak again. She should have spoken up long ago.

She clenched her fists and pushed them into her cheeks as she walked. Decision made, she felt better. Full of heat and fury. Now, she would make things right. Fleetingly, she worried about the consequences, but she couldn't turn back. It was like surfing the crest of a wave.

At last, she came to Farfield's icehouse – a discreet meeting place. The crowds seemed far away now, the laughter and music distant. She padded across the soft grass to reach the brick dome, covered in moss and ivy. It was all that was visible above ground. She used to sit inside as a child. It made her feel safe.

She took a deep breath, pushed the door open and entered, preparing the speech she needed to give, but the past overwhelmed her again. The familiar smell of earth, brick and damp made the years fall away.

It was the sight of the safety grille, illuminated by her phone torch, that brought her back to the present.

It was an iron gate, blocking the entrance to the icehouse's well. It stood open, when it should have been locked shut. She walked towards it, the thirty-foot drop in front of her. It was where they'd packed the snow and ice in olden times. The protective grille swung, creaking on its hinges as she pushed it.

Turning around would have come next, but there was to be no next.

The blow to the side of Kitty's head was shattering in its force. The darkness came a millisecond before the fall.

1

Eve Mallow sat in her seventeenth-century thatched home, Elizabeth's Cottage, wondering what she'd done. For the first time in twenty years, she'd accepted a writing commission that wasn't an obituary. Eve had given up covering living subjects long ago. They tended to interfere. She'd put this point to Portia Coldwell of *Icon* magazine, who'd offered her the work. Portia had been her usual smooth-talking self. She'd pointed out that she was asking Eve to review a new writers' retreat. '*So you won't be writing about a person.*'

But that was baloney. The retreat had been set up by three celebrities. If Eve was going to make the article interesting, their personalities would be crucial. And they were bound to want a puff piece. They'd only approached two publications for reviews. Eve guessed they wanted exclusivity and control.

Once again, Portia had been soothing. '*You'll have a completely free hand. You'll get a nice fee and a week at a luxury retreat that's on your doorstep.*'

The setting *was* an attraction. Eve couldn't imagine she'd get another chance to stay at beautiful Farfield Castle. But inevitably, it was the chance to people-watch that persuaded her. It wasn't the celebrity status of the founders which had her hooked, but the notoriety of one of them. Kitty Marchant's grandparents had once lived at Farfield, and she was at the centre of a village scandal. That, and her return to the castle, made her fascinating.

It was Kitty, her wealthy financier brother Nate Marchant, and her husband, acclaimed writer Julian Fisher, who were behind the retreat. Nate had put up the money, Julian would act as a mentor, and Kitty was to run exercise classes. She'd made her name as a wellness coach. Most women above a certain age had a copy of her book, *Soaring, Grounded*, or the workout DVD that went with it.

Eve sighed and bent to stroke her dachshund Gus, who looked at her with soulful brown eyes. The Marchant scandal was a double-edged sword. The background to the bust-up between Kitty and her grandparents filled Eve with curiosity, but it meant many people in Saxford St Peter were hostile towards the retreat. It left Eve in an awkward position: she was siding with the enemy by accepting the commission. And it went beyond that. A local historian and schoolteacher, Ella Tyndall, had been set on buying the castle until Nate Marchant outbid her. She'd spent months fundraising and applying for grants. She'd planned on using the place as a community facility.

Now the locals would be shut out. Only the very rich would get to see Farfield. Eve sympathised with Ella, whose grandparents had worked at the castle. She, like most of the locals, had had the run of the place. Eve would have to ask what Nate intended to do for the community.

She was curious about him, and most especially about Kitty. The siblings' dad had behaved appallingly, on the face of it. Stood by as his parents fell on hard times. Watched as they lost the castle even though he'd been wealthy enough to help. Unlike Nate, Kitty had sided with her dad. If the tales were true, she'd cut herself off from her grandparents completely. Refused to visit, even when her grandmother was dying. It left Eve puzzled. She'd watched interviews with her. Read about her charity work. She came across as kind. Determined but sympathetic. Eve would give a lot to know what was behind the contradictory impressions.

Eve first encountered Kitty Marchant a few days before her planned stay at Farfield. She and her brother were sitting in the window at Monty's teashop, where Eve worked part-time for the owner, her best friend Viv. Freelance journalism was an uncertain business. The regular income from the teashop was reassuring and besides, it gave Eve the chance to use her organisational skills. Viv was a gem, but utterly chaotic.

Kitty and Nate were huddled over a collection of exquisite chocolate heart cakes when Eve went to serve. Eve hadn't registered their presence, nestled as they were in the corner of the busy café, but as she cleared and relaid a neighbouring table, she heard them behind her, talking.

'Thanks, Kitty. I was completely stuck, but that's the answer. I'm so glad we're working together.'

It wasn't the name that struck Eve. There must be plenty of Kittys around. It was the tone. The man's voice was warm, but there was a hint of triumph, too.

'I am as well.' The woman sounded emotional.

Then the man spoke again. 'You're still thinking about Dad, aren't you?' There was an edge to his voice now.

'I'm sorry, Nate. I invited him to the launch party.' The woman sounded nervous. 'You needn't worry though. He's not coming.'

'Of course he's not, and I'm glad.'

Nate. Kitty. And a launch party. The penny dropped. The official launch of the writers' retreat was scheduled the day after she arrived. It was aimed at the locals and intended to soften them up, Eve suspected. She stole a glance at the pair.

'You need to learn,' Nate replied. 'He's a fraud. Not worth a second thought. I assumed you'd realised that by now. Let's talk about it later.'

Eve dashed to the kitchen, hoping she hadn't been seen. She wondered what objection their father had to the Farfield venture. He'd hated his parents, according to the gossip. Did nothing as they lost the castle. Was that feeling still so visceral that he couldn't bear Nate repurchasing the family home? The siblings arguing over his character made sense; Nate had taken his grandparents' side in the family row. He'd only been twelve at the time, Kitty sixteen. Was Kitty still under her father's spell? And why had she continued to keep her distance when her grandmother fell ill? It seemed so cruel.

'What's up?' Viv broke into her thoughts, tucking a strand of rose-pink hair behind her ear.

Eve filled her in. 'I'd love to understand more of the family history. Why did Kitty and Nate's dad – Benet, I think? – hate his parents so much?'

'The million-dollar question. The Marchants senior were lovely. They lost their money trying to help someone who diddled them. Meanwhile, Benet came into a fortune when his wife died, involving no effort on his part, then gloated as they were forced to sell.'

'But what made Kitty take his side?'

'She'd been living with him, whereas Nate was away at school. She must have been in bits when her mum died. She probably felt protective towards Benet too. But to turn her back on two of the nicest people I've ever met? Not only to applaud her dad's actions, but to cut herself off for years, not even relenting when her grandmother was on her deathbed? That's what gets me.' Viv's hands were clenched. It was rare to see her angry.

'What happened to Farfield after her grandparents sold up?'

Her friend shook her head. 'I never knew the next owners. They kept themselves to themselves. It's changed hands a few times since. Some people say it's unlucky.'

Eve wasn't superstitious, but she knew the latest drama associated with the castle. Moira at the village store had told everyone about the poor woman who'd been forced to sell, just like the Marchants. She'd been swindled too, by her husband. When he died, he'd been revealed as a fraudster, leaving a mountain of debt and a mistress. A lot of it had made the papers. Ella Tyndall had been the widow's preferred bidder, but when Nate Marchant trumped her, she'd had to accept. She needed the money too badly.

'You might as well go and say hello,' Viv said. 'You'll have to deal with Kitty in a few days anyway. I promise I won't listen in!'

'Yeah, right.' But Eve couldn't very well hide for the rest of the afternoon. She went into the teashop again, but found the siblings' table empty, the bell above Monty's door jangling. Tammy, one of their regular student helpers, was picking up the tip the pair had left her.

As Eve cleared another table, she glanced out of the window, towards the village green.

'Uh-oh.' Viv was watching too.

Eve had been thinking the same thing. On the other side of the green, she could see Ella Tyndall leaving the village store. Eve had seen her in floods of tears after her bid for Farfield failed. It wouldn't be easy to make small talk with Nate and Kitty Marchant.

Eve held her breath as the rivals came within feet of each other. Then Kitty approached Ella. Eve tried to imagine what she'd say in her place.

Some customers neared Monty's and Viv dashed to let them in, shamelessly hovering in the doorway.

Kitty put out a conciliatory hand but Eve couldn't hear her words, despite the open door. Ella's response carried, though, her voice cracking with raw emotion.

'You walked away from Farfield! You didn't care about it and you didn't care about your grandparents. And now you tell me I should understand because it's *your* family home? You have no right. No right at all.' She flung out a hand in Nate's direction. 'At least he didn't desert his own family. Sophie and Daniel were like grandparents to me. It isn't just blood ties that count, you know. I hate you!'

She stood there shaking, then threw down the newspaper she'd bought before dashing off, her hands over her face.

Nate put an arm around his sister's shoulders. They didn't look back.

'Ella has a point,' Viv said. 'I hope you know what you're doing, accepting this commission.'

The teashop clientele watched in silence and Eve's cheeks flushed, but turning down the work wouldn't have helped anyone. If she wanted to understand the background, being on the inside was the only way. It wasn't just that she was curious; the build-up of resentment was affecting the whole village. She was sure there was more to the Marchant history than met the eye.

2

The day before her planned visit to Farfield, Eve got up early and walked Gus down the estuary path towards the sea. It was her favourite time of day: so quiet and peaceful with space to think and plan. That morning, though, Eve was preoccupied with her stay at the writers' retreat. Concern for Monty's while she was away sat in the back of her mind, but it was Ella Tyndall who was front and foremost. She was still so upset at losing her bid, despite the months which had passed since. Eve had expected her to have got used to the idea. Of course, she'd put a vast amount of effort into securing the place, but it had been years since Sophie and Daniel Marchant had kept open house. In between times there'd been no public access. Ella must be used to the status quo.

Perhaps having her hopes raised had been too much for her. The blame she put on Kitty was acutely personal. Her strength of feeling made Eve uneasy.

She'd visited Ella and promised to ask Nate Marchant about his plans for the community. Ella had been monosyllabic.

Perhaps it would help if Eve could find out why Benet Marchant had hated his parents and what had made Kitty take his side. If the villagers knew, it might put the situation in perspective. The mystery occupied her as she continued down the path, estuary and mudflats to her left, fields and the village to her right.

A rustle in the reedy ditch caught her attention. Gus scrambled down to investigate.

'No victimising small creatures.' The words were automatic. She was still abstracted. She wondered what was behind Kitty's return to Farfield. Maybe she regretted what had happened. Or perhaps she blamed her grandparents for losing their money, and saw the castle as her heritage.

She called Gus, who backed out of the ditch unwillingly, looking hurt.

'Let's get down to the beach. You can have a proper run there. And tomorrow I'll take you to the castle. Lots of lovely grounds to explore.'

Pets were welcome at Farfield. The brochure talked about provisions for 'animal companions'.

They'd reached the woods that bordered the heath now. Ahead of them, through the trees, the sun was low over the sea, the sky and water tinged pink and orange. Something rustled. Not a small creature this time. Someone was about.

Another dog walker perhaps? She paused, scanning the trees. She saw them then, ahead of her and to the right. Two figures but no dog. They were up early.

Something about them seemed furtive. The man was looking around, and instinctively, Eve ducked behind a tree, catching Gus's eye, her finger to her lips. He knew that sign and was surprisingly good at humouring her.

She felt awkward. She had every right to be there but because of this man and woman, skulking up ahead, she'd started skulking too. It made moving on difficult. It would look as though she'd been watching them.

She could hear their footsteps. They were coming closer. She could only hope they didn't discover her.

As they approached, their hushed voices became audible. '... been saying the same thing for months now.' A woman's voice. From the way she spoke Eve was convinced she'd be pouting.

'I know, darling.' The man who replied sounded oddly familiar. 'But I can't help it! You do see, don't you? We've only just got here. How can I possibly rock the boat now?'

A creeping realisation flooded over Eve. She knew the voice from hearing it on TV.

'And what would brother dearest say?' the man went on. 'He's so protective.'

She risked a quick look, and glimpsed the face of Julian Fisher: rugged and attractive. Arts programmes loved him.

Eve felt a sharp twinge of disappointment. Of suspicions confirmed. She'd liked the look of Julian when she'd first seen him interviewed. He'd seemed straightforward. Good humoured and down-to-earth. She'd seen pictures of him and Kitty together, happy and contented. But when she'd got her invitation to Farfield she'd looked more closely. Found clips on YouTube, read magazine features. Seen him flirt with young female journalists. Noted a look of self-satisfaction in his eye. Now, Julian was reminding Eve of her own faithless toad of an ex-husband.

'I've never known siblings so close,' Julian continued, with a low laugh. 'Not like me and my sister.'

'Don't get off topic!' The woman's tone had switched from wheedling to irritable. 'I'm not a doormat, you know.'

Eve had glimpsed her too. In her late twenties, at a guess, with auburn hair and a curvaceous figure. Her hands had been on her hips, her lips thin. But despite all that she was attractive.

'I know you're not, darling. I just need you to be patient, that's all.'

'I'm not convinced you'll ever leave her.'

'When I could have you? How can you say that?'

Eve didn't want to hear any more. It was deeply depressing. She waited until they walked away, heading south, down the coast towards Farfield Castle. Whatever Kitty Marchant was like, her husband had no excuse to cheat on her. If she was appalling, he should leave her, but as he'd said himself, that wouldn't endear him to Nate, who was funding his shiny new job.

As they left, Eve heard the woman say, with icy determination, 'My patience isn't limitless, you know.'

3
_____

Eve replayed the scene she'd witnessed in the wood as she drove to Farfield Castle on Saturday. She was inclined to agree with Julian Fisher's lover. He had no intention of leaving Kitty. He'd walked a good way at an unsociable hour to ensure he was alone with his mistress. Ergo, he was determined not to get caught. She wondered how many affairs he'd had since he'd got married.

As she parked in the grounds, Eve surveyed the castle. It was an ancient fortified manor house, its south-facing curtain wall and gatehouse dating back to the 1300s. The rest of it was Tudor, the building a mix of stone and whitewashed walls. It looked comfortable and welcoming. Viv's talk of the place being bad luck seemed far-fetched.

Eve liked its name. It made her think of some far-off rural idyll. And the sight of the castle accentuated that impression. It rose out of the past, surrounded by lush trees. The brochure said there was a creek nearby that ran down to the coast and a boat that visitors could use.

It was Kitty who met Eve at the door and ushered her in. Her smile was warm and reached her eyes. There was no hint of it being a veneer, covering something darker.

'Please, come and make yourself at home in your room.' Kitty led the way up the creaking lopsided stairs. 'Then come and find us for tea in the sitting room whenever you're ready.'

'Thank you.'

Kitty left her, and Eve flumped her suitcase on the sturdy double bed. It was unusually warm for May, but the thick whitewashed walls had stopped her timber-framed room from overheating. She felt a burst of pleasure as she looked around, taking in the details.

Gus sniffed their quarters suspiciously, keeping a close eye on the muted-red carpet runner with its floral motif. After that he moved to the polished floorboards, and accidentally knocked a rocking chair, springing back as it lurched towards him. Eve bent to give him a pat, then pushed the chair back and forth to show him how it worked.

He looked unconvinced but drank from the water bowl which had been left for him. Thought had gone into their arrival.

Out of the window, Eve could see Kitty, Julian and Nate, deep in discussion. Beyond the immediate grounds was the castle's old deer park, dotted with oaks, birches, limes and sweet chestnuts. In the distance, there was a hunting lodge.

Nate was gesticulating over the open lawn, his chestnut hair falling over his eyes. Julian Fisher pushed his dark-rimmed glasses on top of his head and peered in the same direction. His wavy, greying hair stirred in the breeze and his white shirt showed off his tan. Eve bet that was deliberate. Kitty Marchant leaned against him. The trademark cowlick in her hair created a blonde waterfall, gleaming in the sun. Julian put a casual arm around her and Eve thought of the woman she'd seen him with in the woods.

Nate nodded at last, turned towards the castle and walked out of Eve's sight.

'Rumour has it he makes more money in a week than I do in

a year,' Eve said to Gus. Nate looked permanently serious. Maybe he was feeling the pressure as the official opening approached. Eve imagined he could afford to lose everything he'd put into the retreat, but something told her the project mattered to him. She thought of his interview on local TV: his intense blue eyes as he'd explained his plans.

As Eve glanced back out of the window, she saw Kitty and Julian were making for the castle now too, strolling slowly. And there, down the drive, was a third figure, loitering. A moment later they stepped into the open. A man with tousled hair, his hands stuffed into his trouser pockets.

The sight gave Eve a momentary shiver. Like her, he'd been watching the trio talk. And he hadn't wanted to be seen.

Eve shook her head. She mustn't start jumping at shadows. A moment later, she left her room and entered a long corridor, with tapestries on its whitewashed walls. Diagonally opposite her room, it opened onto a landing.

Eve turned to descend the stairs with Gus at her heels and found the sitting room. Kitty had left the door open and was looking out for her, her smile slightly anxious. Eve sensed she wanted to make a good impression and wasn't confident she'd succeed. Yet she'd been a big public figure not so long ago. It seemed odd that she was so diffident. Either way, Eve found her impressions hard to reconcile with the villagers' tales. Yet she liked her neighbours too. She'd need to dig to understand.

The sitting room faced west, like Eve's bedroom. It had a huge fireplace with an oak surround and was painted Wedgwood blue. It was lived in but not cluttered. Tranquil. One wall was taken up with polished bookshelves, stuffed with everything from dictionaries to fiction and poetry. Eve would love space for a collection like that.

'Hello!' Julian Fisher was out of his seat the moment she entered, his smile lighting his face.

He was certainly good-looking, but Eve knew what he'd been up to in the woods. She made a firm effort not to be prickly. If she wanted to understand him, she needed to build a rapport.

She shook his hand, and his grip was firm and warm.

Just beyond him in the bookcase she spotted one of his novels. Julian followed her gaze, then turned to her, his head on one side, and laughed.

'I wasn't in favour of having my books all over the place, but Nate said people would expect it. I've insisted his are on display too.'

Eve turned to Nate, and he welcomed her formally, ignoring Julian's comment. She'd known he was also published, by a small literary press. He'd had some good reviews – from Julian amongst others – but hadn't gained the same traction yet. It was Nate's spectacular success on the money markets that had made his name. He was his bank's most successful employee, but thought of as one of the good guys too, supporting firms who worked to make the world a better place.

'Nate's far too modest!' Julian said, getting up and slapping his brother-in-law on the back.

Nate gave him a brief look then shook his head.

'We all know it's luck,' Julian went on, 'who gets noticed and who doesn't. It's a matter of a book landing on the right desk on the right day.'

Talk about labouring a point. Tact wasn't his strong suit, clearly. Yet as he spoke, she saw Nate smile briefly, though Julian had looked away and missed it.

'Would you like some tea?' It was Kitty who offered. There was a trolley laden with crockery and a large white teapot.

'Yes please.'

Eve stepped forward, but Kitty smiled and motioned her to a seat. 'Please. You're our guest.' She wasn't just being polite,

Eve was sure. She wanted her to feel at home. The kindness was there in her eyes.

It felt odd to be waited on, but Eve dropped into the sofa and decided to try to get used to it.

'What part of the States are you from?' Kitty asked as she poured Eve's drink.

Eve explained about her childhood in Seattle. She told them about her American mom and her British dad, her move to London to study and her extended stay in the capital as she'd worked, married and raised her twins.

'They're grown-up now, still living in London. I came to Suffolk for work soon after I divorced and I loved it so much I relocated.'

'It's a beautiful county,' Kitty said. She blinked quickly. 'I spent a lot of my childhood here. Here, here, in fact. Staying with my grandparents. You know it was their place? It's changed hands a few times since.'

Eve nodded and listened as Kitty talked about her and Nate's love for Farfield and how pleased she was to be back. Her feelings towards her grandparents must have changed – it was clear in her wistful tone and the look in her eye as she spoke about them. It was almost too painful to witness.

Eve knew Kitty was thirty-seven now. She'd found fame young and hadn't changed much since her heyday. Her cheekbones were enviably high, her dyed blonde hair natural-looking, her eyes deep blue.

Eve had seen photos of her before she got famous: a punk rocker with hair streaked black and white. Different, but no less arresting. And one of her as a child, with long chestnut-brown pigtails. She was currently wearing a shocking pink and orange shift dress and strappy sandals. She looked chic and Eve was glad she'd packed smart, not casual. At least she'd look halfway decent.

She'd almost finished her tea when a newcomer entered the

room. His eyes flicked from Nate to Julian, his look transparently combative, his jaw tight. But his expression changed when it fell on Kitty, a smile illuminating his face.

Here was the man who'd been secretly watching her, Nate and Julian in the castle grounds.

4

A flicker crossed Julian's expression. A mix of surprise and slight unease. 'Here he is! Eve, meet Luke Shipley of *Cascade*.' The other magazine covering Farfield's new venture. 'His room's opposite yours, so you'll probably bump into each other.' He leaped up to clap the newcomer on the back.

The gesture and the words sounded overly hearty.

Cascade was a shade more upmarket than *Icon*, but they fought for similar readers. Both were known as trendsetters, a fact that embarrassed Eve. She didn't approve of trends. People should make their own choices.

She stood up to shake Luke's hand. It was oddly cold. She'd read somewhere that stress could cause that symptom. He had a relaxed, bed-head look, but there was something uncompromising in his expression.

'You two have met before?' She looked from the journalist to Julian.

Julian beamed but the smile didn't reach his eyes and he gave a tiny shrug. 'Luke met me and Nate at one of those smart parties in London where the great and the good get dragged along.' He laughed. 'They're an awful bore. Luke was there to interview some of the key players. He's kept in touch ever since.'

Kitty looked up, a frown passing over her face. Eve felt uncomfortable too. Julian's words were harmless enough, but his tone said something more. He was telling her they'd met by chance and Luke had clung on, whether they'd liked it or not.

But Luke seemed unaffected. His focus was on Kitty until Nate shook his hand, forcing him to transfer his attention.

'Great to see you again.' Nate flushed slightly.

If he'd handpicked publications to vet Farfield, Eve was surprised Luke and *Cascade* had been invited. There was clearly an undercurrent. She was curious about the cause.

Kitty greeted Luke with a friendly smile. 'It's good to meet you.'

'You too.' His shoulders relaxed a fraction as he focused on her, though his look was intent. Appraising.

'We haven't seen much of each other in a while, have we, Luke?' Julian said. 'I've been so busy.' He shook his head. 'We kept trying to find a date, didn't we, Nate, the three of us? But I kept letting you down. Very bad of me. But now's the perfect time for us to catch up.'

Eve felt it was time to stop rubbing it in.

'All in all, it's amazing you carved out enough hours to commit to this place.' Luke's tone was ironic.

Julian smiled and flopped back onto the sofa. 'True. I wondered long and hard about it, but I'd like to give something back. Pass on my advice to novice writers. Chew the cud with fellow professionals. We might get either turning up.'

Eve had read that Julian and Kitty had run out of money. She'd seen photos of the house they'd left to come here: a two up, two-down in a shabby village called Little Mill Marsh. Eve imagined life at the castle had been appealing.

'I was keen on the idea,' Kitty said. 'And when I realised Nate wanted to base the retreat here, I felt I needed to come.'

'Needed' was an interesting choice of word. Perhaps she meant to face up to the past. Nate put his hand on her shoulder and gave it a squeeze and Kitty's eyes glistened.

'It's beautiful,' Luke said, and Kitty smiled.

They discussed the background to the project. Eve heard how Nate and Julian had met at a literary awards ceremony four years earlier. Nate's firm had been the sponsors and Julian the winner. Nate had introduced Julian to Kitty a short while later. The retreat idea had sprung from Nate's desire to get involved in something that reflected his literary interests. Julian had jumped onboard at his invitation, driven – he claimed – by a noble desire to pass on his insights. Kitty had been all for it: keen to give classes in her and Nate's grandparents' house.

Eve was privately assigning alternative motivations to Julian. He only wrote a book every few years. They came out to rave reviews for their razor-sharp observations, but one of Eve's neighbours had pronounced them short on plot. Eve had read his debut and saw their point. Some of the descriptions had held her spellbound, but they were oddly disjointed, so that you'd just got hooked when the story spun off in a different direction.

They sold modestly, despite the adoration and TV interviews. If Nate was giving Julian a beautiful roof over his head, a generous salary and the chance to show off, Eve doubted he'd taken more than a second to decide he was in.

'Running something like this seems quite a departure for you, Nate,' Eve said.

'I was after a new challenge.'

'You're tired of your work in the City?'

But he shook his head. 'It's exciting. I get a tremendous buzz when my instincts pay off.' His eyes were bright. 'I'm not retiring. Not yet. But my wife's a reporter. She's often away, and I have time to spare. We've employed a manager so I can cope with my day job and this venture.'

'What about your involvement, Kitty?' Luke said.

'It seemed a natural fit.' She turned to him, her smile warm. Eve wondered if she was compensating for the other two. 'It's too easy for writers to spend all day hunched over a laptop. I can teach people to free up all those knotted muscles.'

'I'm looking forward to your sessions,' Eve said. 'I was curious about the morning shake-up.'

'It works extraordinarily well.' Julian leaned across Luke to take Kitty's hand, forcing the journalist to move back. 'Frees up muscles and ideas. It's got me unstuck time and again. I don't know what I'd do without Kitty.'

Julian's move seemed territorial, which was a bit of a joke, all things considered.

Behind him, a woman appeared at the door. A familiar face. The lover from the woods.

'Mr Randall's on the phone, Julian.'

No apology for interrupting and no hanging around. She left as she finished her sentence.

'So sorry.' Julian gave Eve and Luke the benefit of his radiating smile. 'That's Bonnie Whitelaw, my PA. She's not having a good day.' He shook his head and added in an undertone, 'Sometimes I wonder why I keep her on.'

But of course, Eve knew why. Whether it was to keep a secret or to have his cake and eat it, Julian had every reason.

Kitty held her husband's gaze for a moment. Her look was instantly recognisable to Eve. She'd done the same thing herself. Suspected something was off. Thought meeting her husband's eye unflinchingly would tell her if she was right. Because no one could be shameless enough not to react when faced with that sort of scrutiny, surely?

But Julian squeezed Kitty's hand tighter, and Eve saw doubt creep into her eyes.

5

Sitting on a mat learning loosening exercises with Luke next to her was just as awkward as Eve had predicted. She felt conspicuous in her vest top and leggings. She must focus. Her mind kept drifting to Julian and how foul he was, then to her ex, and then to Robin, her current boyfriend who'd restored her faith in men. Everything in the garden was rosy. Well, almost. She sighed. She'd promised herself she wouldn't go through these thoughts again. There was no problem. Their lack of time together was natural after what had happened. Robin was a former police detective who'd been forced underground after uncovering a network of corrupt officers and their criminal contacts. For over a year, he and Eve had seen each other on the quiet. Eve was too afraid of being grilled by her neighbours to go public. She couldn't risk slipping up over his backstory and putting him in danger.

Then, at long last, the police had found enough evidence to take the whole network down. Robin had been able to tell everyone in Saxford his true history and suddenly he and Eve were free to saunter through the village to the local pub and visit each other openly. It had been heaven, that first week. But of course, Robin had other friends and family to reconnect with. And new offers of consultancy work for the police in London. He'd been doing the rounds. If anything, Eve saw less of him now than she had when they'd been secret lovers. Life wasn't quite how she'd imagined it. She pushed the thought away. Talk about self-centred.

She looked up to see Kitty approaching her.

'Let's try that last move again. And while you're doing it, I want you to focus on a colour. What colour would you like to use?'

Eve was unprepared and said 'blue' because it was the colour of Kitty's exercise top. She had a nasty feeling her choice should go deeper than that. She wasn't very good at new-age stuff. But she was determined to be objective when she wrote this up.

'Blue. Perfect. Do the move again and visualise the intensity of the blue. The blue sea. The sky.'

Eve thought of Robin's blue eyes.

'Nothing personal,' Kitty said, as though she'd read Eve's mind. 'Something external. Cornflowers, delphiniums.'

At last Eve unwound enough to follow the instructions. As she performed the move, a seated stretch, she saw the sun sparkling on the North Sea and the distant horizon where an indigo line met sky blue. And then she lost track of time. It was weird. When she stopped, she felt loose-limbed and refreshed.

'Wow. I really do feel more flexible.' She felt almost liquid, but she wasn't going to say that.

Kitty beamed. 'That's what it's all about. But anyone can do it. I still reckon I only got well-known because a journalist produced the "soaring, grounded" quote. They said they felt light after they'd done my workout, full of energy and grace, but also, well,' she blushed, 'more peaceful than they'd ever felt. It was an evening class and I often wondered if they'd been on the sherries beforehand. Anyway, I asked if I could use their words as the title of my book and they were delighted.' She shook her head. 'I had no idea it would take off in the way it did. The power of a slogan.'

Kitty sounded wistful. It must have been hard when her routine went out of fashion.

'You miss the old days?'

But she shook her head. 'Oh, goodness no. Though it taught me some things.' She sighed. 'You get to know a lot about your friends and family when that kind of fame picks you up and spits you out.'

Luke leaned forward. 'Some people weren't pleased for you?'

'Nate practically carried me around on his shoulders. But some people were less impressed.' She stood up suddenly. 'It's not important. I'm where I need to be now, doing what I love. If only I hadn't—' She stopped herself, but Eve didn't miss the tear she blinked away. She could see the regret. Kitty took a deep breath. 'The main thing is that I'm back at Farfield. Nothing else matters.'

Eve wondered how long her fragile world would last. She was still convinced Julian wouldn't bring it crashing down. He seemed the sort to choose the easiest path every time. And besides, philanderer though he was, he'd married Kitty after her career had faded. He couldn't have been driven by her income. He must care about her on some level.

But the PA was another matter. Bonnie Whitelaw had said she was running out of patience.

Eve didn't like the sound of that.

At suppertime, Gus, who'd already eaten, was allowed to potter in and out of the communal dining room. It was an informal space with an oak refectory table and chairs. It had alcoves to the left and right of the fireplace and a hatch, connecting to the kitchen next door. Eve could see shelving through it, and a window in which was framed a dramatic-looking dead tree, dark and gnarled against the blue sky. It looked like something from a film.

Julian engaged Eve in discussion as she ate a seared tuna salad served with chilled white wine.

'The food's amazing.'

'The cook comes in from one of the villages, or so I'm told.' He didn't sound interested. 'Now, ask me anything, anything at all. People often feel hesitant if I've written something they don't understand, but no question's too silly.'

Eve relied on the one book she'd read and asked him how he managed such accurate portrayals of intimate family life.

He tapped his head. 'Observation, of course, but it's the ability to stand in someone's shoes that really counts. The more I work, the more the words pour onto the page. It takes years for a story to build. You can't rush these things. I wait for characters to speak to me.'

Whatever it was, Eve had to admit it worked. She might have missed a page-turning plot, but she'd bought into his scenes one hundred per cent.

'What about your latest book?' Luke said from across the table. 'Reviewers have been raving over the power of certain sections.' His eyes gleamed and Eve sensed trouble. 'It's interesting. Your second novel was considered disappointing compared with your first, but your third was lauded. Reviewers often wax lyrical about certain scenes, implying others are... less successful.' He glanced at Kitty and took a deep breath. 'Does it frustrate you that your work's seen as hit and miss?'

Julian reddened and blinked. 'There are as many opinions as there are reviewers,' he said at last. 'I don't pay much attention.'

Eve doubted that was true.

Luke leaned forward. 'But I'd be interested to know why you think your effectiveness waxes and wanes given you—'

He was interrupted by a crash. Kitty leaped up. Julian's glass was in smithereens on the floor.

The writer sighed heavily. 'How the blazes did that happen?' He got to his feet. 'I'll fetch a dustpan and brush.'

Was he really so thin-skinned that he'd smashed the glass deliberately? It felt almost like panic. Eve would have to read his latest book and see what Luke was talking about.

After supper, Eve took Gus to explore the gardens. The building was beautiful in the sunset, with its imposing stone-clad gatehouse and corner towers. The evening was warm and still, the air scented with grass and shrubs.

As she walked round the north side of the castle, she saw a mound rising out of the ground. For a moment, she couldn't imagine what it was.

And then it came to her. It must be an icehouse. It was an interesting relic and Eve had a peek inside but she couldn't get far. The well was at the rear of the brick-built structure, but a locked metal grille kept stray visitors away from the drop.

After that, she took Gus towards the creek and found the boat she'd heard about, in amongst the reeds. The cries of the gulls and the gentle sound of lapping water filled her with a sense of peace. It really was the perfect place to come and write if you could overlook Julian. But of course, he'd be part of the attraction for people who hadn't met him. They'd hope his artistic success might rub off on them. Maybe that was what Nate wanted too.

As she turned back towards the castle, she glimpsed movement at the rear of the majestic building, by the hedges that bordered the formal gardens.

She stood still and peered, eventually using the camera on her phone to zoom in on the scene in front of her.

It was Luke Shipley.

There was no way Eve could get closer without being seen; it was open lawn between them. Luke was tucked away in a small gap between two bits of yew hedge. What was he up to?

'It's no good, Gus,' she said, bending down. 'If we want to know more, we'll have to spy on him from upstairs.'

Her dachshund looked disapproving. Or perhaps it was just Eve's conscience that made her think so.

She went back into the castle, deposited Gus in their room, then walked to the very back of the building. The floor, which sloped, creaked with every step and she wondered where the others were. But if she was spotted, she could say she'd wanted to see more of the place. It wouldn't be unnatural.

At the end of the corridor, she reached the mullioned window and peered out.

Down below, Luke was hidden by the yew hedge, but she could see what he'd been looking at. Or rather who.

Kitty Marchant.

Eve had already noticed Luke's interest in her. It hadn't seemed odd. Kitty was beautiful, welcoming and easy to talk to.

But spying on her was another matter, and it was the second time she'd caught him at it, assuming Kitty had been his focus earlier. Eve wondered what he was after.

Maybe he'd admired her ever since she became famous. Or perhaps he was out to make trouble because he didn't like her husband.

For a second, she wondered whether to warn Kitty, but she might be overreacting. She'd keep an eye on things, then decide.

6

The following morning, Eve and Luke had been promised a tour of the castle. The fact that Julian was giving it was off-putting, but in the end, she was fascinated. She got to see the oldest parts of the structure. The upper-floor guard room still had its original stone fireplace. In the Tudor wings there were lots of spaces with desks so writers could choose to work in shared rooms or on their own. Eve loved the gilt-framed mirrors and the sound-proofed music room.

'There's plenty of capacity. No one will have company forced on them,' Julian said. 'I'll be on call for certain hours during the day, then around at dinner. I don't intend to over-whelm anyone.'

That was something.

'How will you cope if you find a visitor who hasn't read your books?' Luke said, smiling.

Eve had wondered too but had decided discretion was the better part of valour.

Julian laughed, but she could see the irritation in his eyes. 'I'm not here to judge their tastes. I'll be around for everyone.'

When the tour ended, Luke disappeared upstairs, taking the steps two at a time. Even that seemed like a message.

Eve looked after him. 'Did you know *Cascade* would send Luke?'

There was a slight nervousness to Julian's laugh. 'Yes. Yes, we did.'

'He seems a bit scratchy.'

Julian rubbed his chin. 'Oh, I don't think so especially. It's just his manner.'

Yeah, right.

Nate walked past as they spoke and exchanged glances with Julian. She suspected it was her question which had triggered the look. They'd probably discuss it next, and she was more than curious to know what they'd say. Why had they welcomed Luke's visit?

Julian turned to her. 'Excuse me. I must just attend to something.'

Eve started towards the stairs, but as his footsteps receded, she changed course. A moment later she was following him at a discreet distance. She saw him disappear into one of the castle's many cosy rooms and crept after him, treading lightly on the tiles, then standing as close to the door as she dared.

'I can't think what the hell's got into Luke.' That was Julian. 'I could tell there was something up the moment he arrived. Talk about looking daggers. What's happened to the obsequious hanger-on we know and hate?'

So the attitude was new. That explained why they hadn't hesitated to get him involved.

'Don't talk like that. I suspect that's what got us into trouble in the first place. You were cruel about him, and I think he overheard.'

'*I* was cruel about him? What you said was far worse.'

'It was a knee-jerk reaction after what you told me about his cloying behaviour. I shouldn't have come out with it.'

'Well, it's too late now. And we don't *know* he heard us.'

'He's behaving like he did. And that's all we need with the first proper guests coming tomorrow. Thank goodness *Cascade* said we could vet his piece.'

Eve stiffened. Had Portia lied when she'd said Eve would have a free hand? If *Cascade* had made that promise she bet Nate had pushed *Icon* to follow suit. All her misgivings came flooding back. Thoughts of a full and frank discussion with Portia filled her mind.

As Eve edged back along the corridor, she wondered again about Luke and his relationship with Julian and Nate. Why had his behaviour been cloying? Had he been after something when he'd sought their friendship? And if he'd failed to get it, could he be transferring his attentions to Kitty?

Or perhaps he was out for revenge if he'd heard Nate and Julian bad-mouth him. That might include making up to Kitty, purely to annoy Julian. But if that was the case, why the need to watch her in secret?

After a moment's thought, she went to fetch Gus, then sought out a room with a desk to write up some notes. Out of the window she could see preparations for the launch party, and beyond, Luke examining the icehouse just as she had, his reddish-brown hair gleaming in the sun. He stood next to the mound for a moment, seemingly lost in thought, then disappeared through the entrance.

For fifteen minutes, Eve worked on her notes, before her attention returned to the hubbub outside. A marquee was being erected and wine glasses and champagne flutes being laid out. It seemed every effort would be made to woo the villagers. Some would take a lot of convincing. Ella would never be reconciled, that was clear, and Moira from the village store had been full of righteous indignation each time the topic came up. She was still attending, though. She claimed she wanted to take the retreat team to task. Eve suspected the free food and drink might have played a part.

Kitty dashed to and fro with trays of plates. The automatic urge to offer help was overwhelming. Eve knew she was a guest, and they'd turn her down, but she went anyway. As she stood up, she saw Luke leave the icehouse. There wasn't a lot to see. What the heck had he been doing in there?

7

Kitty did refuse to let Eve help, of course, then Luke appeared and he and Eve were invited to watch a video about the history of the castle, then rest until it was time for the party.

Eve watched Luke in the low-lit room. He was leaning forward, engrossed, writing notes. Nothing about him rang alarm bells now.

When the video finished, Eve found Gus and returned to the writing room she'd used earlier. She went back to her work, but glanced up periodically to monitor progress in the grounds.

Kitty Marchant was talking to Freya Hardwicke, the woman who'd sold Farfield to Nate after the death of her fraudster husband.

There was something odd about Kitty and Freya's body language. Eve had seen them prowling around each other for a while. First Kitty noticing Freya and stepping back, almost as if she didn't want to be seen. Then Freya performing similar moves while Kitty's back was turned.

At last, they came face to face, Freya's hands on her hips, Kitty defensive. They parted, then spoke again twenty minutes later and it was the same. Each time, Freya looked controlled but angry and Kitty anxious.

Eventually, Eve abandoned her notes, put her laptop in her room and left Gus there too.

'I'll be back very soon. And then you'll get to see Viv and everyone from Saxford. I just need a short time on my own first.'

He slumped on the floor, resigned, as she patted him.

A minute later she was outside, weaving around the temporary waiting staff and guy ropes, ducking behind a barrow full of ice and champagne. If she was spotted, she hoped people would imagine she was soaking up the atmosphere for her article. In fact, she was driven by the desire to understand Kitty's character. She liked her. She seemed kind, modest and sensitive to people's feelings. If she had a failing, Eve would have said it was lack of confidence. So why was Freya Hardwicke antagonistic towards her, just like many of the villagers? Eve doubted it was the Marchant scandal; Freya hadn't lived in the area back then.

At last, she saw the pair again, and caught Kitty's words. 'Please, Freya—'

There was desperation in her tone, which made the situation all the more curious. It struck Eve that this wasn't a sudden row over some small detail.

Freya strode away from the main group and Kitty followed her. Eve kept on their tail, skirting around the marquee and past a bank of portaloos towards the formal gardens where Luke had watched Kitty. It was a secluded area. Perhaps they were planning to air their feelings more frankly.

It was lucky that the yew hedge had gaps. She could occupy one just as Luke had, looking beyond, into the shrubbery where Kitty and Freya stood.

She caught the end of Freya's sentence. '... too late, now. If you wanted to say something you should have done it three years back. I thought we were friends! I never guessed you had such a hateful ulterior motive.'

Kitty had her hands up to her face as she replied. 'It's far more complicated than that.'

'I don't see how it could be. Either way, you should have had the guts to be honest.'

'It's not as it seems. Let's talk now. Please!'

Freya's face was flushed. 'No, thank you. I've got nothing to say.' She turned smartly and walked back towards a different gap in the yew hedge.

Eve would be visible if Freya turned left, and Kitty was on the move as well. Eve stood stock-still and hoped.

She was in luck. Both women were too upset and distracted to focus on anything but their quarrel.

As Eve went to fetch Gus and change into her dress for the launch party, she considered what she'd heard. So, Kitty and Freya had been friends but there'd been a bust-up and now they'd been thrust together again, because of the sale of the castle. Eve remembered hearing that Freya had hoped to sell to Ella, but in the end, she'd had no choice but to accept the highest bidder. Her late husband's debts were huge. She wondered how Kitty had offended her. What was the ulterior motive Freya had mentioned? It couldn't be Kitty's desire to live at the castle; Freya implied the root of their argument went back three years. And Kitty hadn't been her husband's lover. That woman had been identified. Unless he'd had more than one and Eve had seriously misread Kitty's character. It was one more mystery to fathom out.

Eve had chosen a high-necked blue floral dress for the party, with a short-sleeved blue jacket. Robin had said he liked her in it, though that was irrelevant as he wouldn't be coming. He was staying in London to testify against his old enemies. Eve couldn't think beyond the trial. She'd been told countless times that there was no way the network would get off, but it was like a brick wall looming in front of her. She was desperate for it to conclude, but also more scared than she liked to admit. Robin had just called with his daily update. She hated not being by his side but he hadn't suggested it. She'd felt the nerves coming off him and sensed he wanted to hunker down. Shut out the wider world.

As she descended the stairs, she saw Viv standing at the bottom, her rose-pink hair glowing in the light that poured through a nearby window.

'There you are!' Viv was instantly mobbed by Gus, who got a thorough tummy tickle in return. She looked up at Eve. 'Reporting for updates! What a place this is! I still can't believe Benet refused to help save it. What's it like, staying here?'

'Even more fascinating than I'd expected.'

Viv gave her a knowing look. 'Tell all.'

'You first. Is everything all right at the teashop?' She had to ask.

Viv waved an impatient hand. 'Fine, fine. There was a spot of bother over— No, actually, forget it. Lars mopped it up in no time and it wasn't even that hot. Pam Crocket was dry before she left.'

Eve opened her mouth but Viv held up her hand. 'You need to let go.'

They went into the garden to fetch glasses of champagne and Eve tried to switch off.

Back in the house, where things were quieter, she filled Viv in on Julian's affair with his PA, Bonnie Whitelaw, Luke Shipley's strained relationship with Julian and Nate, his pronounced interest in Kitty, and Kitty's row with Freya Hardwicke.

'I told you she'd be trouble,' Viv said, but Eve shook her head.

'Honestly, Viv, I like her. I really want to understand the row with her grandparents. I just don't know her well enough to ask yet.'

As they talked, they walked the length of the west wing corridor, which echoed the one upstairs. At last, they opened a door leading to the formal gardens. As they stepped between the flower beds, they found a group of Saxfordites: Moira from the village store, Jim the vicar, and Eve's beloved neighbours, Sylvia and Daphne. Moira's friend and rival from the amateur dramatic society Deidre was there too. She'd just returned from nursing a sick relative in Wales.

'Ah, Eve, dear.' Moira bustled up, dyed auburn hair bouncing. 'I'm still rather disappointed that you agreed to come and write about the retreat. I can't forgive Kitty for the way she hurt her grandparents, and as for her brother, swiping Farfield from under Ella's nose...'

Moira looked out onto the grounds, where Ella was talking to Viv's brother and his wife. Eve was surprised to see her there after the scene in the village.

Moira was still sighing at the injustice of it all. She'd bemoaned it before. Several times. And Eve sympathised. The Marchants senior sounded lovely and she'd wanted Ella to buy the castle too. But there wasn't a thing they could do about it now. She wasn't going to stand there justifying herself to Moira.

'I understand,' she said instead. 'We don't have to talk about my work.'

Everyone apart from Moira suppressed smiles.

'Oh, I didn't mean that,' the storekeeper said hastily. 'You know me, Eve. I'm not one to bear a grudge. Didn't I hear you mention Freya Hardwicke?'

She must have caught Eve's last sentence as she'd exited the corridor. Ears like a bat and a radar for gossip that was second to none.

'Only that I saw her just now,' Eve said cautiously.

'I heard something most interesting about her today,' Moira said. 'We all know, of course, that she sold the castle to pay off the debts her husband ran up. It must have been such a shock when he died and she realised the corners he'd cut with his export business. Quite criminal, I'm told.'

She went into a long explanation about his fraudulent activity. She'd already told them all before, of course, but Deidre was fresh meat. Half Eve's mind was on Gus. He'd accepted some tickles and pats from the vicar but was now staring at some carp swimming in the pond. Rather too intently for Eve's liking.

Moira broke into her thoughts.

'Do you know, it turned out he'd spent a hundred thousand pounds on a sports car for his mistress?' She gave a deep sigh, reflecting deep satisfaction at the quality of the gossip. 'It's understandable that Freya had to accept Nate Marchant's offer on the castle.' She sniffed. 'It wasn't her fault that poor Ella lost out. Such a shame, after *all* her hard work. To think this place could have been open to the public.'

They knew all that already too.

'It was very stubborn of Nate, Kitty and Julian to insist on bidding for Farfield. I know it was the Marchant family home, but Ella spent as much time here as any of them. Her grandparents worked for Sophie and Daniel and they treated her like family.' She spoke as though the Marchants senior had been her close friends. Eve happened to know that wasn't the case. 'Kitty strikes me as cruel and spoiled. Used to getting her own way. And her brother's the same, no doubt, though at least he kept in touch with his grandparents. As for Julian—'

Julian rounded the corner at that moment, clutching a tray of champagne flutes.

'How wonderful to see you all here. Please, have some champagne. And Nate and Kitty are on their way with the canapés.'

Moira blushed puce and took a flute rather stiffly.

'Are you Moira Squires, by any chance?' Julian said, his focus on the storekeeper.

'Well, I am, as a matter of fact.' She sounded unwilling to confirm it.

'Ah, I'm so very pleased to meet you. I've heard all about your key place in Saxford St Peter. I understand you're the person to ask for advice about the most idyllic spots for our clients to visit. A little bird tells me you know every last detail about the area.'

'Well,' Moira blushed again, 'I suppose that's true. I don't know who told you. I don't like to boast.'

Viv caught Eve's eye and mimed a Pinocchio nose. Sylvia snorted and Daphne put a restraining hand on her arm.

'Your reputation's bound to travel,' Julian said. 'You'll meet our clients personally, of course, when they come to your shop. We'll be recommending it. Could I possibly steal you away for a quick chat?'

As they left, Eve heard Julian say: 'We'll be conducting tours for everyone later in the evening, but I'd like to escort you personally, if I may.'

Deidre scuttled after them, but Eve was afraid she'd been forgotten.

Sylvia and Viv gave way to suppressed laughter as soon as they were out of earshot, Sylvia's long grey plait falling forward as she doubled over.

'I knew Moira would crack, but I think that was a record.'

Daphne shook her head. 'I expect they'll work on Jo too.'

'They won't get much change out of her,' Sylvia said.

Eve had imagined the same. Jo was the fierce cook at the local pub and nobody's fool.

'Sophie and Daniel Marchant meant a lot to her,' Sylvia went on. 'You can imagine what she thinks of Kitty. Even with Nate at the helm, she suspects they'll fail to live up to their grandparents' standards.'

'What made them so close?' It was news to Eve.

Daphne's eyes met Sylvia's.

Sylvia shrugged. 'It's going back a bit, and it's common knowledge.'

Daphne nodded at last. 'Jo lost a baby, late in her pregnancy. She was very young. It was years ago now, before they took on the pub. It was a terrible time for her of course and she didn't have the space to recover. Villages are like that. So Sophie Marchant asked if she'd like to stay at Farfield. Matt came with her for a few days.' Matt was Jo's husband. He ran the pub jointly with her and his brother. 'After that, he felt strong enough to go back, but Jo stayed for longer. She said Sophie just let her be. She was company when Jo needed it and would fade into the background when she wanted to be alone. There's so much space here, of course.'

Eve felt awkward for having asked. It was such an intimate bit of Jo's past. The haven the Marchants had offered must have been a godsend.

Sylvia shook her head. 'Jo's feelings about Farfield are complicated. She said from the start that Sophie and Daniel would have loved the thought of their grandchildren coming home. They never stopped loving Kitty, in spite of it all. But it was Ella Tyndall's vision that matched their world view. They welcomed everyone when they lived here.'

'What do you think of the present household?' Jim asked Eve.

Now Moira had departed it was safe to confide without fear of being quoted. 'Honestly? I like Kitty so far. I can't begin to imagine why she refused to see her grandparents. It seems alien to her nature.'

She was worried they'd pooh-pooh her assessment, but Sylvia's surprised eyes became thoughtful. 'Families. They're nothing if not complicated.'

Eve nodded. 'Something makes me sad for Kitty. She doesn't have much confidence in herself, despite her success. Nate seems all right, but tense and hard to read. As for Julian,

I'd say he's a total fraud who's good at manipulating people. But you don't need me to tell you that, having seen him in action.'

'No, indeed,' Sylvia said with another snort. 'It's frustrating that Moira never passed on the gossip about Freya Hardwicke. She wasted all that time repeating what we already know instead.'

'Poor Freya,' Daphne said, sighing.

'I think I know,' Viv said unexpectedly.

'Is it fit for a vicar's ears?' Jim asked, raising a bushy white eyebrow, a smile quirking his lips.

Viv laughed. 'Perfectly. Sorry to disappoint. It's interesting, though. She's accepted a job as manager here, apparently. She's at the launch party in an official capacity.'

'Really?'

Viv nodded. 'She preferred Ella's bid, but I guess beggars can't be choosers.'

'Yes, I can understand all that.' Eve wondered how much to say. 'But it seems she and Kitty had a major falling-out a while back. It makes me wonder why Freya's accepted a job here.'

Surely she could have found one somewhere else?

8

In between chatting to her fellow villagers, Eve photographed the party. *Icon*'s official photographer would come and take shots for her article, but she wanted some informal ones to remember the occasion.

Freya had things running like clockwork at first. Eve could see why Nate would want to employ her, even if her accepting was a surprise. But at some point, the hired staff overseeing the drinks had been distracted by a small child who'd fallen from a tree. The child was okay but by the time they returned, the civilised bar had turned into a free for all. Eve saw multiple villagers make off with champagne bottles and flutes. Julian looked momentarily miffed, but then laughed, took a bottle himself and started topping people up.

'After all, it's what it's there for,' Eve heard him say to Moira. 'Let's make merry.'

Moira was positively beaming now.

Honestly.

Eve was back with Viv again when she saw Freya Hardwicke dashing after Bonnie Whitelaw. Was this the new manager trying to grab a word with the PA who'd been holding the fort? Or did she want to say something personal? Either way, Bonnie seemed intent on keeping her distance. It was obvious enough to be embarrassing.

'Bonnie!' Freya was met with the woman's retreating back.

Viv mouthed 'awks' as Eve caught her eye. Then Freya became aware of them both and reddened. She looked annoyed.

'That is Julian Fisher's PA, isn't it?'

Eve nodded.

'We haven't met before, but someone pointed her out. I'll be doing a handover with her tomorrow; I thought I could at least say hello.' She frowned. 'Maybe she resents me. She's been doing some of the paperwork while the manager role was finalised. But I gather she knew it was temporary and I was told she didn't want to switch jobs.'

Eve wondered if Nate could have promised Freya the post as part of the package in exchange for Farfield. But it still seemed odd that she'd want it. Surely returning to her old home, where she'd lost her husband and discovered he'd double-crossed her, would only bring back painful memories? *And* she'd argued with Kitty. It was peculiar.

'Maybe Bonnie's just distracted,' she said to Freya. 'She seemed a bit tense earlier.' Too busy thinking about her affair with Julian to worry about the retreat, probably. Eve could feel her lips thinning.

'Maybe.' Freya was still frowning. 'Someone mentioned she was high maintenance, so I was already wary. She's down to do some of the admin here as well as her work for Julian.'

Eve felt a wave of sympathy. She wouldn't fancy Bonnie as a colleague.

Freya left, and by the time they'd refreshed their drinks, Bonnie Whitelaw had reappeared. She was standing at the edge of the room, glancing this way and that, fiddling with the necklace she wore. Eve liked it: it was rectangular and art deco in style, black onyx with detailed silverwork, and what might or might not be a real diamond at its centre.

Eve would have worn it herself and was surprised to see Bonnie sporting it. It didn't match her style. Her earrings were modern, delicate and gold, as was her bracelet. The necklace didn't marry well with her low-cut fitted dress either.

As Eve continued to watch, she guessed it must be valuable. A present that she was proud of, perhaps. She kept touching it, making sure it was perfectly placed, pretty-side outwards. Bonnie was the sort to show off what she had, both physically and materially. Eve told herself off for being cynical.

She and Viv ventured outside.

'I take your point about the tensions here,' Viv said, 'but it is beautiful, isn't it?'

The sky was turning pink and orange as they looked west over the castle's roof, a mix of steeply pitched Tudor tiles and medieval crenelations. Gulls swooped overhead towards the coast.

'You will ask them about access for locals, won't you?' Viv said. 'Simon and I used to run about the old deer park here in the summer holidays and bring picnics. The Marchants were so nice. If they were playing croquet or had the archery kit out they'd always invite us to join in.'

Simon was Viv's brother. 'I will. I'm hoping Nate will want to carry on the tradition in some way. And Kitty too. Honestly, Viv, if you chatted with her, you'd see what I mean.'

A short while later, Eve nipped back inside to go to the bathroom. She left Gus with Viv and her brother and hoped they remembered to supervise. She didn't trust him not to beg for the chipolatas which were being handed round on silver trays.

'It would count as cannibalism, Gus,' she heard Viv telling him as she cut across the grass. 'You're a sausage dog, don't forget.'

Inside, she came across a repeat of a scene from earlier in the evening. This time it was Kitty calling Bonnie, and Bonnie not responding. She was giving Kitty exactly the same treatment she'd given Freya. Perhaps she only heard selectively.

But Kitty was more determined than Freya. As Bonnie mounted the old oak staircase, Kitty kept after her, calling her name.

Eve carried on towards the bathroom, but glanced over her shoulder to see what happened next.

At last, Bonnie turned to face Kitty. Eve saw the defiance in her eyes. And amusement too.

Kitty gasped and Eve could hear her pain. Her hand was up to her face.

Eve saw the twinkle of pure malice as Bonnie turned and carried on climbing to the upper floor.

There was a moment's pause before Kitty went after her. Eve heard their footsteps thumping along the corridor above.

9

As Eve washed her hands in the spacious downstairs bathroom and dried them on a fluffy towel, she felt nonplussed. Why had Kitty reacted like that when Bonnie turned round? There were too many secrets at Farfield and too much suppressed emotion.

As she left the room, she saw Kitty had come back downstairs and was dashing down the corridor towards the rear of the castle.

Eve was tempted to check she was okay, but she'd headed to a quieter part of the grounds. Maybe she needed some time alone.

As Eve passed the door to the main area outside, someone in the marquee tapped a wine glass, and people hushed.

'We'd just like to say a few words.' Julian's voice.

She'd better go and listen. She might want to put something he said in her article, and if speeches were coming, Kitty would probably reappear for them.

'We're all so grateful to you for coming tonight,' Julian said. 'We know Farfield is dear to your hearts, and we hope to hold a party like this at least once a year so that you can keep in touch with the place.'

Eve was standing close to Moira and watched her simper. 'That really is very decent of them,' she said to Jo from the pub. Jo had one eyebrow raised, unconvinced, but Moira seemed oblivious. 'I'm most reassured now that I've actually talked to dear Julian personally. It does make a difference, doesn't it?'

'A party once a year's no good,' said Jo darkly. 'They've got a lot to live up to.'

'To be fair, Freya never invited people to use the grounds,' Moira said, hesitantly.

'No reason for her to. She wasn't family. If Nate and Kitty don't do it, it's a betrayal. Though that's nothing new in Kitty's case.'

Moira had the sense to shut up at that point.

Eve picked out Ella Tyndall's face in the crowd. Still, sad and determined.

It was true, a party once a year was a far cry from permission to wander at will.

It was Nate's choice of course, as the new owner; there were no rights of way. The Marchants had treated the villagers like guests and they'd gone hither and thither, without establishing regular routes that might have a legal standing.

Nate said a few words too and mentioned literary talks in Saxford.

'They'll have to do better than that if they want the Cross Keys as a venue,' Jo said.

Eve slipped closer to her. 'It could be a way to open negotiations. I can't believe Nate and Kitty will be unsympathetic, given their grandparents' attitude. And I think Kitty's changed.' Either that or she was misunderstood from the start.

Jo gave her a sidelong glance. 'Time will tell. Even if she has, I don't trust Julian Fisher. He won't want to mix with the hoi polloi.'

Moira, who'd been bad-mouthing him solidly up until that evening, looked shocked.

Kitty didn't appear and though Julian looked around vaguely, he didn't seem bothered. That didn't surprise Eve one bit.

It was some time after the speeches that Eve became aware of a disturbance inside the castle. The weather was warm, and the casement windows were open. Whoever was in there must be aware that half the residents of Saxford St Peter would overhear them. If they were thinking straight. But perhaps their upset had blinded them to the fact.

'What the—?' Close to a roar. A man's voice. Luke Shipley? 'I don't believe it. Is this your idea of a joke? I knew it! I knew there was something.'

Eve and several others moved towards the door to the castle.

'But you didn't though, did you?' That was Bonnie, Eve was sure. 'You had no idea. Not until now.' She was crowing.

They heard a chair scrape, then a cry and a crash.

'Oh, very well done,' Bonnie said, 'but it won't do you any good. And you know that.' She laughed.

A door slammed and there were footsteps. Not running, but hurried.

Eve was in time to glimpse Bonnie Whitelaw disappearing into Julian's study. She was still laughing but it was uncontrolled, and her hair had come down. 'Poor fool,' she said, over her shoulder.

Eve watched as Luke appeared, hands shoved into his pockets as though to stop them shaking. He was pale.

He took one look at Eve and turned towards the castle's west wing without a word.

Julian arrived, frowning. Someone must have reported back to him. 'Excuse me one moment,' he said to the small group nearby.

Eve returned outside as Julian closed the window to his study.

'Oh, dear me.' Moira had appeared. 'What an unexpected

turn of events. You'd think Julian Fisher's PA would behave herself on such an important occasion.'

Eve could hear the low rumbling of an angry discussion inside.

'I'm sure we can't blame dear Julian for being upset,' Moira said.

Eve couldn't bring herself to reply.

A moment later, Julian came back out. Eve and her group chatted busily as he walked past.

Then, down near the formal gardens, Eve saw Bonnie, striding across the lawn, her jerky, angry movements visible even at that distance.

There was a string quartet getting ready to play in the marquee.

'This really is quite lovely, isn't it?' Moira said.

Eve caught the vicar's eye and tried not to laugh. But a moment later, she was distracted by Gus. She'd been alert to the danger the moment the string players had begun to tune up. They'd started now, and Gus was joining in. It often happened in church, where Jim was remarkably accepting of the dachshund's efforts, but it wasn't quite the same here.

'C'mon, Gus,' Eve said, moving round to usher him away from the tent. Insultingly, the dachshund took no notice until Viv spotted Eve's desperation and called him too.

'Who is it, Gus, who buys your food and gets up to walk you at the crack of dawn?'

But Gus was scampering happily after Viv, who was running away to encourage him, and laughing as she went.

Fine.

They were beyond the formal gardens when they heard the scream.

And then they saw a figure running across the lawn towards the castle. Bonnie? Eve was reliant on moonlight but from the hair and dress she was sure it was her.

'Where did she come from?' Viv said.

'Somewhere beyond the trees.' Eve was already running as a shadowy figure appeared from a similar direction.

As she got closer, she saw it was Nate Marchant. What on earth was he doing here?

'I heard someone scream.' He stood there, slack-jawed. 'What happened?'

'We don't know.'

Other villagers were dashing over the lawns towards them now and the three of them ploughed through the trees.

Beyond them stood the icehouse.

As Nate ran ahead, Eve thought she saw movement through the trees to her left. Someone creeping quietly away?

She turned but a cry yanked her attention back. It was Nate, inside the domed structure.

'No, no, no.'

Eve and Viv's eyes met. Jim Thackeray had arrived too. He was quick on his feet despite his years. He approached the icehouse, heading inside after Nate.

A moment later he reappeared, his arm around the man's shoulders.

Nate was sobbing. 'There's been an accident. Kitty must have opened the grille to the well. She's... she's fallen. I think she's dead.'

Eve dashed forward. 'It's only thirty feet deep, right? Maybe she's just unconscious. We need to get down there.'

She went to look, the vicar dashing after her. 'Be careful. It's a sheer drop.'

Eve used her phone torch. Down below lay Kitty. Her eyes were open, but they were unblinking.

10

_____

Jim Thackeray managed to find coverage to call the police then stood quietly next to Nate, though he stepped forward when Julian arrived. He was surrounded by a sea of villagers, their faces slack with shock.

'Is it true, what they're saying?' Julian's words echoed ones Eve had heard in countless television dramas, but that didn't mean they weren't genuine. It was common for bereaved relatives to fall back on stock phrases. Eve put it down to shock.

'I'm afraid it is.' Jim's tone was gentle. 'I'm terribly sorry. Kitty's had a fall and she's dead.'

After a moment, Julian put a hand to his forehead and turned on his heel. It looked theatrical. 'Excuse me. I think I'm going to be sick.' He stumbled over the grass towards the castle, presumably to the bathrooms. It was a long way to go, and Eve watched and wondered as he went.

The rest of them edged back a little from the icehouse, the enormity of the situation sinking in. People were shivering, despite the mild weather. Villagers were hugging each other and talking in whispers.

Only Jim and Nate Marchant remained close to the

icehouse, Nate shuddering in his blue jacket. Shock must be setting in.

'This is terrible,' Viv whispered, as she and Eve backed away. 'Do you think it was an accident?'

Eve gave her a sharp look. 'I'm not sure. What makes you ask?'

'She was virtually brought up here until the estrangement. She must have known she had to be careful in the icehouse.'

'I agree. And the safety grille in front of the well was locked when I went in there yesterday. Why would it be open now? And why would Kitty lose her footing? It's not like it's wet or icy.'

Viv's glassy eyes met hers. 'It's so shocking.'

Eve nodded. 'I hope to goodness we're wrong. If it *is* murder, it was a chancy method to choose. She could easily have survived the fall. The well's not that deep.'

Eve knew she'd get the lowdown eventually, via Robin. DS Greg Boles, who served on the local force, was married to Robin's cousin and they tended to discuss cases. Greg's boss, DI Nigel Palmer, drove him to it. He was lazy, narrow-minded and always operated with an eye to his career. Eve had written the obituaries of several murder victims and each time Greg's inside knowledge had helped keep her safe. Him sharing details would be a sackable offence, of course. Eve could never let on she had a police source, not even to Viv.

She cast her eyes over the crowd, automatically scanning for Kitty's key contacts and fixing people's movements in her memory. Nate had appeared through the trees, close to the icehouse, just after Bonnie dashed off, presumably having found Kitty's body. They'd both been near enough to be involved. Julian had seemed to come from somewhere beyond the marquee, before dashing off to the castle to be sick.

She thought she could see Luke Shipley in the glow of the

lights festooning the marquee. He was absolutely still, staring ahead.

And a shadowy figure walking past the end of the formal gardens proved to be Freya Hardwicke. Eve still couldn't see Ella Tyndall.

But realistically it meant nothing. The place was busy, and Kitty could have been killed earlier, when no one was paying attention.

'Don't look now, but our least favourite policeman's just arrived,' Viv said, nudging Eve.

Eve watched Palmer stride across the grass. There were paramedics as well, of course, but it was clearly too late. They stood just inside the entrance to the icehouse, issuing instructions about ladders and equipment.

'Stand well back, everyone,' Palmer said. 'We'd like to see you all over in the marquee. Make your way there in an orderly fashion.' His eyes lit on Eve and his mouth soured, his shoulders tensing. 'Ah, Ms Mallow. We meet again. Why am I not surprised? Trouble seems to follow you around.'

He turned and walked towards the marquee, leaving some colleagues with the paramedics.

Viv gave Eve a sympathetic glance. 'He's such a moron.'

Eve sighed. 'He's right though, isn't he? Who'd have thought there'd be so much death and malice in a quiet corner of the English countryside?'

'Simon says people have long memories and intense feelings round here,' Viv replied. 'The Marchant family row caused people to take sides and Nate's purchase of Farfield was controversial. Maybe it's got something to do with that.'

Eve gave Viv a look. 'You think Ella Tyndall could have done it?'

Viv didn't rise. 'Of course not. I like Ella. She's one of Monty's best customers. But you know what I mean.'

But Eve had seen how upset Ella had been at losing her bid.

And she'd lashed out at Kitty in particular. They couldn't discount her because of her taste in cakes.

When they reached the marquee, the villagers were asked for their contact details so the police could follow-up if necessary, but Eve was sent to sit with the castle's inhabitants. Julian had reappeared and sat staring at the floor. Nate was next to him, his head buried in his hands. Bonnie was on Julian's other side, staring straight ahead. She was wrapped up now, swathed in scarves and shawls. Night had finally fallen, and her face was pale in the artificial light. Luke was looking blank, but Eve guessed he was working hard to keep it up. Every so often she saw him wipe a tear from his eye. It was natural to be upset, but he was a virtual stranger, supposedly. His reaction and his desire to hide it made her wonder about that.

As they waited, Eve watched her friends and neighbours give their names and addresses. Ella Tyndall had appeared now. Her hand shook as she lifted a glass of wine from the table next to her and sipped it. It wasn't hers. Eve had seen it sitting there when Moira gave her details.

Freya was talking to a young constable who directed her to where Eve and the other household members were sitting. She must count as one of them now, with her new job as manager.

A moment later, a breathless uniformed officer came jogging over the grass and spoke to Palmer.

The DI's shoulders sagged. He stood up and cleared his throat. 'Ladies and gentlemen, I'm afraid we'll have to keep you a little longer. We're treating Kitty Marchant's death as murder.'

11

Eve watched the reactions of her group. She felt Julian was deliberately hiding his, keeping his eyes down, putting both hands over his face. Nate seemed to crumple, sinking in his chair. He pulled out a tissue. She could see the tears were genuine.

Whereas Bonnie looked angry. Her unflinching stare came across as defiance. Eve wondered what had caused it. If she'd been livid with Kitty, her death would have defused her rage, surely, whether she was guilty or not? Her emotion would have transformed into something else. Regret, guilt, fear or triumph. If Eve's thinking was right, Bonnie was livid about something else. Eve wondered what.

Luke was looking down now, shaking his head. A periodic tear still fell into his lap. What was he hiding? The memory of him visiting the icehouse filled Eve's head. He could have been there to plan. If he had reason to want Kitty dead, he could have been softening her up from the start. Lulling her into a false sense of security. But Eve couldn't imagine what motive he might have.

Freya was biting her nails, her chest rising and falling

quickly.

Palmer approached her. 'You'll need to contact your guests for the coming week and delay them. PC Griffiths will accompany you. We'll speak to you when you've finished.'

She nodded and got up as though in a trance.

Bonnie turned, her shawl falling open slightly, and Eve noticed her necklace was gone. Maybe she'd taken it off when she'd fetched her extra layers.

At last, the CID team came to talk to them: Palmer with Greg Boles and DC Olivia Dawkins.

Eve got Dawkins, and breathed a sigh of relief. She was thorough and conscientious.

'People were milling around. There were all kinds of inter-actions that are probably irrelevant,' Eve said. She was worried about what she'd overheard. If she passed it on it was bound to put pressure on innocent people who were grieving. She couldn't feel much sympathy for Julian, but it was different for Nate. Eve was grateful for Gus's reassuring presence, warm against her legs, his sympathetic brown eyes looking up at her.

'Please just tell me everything.' Dawkins gave her a sympa-thetic smile. 'I'll make sure it's followed up tactfully.'

So Eve told her the lot. The scenes came back to her vividly, from Kitty and Freya's conversation about their broken friend-ship, to Kitty's upset with Bonnie as she turned on the stairs. She explained how Kitty had dashed after the PA, only to reap-pear minutes later and hurry down the west wing to the rear of the castle. It was the last time Eve had seen Kitty alive.

'Did you notice the time?'

Eve grimaced. 'I'm afraid not. Eight forty-five, maybe? But it was immediately before the speeches, so that might help.'

Dawkins nodded. 'And she didn't come to them?'

Eve shook her head. After that, she told Dawkins about Bonnie and Luke Shipley arguing. She didn't see how it could be relevant, but other people were bound to mention it.

'Can you think of anyone who might have wanted Ms Marchant dead?'

Eve hesitated, but she had to come clean. Julian's affair with Bonnie Whitelaw was too important to hide.

She explained what she'd overheard. 'It's awkward. I know DI Palmer will think I was snooping, but seeing them together was pure luck.'

'You're sure it was Ms Whitelaw and Mr Fisher? You'd never met them before, and Ms Whitelaw's not a familiar face.'

'That's true, but I'm sure.' Eve could imagine what Palmer would say. Day had only just broken and they'd been in the woods, which were dark at the best of times.

'Did you hear either of them address the other by name? Or mention Farfield?'

Eve tried to remember. 'I'm not sure.' She could feel the situation slipping away.

Dawkins nodded.

'And is there anything else, however small, that you think might be relevant?'

Once again Eve was torn about what to say. Pointing the finger in a murder investigation was a serious business.

'Luke Shipley seemed to admire Kitty. He lightened up in her presence and I... well, I saw him secretly watching her in the gardens.'

But had that scene been as creepy as Eve thought? Eve wondered if Dawkins would think she was as big a drama queen as Palmer did, but the detective constable just nodded calmly.

On impulse, Eve added: 'I don't suppose it's relevant, but Bonnie Whitelaw was wearing a rather nice pendant earlier. It's missing now.'

She described it. If Dawkins ever had any faith in Eve's credibility, she was probably doubting it now. But Eve couldn't help wondering where it had got to and why Kitty had been so upset with Bonnie on the stairs. It had been when Bonnie turned around. Could the sight of the necklace have made her lose control?

The police sealed off the east wing of the castle where Julian, Nate, Bonnie and Freya had rooms. They'd have to move to the west wing overnight. It would be weird enough for Freya to live on site again after her husband's death, and now this.

The villagers had long since gone when Eve finally went to her room, Gus behind her, almost too tired to mount the stairs. The police had spent longer with her, Luke and the permanent residents than anyone else. It made sense, given their close contact with Kitty in the run-up to her death. After Palmer had finished, he'd asked them all to stay on site until they were given permission to leave. He'd grovelled embarrassingly to Julian and Nate, sneered at Eve, and been perfunctory with everyone else. Apparently, he needed to 'process their paperwork' before he could let them go. Eve hoped he was going to think about what they'd said too.

The image of Kitty still filled her head. She'd finally returned to her family home. Felt comfort, Eve guessed, but also pain at the loss of her grandparents. Her time to face up to the past had been so short. It was achingly sad. She wondered how the police had decided it was murder and who had opened the safety grille.

There were so many questions, both about the past and the here and now. She messaged Robin before she went to bed to tell him what had happened, then sent Portia Coldwell at *Icon* an update. She could still write the feature on Farfield if the business went ahead, but the immediate job now would be Kitty Marchant's obituary. Many of her closest contacts had something to hide. Perhaps Eve's interviews might reveal the killer. The thought filled her with unease, but she couldn't turn her back. Not when she'd seen so much.

12

Eve's mobile rang early the following morning. She'd left it on top of a chest of drawers; the best place to catch what coverage there was.

She leaped up to answer. A moment later, Gus was scampering around her ankles. He must have heard Robin's voice faintly down the line. She patted him with her free hand.

'*You're still at the castle?*' he said after checking she was okay.

'Yes. I haven't seen anyone this morning. It's very quiet but the CSIs are still down in the grounds.' She'd seen them going to and fro.

'*I'm coming back.*'

'There's no need. You've got more than enough to contend with.'

'*I don't have to be in court again until tomorrow morning.*'

It would be so good to see him. So nice not to have to wait. But she pulled back from the brink. 'Honestly, Robin, I'm fine. You'll be back the day after tomorrow if everything goes to schedule.' As ever, thoughts of the trial made her feel sick. She took a deep breath and focused on the matter in hand. Their relationship wouldn't work if she lost her independence, or if she held him back. He'd waited for years to bring this network to justice. What if a lack of preparation time today affected the outcome? And besides, she resented it if people took her for granted. She couldn't bear it if Robin started to feel like that about her. 'I'll be careful. I promise. I imagine the police will send me home today. I can't see the retreat opening for a while after what's happened either.'

There was a long pause. '*Okay. But please keep me posted. I'll let you know what Greg says.*'

'Sure. I love you.'

'*I love you too.*'

After they'd hung up, Eve saw she had a voicemail waiting – it was DC Dawkins, confirming that she was free to leave the castle if she wanted. As Eve showered and got ready for the day, she was full of mixed feelings. Part of her was desperate to get home, away from the tragedy that had engulfed Farfield. But she knew she'd be more likely to find out the truth about Kitty's death if she stayed put. Observing the household might make all the difference. And on a practical level, it would work well if Portia gave her the go-ahead to write Kitty's obituary. Most of the people she'd want to talk to were right here. She sighed. Agonising over it was pointless. It wasn't her decision. Julian and Nate would likely want her and Luke gone.

It was still warm, and she put on a sleeveless fitted cotton top and wide-legged trousers before taking Gus for a quick walk in the grounds. She saw no one on her way out and kept away from the areas where the police were at work, walking through the old deer park on the west side of the castle instead. She could see the hunting lodge in the distance. Eve gathered it had been sold off decades earlier and a young couple with a baby lived there now. It was an isolated place. They must be wondering who was guilty, and if they were in danger.

Back inside, she found the dog bowls and pet food in a

cupboard in the boot room. The previous day they'd been put out ready and she wondered if that had been Kitty's careful attention to detail. She couldn't see Bonnie going anywhere near dog food.

Eve found the lovely informal dining room again and cereal on the dresser together with milk in a fridge next door. She couldn't help imagining the place when Kitty and Nate were little. Their grandparents beaming at them as they ate their breakfast. Feeling lucky to have them during the school holidays, with no idea of the trouble that lay ahead.

And Freya Hardwicke too, sitting down to eat with her husband before he died.

Before everything went wrong. And now it was a million times worse.

After she'd eaten, she washed up, Gus pottering after her, his paws clicking on the tiled floor. The castle was utterly quiet. She wasn't surprised no one had appeared. Maybe she could find Bonnie and see if Nate and Julian had made any decision about her and Luke's presence.

She walked towards the reception area and heard a kettle boiling in a room next door. The door was ajar and she knocked.

Bonnie appeared, smart in a high-necked figure-hugging dress, a gold chain around her neck. It was much more her style than the art deco pendant she'd worn the day before. Eve could see office equipment behind her and two workstations. A moment later, Freya Hardwicke appeared from the direction of the bathroom and blinked at Eve.

'Oh my goodness. I'm so sorry. Have you found some breakfast?'

So she'd started as planned then, despite what had happened. Eve nodded. 'Please don't worry. You must all be in shock.'

At that moment the phone rang, and Freya picked up. There would be plenty to deal with. The press – who were on the line now, by the sound of it – and quite possibly cancellations too. The rural hideaway the retreat offered was in jeopardy.

'We simply don't know yet,' Freya was saying. 'No, I'm sorry. There's nothing I can tell you.' Eve wondered how many times she'd had to repeat it and if Kitty's death would be enough to ruin the business before it got started.

Could Ella Tyndall have killed Kitty, anticipating that very thing? It seemed unthinkable. Eve thought of Ella the school-teacher, mucking in with village events, bringing her class on walks around Saxford.

But in the background Eve also remembered the way she'd lost control when her bid to buy Farfield was trumped. How she'd screamed at Kitty on the village green, then broken down.

Eve shifted her focus back to Bonnie. She wanted to find out where she stood, and to understand the PA's role the previous night.

'How are you?' She looked into Bonnie's eyes. She'd been huddled up the night before, as though trauma had left her cold and shaky, but she'd looked angry. 'It must have been terrible, finding Kitty's body.'

'It was an awful shock, but I'm better now, thank you.' Bonnie's chest rose and fell quickly, but her expression was cool.

Eve wondered about the emotion she was clearly suppressing. Was she guilty? She might have wished Kitty dead plenty of times. She certainly wanted Julian for herself, but he was stalling. She had a motive.

'It's probably too soon to ask, but I wondered about my position here. The police have cleared me to leave, and I imagine Farfield's opening will be on hold indefinitely, but I'm happy to see out my stay if you'd still like me to prepare my article.' She lowered her voice. 'It's likely I'll be tasked with writing Kitty's obituary too. I could do that from home, but a lot of the people I'll want to interview are here.'

As Eve stood, waiting for an answer, her desire to stay intensified. She'd seen and heard things in the last days that no one else had. She'd passed most of it on to Olivia Dawkins, but that was no substitute for witnessing it first-hand. If she stayed on site, what she saw next might link with what she already knew. But it was more than that. Kitty had been wronged and Eve knew it. Blasted Bonnie and horrible Julian had been carrying on behind her back, taking advantage of her trusting nature. Eve felt for her, remembering her own pain when she'd discovered her ex had been cheating. She hadn't managed to help Kitty when she was alive. Justice for her mattered.

Blasted Bonnie wrinkled her nose. 'I don't know yet, but Nate and Julian told us to postpone guests who're booked in next week as well as this. Some of them have cancelled of their own accord. Nate said they'd make a decision later this morning.'

Eve nodded. 'Thanks. I need to nip home for a couple of things, but I'll be back to find out what they think. Please pass on my condolences in the meantime.' She was keen to talk to some of her neighbours about the night before. If they had useful memories, it was best to get them fresh.

Bonnie nodded.

'I like your necklace, by the way.'

The PA gave her an odd look. 'Thanks.'

Eve felt like a continuity announcer, desperately trying to make a tenuous link, but she needed to ask. 'I really loved the pendant you wore last night, too. Art deco, wasn't it? But you'd lost it by the end of the evening.' She let the sentence hang.

Bonnie frowned. 'It fell off somewhere. I expect it'll turn up, though I'm not worried. It's not one of my favourites.' She gave Eve a long look. 'The police asked me about it too.'

Behind Bonnie, Eve saw Freya glance round, then busy herself with some papers.

'Really? That's odd.' Eve assumed Olivia Dawkins had kept her name out of it and silently thanked her.

'It's not impossible someone walked off with it,' Bonnie added. 'Julian's laptop went missing last night too. With that number of people and an open invitation, what can you expect?'

The phone in the office rang again and Freya picked up.

Eve felt affronted on her neighbours' behalf. She had an open house twice a year in aid of children's charities and had never had anything stolen. But here there'd been a murder and at least one theft, all on the same night. It would be a heck of a coincidence if they weren't related.

13

Eve said goodbye and set off for Saxford St Peter with Gus. She'd messaged Viv earlier and arranged to meet her at Monty's teashop.

'You can scamper around in Viv's garden,' Eve said as she put Gus in his travel harness. 'And then I'll take you for a walk around the village green.'

There was a giddy look in his eye and his tail thumped. Viv's cottage was next door to the teashop and the gardens adjoined. The only downside was her cats, but they tended to keep their distance when Gus was around.

Half an hour later, Eve was sitting opposite Viv in Monty's garden. They were being waited on by Lovely Lars. He was supposed to be travelling around Europe but had lingered in Saxford for over a year now, thanks to the charms of Tammy. Eve was anxiously anticipating the summer, when Tammy's course would finish. They might lose both of them at once.

Eve and Viv's table had a rose-pink cloth, matching Viv's current hair colour, and a ribbon-decorated jam jar at its centre, full of pink hardy geraniums. Memories of her first visit to Monty's about four years earlier filled Eve's head. She'd felt at home the moment she'd stepped inside and seen the cheerful mismatched crockery and Viv, standing behind the counter in her tie-dye top and jeans. She'd been so open and welcoming that they'd gelled within half an hour. It had been late May then too, in the wake of another murder...

Also round the table today were Eve's neighbours, Sylvia and Daphne.

'We bumped into each other outside Moira's,' Daphne was saying, 'and Viv said you were after everyone's memories of last night.' She shook her head. 'The writers' retreat's caused so much division in the village and now this. I was so disappointed when Ella's offer was turned down that I got a bit tearful. To have the promise of beautiful walks around there torn away like that. Now I feel terrible. Almost as if I'd ill-wished the place.'

'We all did,' Sylvia said robustly. 'If ill-wishing was that effective, I'd be surrounded by dead bodies. Kitty was in an odd position, of course, coming back to a family home that was sold from under her grandparents' feet.'

'She was young when it happened,' Daphne said. 'And grieving for her mum. It wasn't her decision.'

'But she never protested against it, unlike Nate, who was younger still. And she never made up with Sophie and Daniel. I can still remember hearing about her and her dad watching as the vans came to take their stuff away. Jo said she looked triumphant.'

'There must have been a powerful reason behind that,' Eve said. 'Even if it wasn't justified.'

'You'd better ask Jo this evening.' Viv took a mouthful of tea. 'I've got us booked in for a Holmes and Watson session at the Cross Keys.'

'Nice of you to let me know.' Eve counted to ten.

Sylvia laughed, but then sobered. 'All I know is that Sophie and Daniel would never have a word said against Benet. If anyone alluded to the situation, they'd say it was a misunderstanding, and that he was grieving. From my perspective, that excuse had to do some very heavy lifting.'

Daphne shook her head. 'I visited Sophie and Daniel at the house they moved to after Farfield. It was a tiny, run-down place with just enough room to accommodate them and Nate. I spotted a handful of photos of Kitty once. They must have been reliving happier days. It was awful, because I caught Sophie's eye and neither of us knew what to say. She turned away and I could see she was trying not to cry. It was such a pity.'

'That's families for you,' said Sylvia. 'And the longer an estrangement goes on, the harder it is for anyone to make peace. Then the older generation shuffles off and it's all too late.'

'Very cheery,' said Viv, taking a bite of the fruit tart she had in front of her.

Sylvia laughed again.

'I think you're right, though,' Eve said. 'I suspect Kitty regretted not making a move. She said she *needed* to be back at Farfield. I wonder if she felt she had to. To face up to what happened. Not let herself off the hook.'

They were silent for a moment.

'Any idea which of them did it?' Sylvia asked at last, picking up her teacup.

Eve took a bite of tart. The sweetness of the pastry and the tang of fruit helped her focus. 'There are plenty of people with motives.' She filled Sylvia and Daphne in on what she'd seen, then sighed.

'Bonnie's top of my list. She told Julian her patience wasn't limitless. Killing to achieve her goal would be extreme, but there was such a look of malice in her eye when Kitty caught her on the stairs last night.' Eve couldn't begin to imagine crossing that terrible line, but if Bonnie had lost faith in Julian's promises, she could see her losing control. She seemed the sort who expected to get her own way.

'Ella's problematic too. She was deeply invested in her own

vision for Farfield and I think she loved Sophie and Daniel. I've always liked her, but likeable people can do terrible things.' Robin reminded her of that constantly. 'She could go either way. On a practical point, she knew the house well when the Marchants lived there. She might know where they kept the keys to the grille and it's possible they're still in the same place.'

'Good point.' Viv sipped her tea.

'As for the others, Freya and Kitty's rift sounds old. I've no idea if it amounted to a motive for murder, but even if it did, why act now? I'd like to find out more, but she's not high on my list.

'And then Luke's antagonism towards Nate and Julian and his interest in Kitty leaves me wondering. Something's off. I saw him go inside the icehouse yesterday afternoon. He took ages to reappear. I can't help wondering if he was examining the safety grille. He was crying after they found Kitty's body, but I don't know why he'd want her dead.

'As for Julian himself, I don't like him, but that doesn't make him a killer.'

'He'd have found it hard to divorce Kitty and keep his job at Farfield,' Viv said.

'True. If he wanted to marry Bonnie, he might figure he could fake an accident for Kitty and get away with it. But I doubt he wants to make the relationship permanent. Bonnie seems keener than him.'

'What about money?' Viv asked. 'Any financial angle?' She'd taken out a notebook and pen, a habit she'd only adopted in the last year or so. It had been an unexpected development and a leaf out of Eve's book. Eve ought to approve, but secretly, seeing all the scribbles and crossings out made her twitch.

'Possibly, though I'm not sure how much Kitty had to leave. She and Julian had been living modestly until Nate bought Farfield. It makes me curious about Bonnie. I wonder how Julian could afford her.'

Eve had already made a note to investigate financial motives in the spreadsheet she'd started on her laptop.

'There's nothing suspicious about Nate?' Viv was still making notes.

'Not as far as I know, except he was close to the icehouse when Kitty's body was discovered. Going back to Julian, I'd swear he was acting, when he heard Kitty was dead.'

'You don't think it was a surprise?' Viv gave a passing bee a gentle steer out of the way.

'I'm not sure. He kept hiding his face. But I don't believe he was upset. And dashing to the bathroom to be sick felt fake... If he was that overwhelmed, you'd think he'd make for a nearby bush.'

Daphne frowned. 'That's what he said he was doing?'

Eve nodded.

Her neighbour's face creased with worry. 'That's odd. I was in the bathroom when Kitty was found. I had no idea what had happened until I went outside, but Julian Fisher dashed past me. He went to his study. I remember because I heard him cursing. When I realised Kitty was dead, I assumed he hadn't heard. But he must have. He sounded angry. Scared perhaps. But not upset.'

14

When Eve got back to Farfield, she saw a small pile of floral tributes outside the castle gates. It seemed the locals had started to forget their entrenched feelings in the wake of the tragedy. She stopped her car for a moment and got out to look.

In loving memory, Mark and Jill.

Remember seeing you here as a child.
Rest in peace, Fiona and Bob.

Sleep well. The Grahams.

Eve shivered. It made her uneasy when people called death anything other than what it was. To her the idea of a permanent sleep from which you never awoke was more frightening than simply not being there anymore.

Freya Hardwicke came to meet her on the drive.

'Nate and Julian have been talking about how to proceed. They'd like to see you in the sitting room. I've called Luke Shipley in too.'

'Of course.' Eve locked her car and walked into the castle with Gus. Luke must have been waiting on their decision as well.

Nate looked almost as pale as the white sofa he sat on.

'I'm so very sorry for your loss,' Eve said to him and Julian, who sat in an armchair to his right.

They both nodded. It was Julian who thanked her.

Luke entered just after Eve. He looked ashen and his eyes were bloodshot. He didn't express his sympathy, but dropped into a seat. He glanced from one of them to the other, his gaze sharp.

'As you can imagine,' Nate said, 'it's been hard to decide what to do. I can't think of opening until Kitty's killer's caught. We'll offer guests postponed slots with extras thrown in to compensate for the inconvenience. Some of them may pull out altogether, which is understandable, but we think, in the long term, we'll be able to continue.' He put his head in his hands. 'It's horrible to have to think so coolly, but the decisions need making now.'

Julian patted him on the arm.

'We won't want your splashes going out imminently, of course,' Nate said, 'but you're welcome to stay and write them up in advance if you feel you can. The police are still busy in parts of the house, but they've said it's okay.' He turned to Luke. 'I know they've asked you to stay local anyway. The least we can do is put you up.' Then his eyes fell on her. 'I realise you're close to home, Eve. You might prefer to go, but we're happy to have you.'

It was the last thing Eve had expected. It didn't make sense. Why get them to stay on in an empty venue and in the strangest of circumstances? Did they think she or Luke might be guilty, and want to watch them? Or was one of them a killer, too nervous to let them go in case they'd seen something? If they became a threat, it would be easier to deal with them on site.

'Ella Tyndall was due to give a history tour tomorrow,' Nate went on. 'We'll ask her to come anyway, so you can see what the guests will see.'

'Ella's giving a history tour?' *What on earth?* Eve would have thought she'd see it as colluding with the enemy. But it had been Kitty who'd borne the brunt of her anger, and she was dead.

Nate nodded. 'She knows this place inside out. It feels wrong to carry on in some ways, but taking a step back, I think it's better. I need a focus until we can sort out the funeral. I expect it's the same for you, Julian. And you won't have to do everything twice,' he added, turning to Eve and Luke. '*Icon* and *Cascade* can hold back publication to coincide with the delayed opening. Does that suit you both?'

Luke was nodding slowly, as though he was processing some thought or plan. Was he guilty and trapped, or innocent, and after information? 'As a friend, I'd like to be here with you.' There was something slightly threatening in his tone.

Perhaps he'd work on a gossip piece, now the only member of the household he'd seemed to like was dead. Allowing him to stay seemed like a big risk, given his animosity towards Nate and Julian. They must have an ulterior motive.

'That's fine by me too.' Eve kept her voice neutral. 'It might be helpful, because I'd like to interview you about Kitty, if I may.' She hesitated. '*Icon* have asked me to write her obituary.' Portia had texted to confirm it now.

Julian blinked and Nate's mouth opened. Eve wasn't surprised and wished there was a gentler way of asking. They'd been dealing with the police, the press, business decisions and the like. Now Eve was forcing their attention on what they'd lost. Nate blinked away a tear.

'Of course. It would be good to pay tribute to her,' he said.

'Oh, for sure,' Julian added.

Eve saw the look Nate shot him. Doubt. They might be

friends, but he was troubled. Eve wasn't surprised. Julian wasn't hitting the right tone. Whereas there was no suspicion in Julian's eyes as he looked at Nate. Either he was guilty himself or convinced Nate had to be innocent for other reasons.

Eve watched Luke ahead of her as they left the room. She'd need to talk to him too. He'd only just met Kitty – he wasn't a natural interviewee – but she'd find a way.

It had been clear from the moment he'd arrived that he disliked Julian and Nate. Hated them maybe. Was there any chance he'd tried to get close to Kitty then killed her to hurt them? But if so, what had caused the hatred in the first place? If Nate was right, he'd overheard them insulting him, but surely that wasn't enough. There was a lot more to find out.

There was just time to start some research into Kitty's life before lunch. Eve sat in one of the writing rooms, her laptop on an old oak table, the sun streaming in, dust motes stirring in the air. The smell of old furniture and polish. Outside, the scene was as tranquil as ever: the lawn such an intense and beautiful green. It made the sight of Kitty's face on Eve's computer screen even harder to bear. She ought to be there, wandering the grounds of her grandparents' house, pottering in and out of the exercise rooms. Making her peace with the past.

Eve shook her head and started googling. The only way to help was to dig for every detail and try to work out who'd done this to her.

Her Wikipedia page told Eve she'd lived in a commune with her father after the loss of her mother, who'd died of an overdose. Kitty had just turned sixteen. Farfield had been sold just under a year later. There was a photo of Kitty during her punk phase at eighteen, so different from how she'd been later. She'd worked in a boxing club back then, running classes for a charity focused on young people at risk, and started to develop exercise programmes there.

'The boxing was a fantastic way to bring people together

and let them lose themselves, working out all their tension,' she was quoted as saying. 'But it didn't suit everyone. I started other classes to draw people in.'

Eve watched a clip of her on YouTube. *'We've all got stuff stuck inside us,'* she said. *'Problems, things we regret, frustrations. Talking helps, but letting rip with a punchbag or running like your life depends on it can be good too.'* She looked serious and Eve was sure she'd battled her own demons. But of course, her thoughts were coloured by what she knew. The family rift.

Kitty had become famous when she was only twenty-three, a year after the death of her grandparents, one from a heart attack, one from cancer. She must surely have felt that loss, despite the estrangement.

Eve read about her rise to stardom. She remembered Kitty's self-deprecating story about the journalist who'd coined the 'soaring, grounded' phrase. She found the same tale online, and the original review by the journalist. Kitty had been invited onto a regional news programme to talk about her charity work, then a national outlet had got her to do a demonstration on TV. One of the presenters had used the soaring, grounded quote and endorsed Kitty.

After that, things had moved quickly. She'd got a publishing deal and a TV programme and her style had gone mainstream. Eve wondered if the TV producers had told her to lose the punk image to broaden her appeal. Looking at the photos of young Kitty, she found it hard to imagine her accepting their interference. She seemed a world away from the anxious, diffident woman she'd become: fierce and determined, nobody's possession. What had changed her? Eve would have to find out.

By the time she was thirty she'd sold hundreds of thousands of books, but her exercise programme was going out of fashion. Someone had started a hula craze and CrossFit was all the rage. The contracts for books and TV dried up but she was still a known face. She must have amassed plenty of money. There were no signs she'd lived an extravagant lifestyle.

She'd married Julian Fisher at the age of thirty-four, just three years earlier. He was sixteen years older than her. Eve couldn't imagine him wooing her, but hindsight was a wonderful thing. Julian was good-looking and he could be charming. Plus, he was revered.

They'd lived in France for a year in a beautiful villa in the countryside. There was a photograph of it in a colour supplement. Eve wondered if it was Julian or Kitty's money that had paid for it. On their return to England, they'd occupied a London flat for a further twelve months, then moved to the two-up, two-down in Suffolk. By that point, Kitty had been making a living teaching local classes.

Eve found reports that she'd been planning to set up a drug rehab charity, returning to her philanthropic roots. Perhaps she'd saved some money from her heyday with the project in mind.

'She was planning to use a trust fund set up by her maternal grandparents. She only came into it when she was thirty-five.'

The voice made her jump out of her skin.

15

Eve looked behind her.

'I'm sorry, I didn't mean to startle you.'

It was Luke Shipley, the slanting sun emphasising his sculpted cheekbones and reddish hair. Eve had left the door open as she worked, hoping to hear what went on in the castle, but her research had had her absorbed. She was shaken not to have noticed him enter the room.

She took a deep breath. 'That's okay. What did you say?'

'Kitty was planning to use a trust fund from her mum's parents to set up the charity you're reading about. She wanted to ring-fence the money for the project, make it legally binding. I don't know if she got that far. Julian will be a rich man if she didn't.'

He said the words slowly and with emphasis. Because he hated Julian, or because he was deflecting attention? Eve was sure the former was true. She didn't know about the latter.

'She told you about it? But wasn't this the first time you'd met?'

He nodded. 'That's right. But she was easy to talk to. She explained the whole thing. It's a lot of money, I gather.'

Yet she and Julian had been living frugally before they'd come to the castle. Eve bet that had irritated him.

'You don't seem to like Julian and Nate very much.'

He shrugged. 'Just personal taste.'

Eve remembered their conversation about Luke. How he'd probably overheard them insulting him.

'But you keep in touch.'

'We run into each other from time to time. Julian assumes I'm desperate to maintain the friendship because he's so big-headed.'

But Julian had made it clear that Luke's behaviour towards him and Nate had changed on this latest visit. It rang true; she'd seen his surprise.

'Do you know if Kitty was planning to put some of her past earnings into the charity too? It'll be relevant for the obituary I need to write.'

'I'm not sure, but I read somewhere that Julian had debts. I suspect she helped pay them off before she found out what he was really like.'

'You think she regretted her marriage?'

He raised an eyebrow. 'Wouldn't you?'

No question.

He just nodded when she didn't reply.

Eve hesitated. 'I saw you watching Kitty while she sat in the formal garden.' She wanted to see how he'd explain it.

He paused too. 'I wanted to talk to her. I felt sorry for her, but I wasn't sure if I was doing the right thing. I went for it in the end.'

He sounded honest, and it was plausible. But that wasn't her only worry. Why had he spent so long inside the icehouse when there was nothing to see except the grille that blocked off the well? And why had Kitty told him about her charity plans? Eve couldn't help wondering if they'd met before, despite what Luke claimed.

There was something he wasn't telling her, and it must concern Julian, Kitty, *and* Nate. But was it relevant to Kitty's death?

Some in-depth research was called for.

Freya had somehow found time to sort out lunch. Perhaps the local cook Julian referred to had brought food in. There was a cold collation of freshly baked rolls, artisan cheeses, Italian meats, olives and salads. Luke didn't appear, though. Eve could see him through the window, pacing the grounds, head down, shoulders hunched.

Beyond the open doorway, Freya was exchanging quiet words with Nate. Behind them, Bonnie tried to catch Julian as he passed, but he ploughed on. Eve wondered about the state of their relationship since Kitty's death.

She started to research Luke on her phone as she ate, Gus sitting at her feet. It wasn't much help. His LinkedIn told her he'd studied English at Oxford University, then written features for a local magazine, before moving to a lesser-known national and then to *Cascade*. She couldn't find anything that indicated he'd met Kitty before coming to Farfield – no connections on social media or joint mentions. But that didn't mean anything. She needed more. Her mind drifted to Portia Coldwell. She operated in the same world as Luke. Perhaps she could put out feelers. See if there was any gossip floating around. Eve could claim it was for the obituary. Understanding Luke and Kitty's relationship was a reasonable goal. She sent off an email, then got ready to walk Gus.

It was a relief to get out of the castle. Eve went across the grounds and through the old deer park until she reached the former hunting lodge. On her way through a field, using a public right of way, she came across a fresh bouquet of flowers. There was no mistaking the way it had been put, upright against a tree. It was a memorial, just like the ones she'd seen outside the main gates to Farfield, but without the traditional note attached. Was this from someone looking on from afar who didn't want to approach the castle? Or a Farfield insider who felt compelled to leave a tribute but wanted to do it secretly? Luke Shipley sprang to mind. Maybe he *had* known Kitty before he came to Suffolk. Perhaps they'd had an affair. It would fit with his level of upset, but after a moment she dismissed the idea. If he was that familiar with her, why would he stand watching her like that from the yew hedge? They'd arrange to meet somewhere secret.

But he could have been obsessed with her. Perhaps he'd killed her, then left the flowers privately as he dealt with his guilt.

Back at the house, Nate met Eve in the hall.

'You said you wanted to talk about Kitty. Would now be a good time?'

'That would be perfect, if you're up to it?'

He nodded. 'I'd like to. I can't think of anything else, anyway.'

They made their way to the sitting room with the squashy white sofas again, crossing paths with Julian as they walked through the reception area. Eve saw Freya turn her back on him as he approached. It was Bonnie who dealt with him, though the atmosphere between them prickled with tension.

'Forty-three calls so far...' Eve heard her say.

The looks they exchanged were full of hostility, their movements stiff. Eve wondered if it was temporary, and down to the strain, or if their affair was over.

'It must be so hard for you,' Eve said to Nate as he closed the door behind them. 'I'm very sorry.'

He nodded. 'Kitty's always been there. Throughout our

childhood she'd do anything for me, even though we' – he hesitated – 'we took different directions.'

The family rift. 'Could you tell me about that?' Eve took out her notepad.

He paused but then nodded. 'I don't often repeat the story, but you need to understand.'

16

Nate sat forward on the sofa, his shoulders tense. 'My grandparents ran an open house here. If a local was in trouble, they were invited in. Neighbours who'd fallen on hard times, friends who needed sanctuary for whatever reason. It's not as if Farfield lacks space. But Dad hated it, growing up; he was jealous, plain and simple.' He sighed. 'My father's never liked sharing. He used to tell me stories of Granny and Gramps's "waifs and strays". I could almost see the bile dripping from his lips.'

It was a vivid image. Nate's dad wasn't the only one who was bitter, though perhaps Nate had good cause.

'Your grandparents sound like good people.'

'They were. I loved them so much.' There were tears in his eyes. 'They tried to build bridges with Dad when he married Mum. They were desperate to shore up the relationship.

'Mum was sweet but troubled. Her parents were rich too, but not loving like Granny and Gramps. They had strings of affairs and spent their time arguing and travelling. Mum barely saw them. She got miserable and fell in with a bad lot at her posh school.' He looked at Eve, his eyes huge and sad. 'Drugs.

She got hooked, then clean before she met Dad. But when their marriage got rocky, she relapsed. I was only young, but I could see Granny and Gramps were worried sick. They tried to help, and that was when things got worse.'

'But why?'

'Mum was far gone. Granny and Gramps got professional advice, then offered to pay for residential care. A place for Mum to dry out. She had money of her own, but she lacked the will and Dad wanted her at home. I believe she might have lived if he'd let them talk to her. She liked them. I think she'd have gone with their plan. They would have looked after us too, if Dad wanted.'

'He wouldn't entertain the idea?'

Nate shook his head. 'He told us Granny and Gramps wanted to lock Mum up. Split the family. That they'd never loved him and never liked her.'

'And Kitty believed him?'

'I'm afraid so. It was like she'd been brainwashed. But she was constantly in his presence. It was different for me. Granny and Gramps paid for me to go to boarding school. I was out from under his thumb. They offered to fund Kitty too, but she refused. Thought she was striking out on her own. Staying true to her teenage socialist principles. Dad applauded her decision and hated me for leaving. He said it had been another attempt to divide us. Well, I guess it did, but it needn't have. Every crack in our family was made by my father.'

He shook his head. 'I was desperately homesick at school and oh boy, did Dad make me feel his disapproval. I let his attitude affect me in those days.'

He still did, judging by his white knuckles.

'Dad was failing to make a living as a modern-day beat poet. Teaching the odd evening class. But we weren't hard up, because of Mum's money.

'It was Kitty who kept me from going off the rails at school. She was four years older than me. We wrote and called and she told me all the goings-on in London.

'When I was twelve, my mother died of an overdose. We were all devastated, Dad included. They might have rowed, but he relied on her emotionally. I came home from school for a bit, but I was so angry. His selfishness had contributed to her death.' His head was in his hands. 'Dad said I should switch to the local school. And he decided we should move into a commune.'

'Ah.' Each to their own, but it would have been another massive change on top of everything else.

'I know. It was in a huge London house and full of friends of his and my mother's. He said he needed the support. My grandparents were aching for him. I could see that. They wanted us all to move here. They went to check on the commune and asked some surreptitious questions. That got back to Dad and all hell let loose. He went at them with all kinds of accusations: that they were trying to control his life and our lives too. That they were spying on him. He said life at Farfield growing up had been "just like living in a commune".' Nate was breathing hard. 'I honestly wondered if he'd decided to move simply to make that point. With the cash Mum left he could have bought us a castle of our own and more.

'It was just under a year later that the final bust-up happened.'

Eve waited for him to continue.

'Granny and Gramps had tried to help so many people over the years. In every other case, the recipients had been wonderful, but then they met someone who took advantage. I won't bore you with the details, but this guy ripped them off for every penny they had. It was true that they were unguarded. That's just what they were like. Suddenly, they had nothing. They had to explain the situation to my dad via a solicitor. He wouldn't even see them. They told him they'd have to sell Farfield. They were happy to know he was well provided for. My mother left him everything, and it was a lot, believe me. They didn't expect Dad to bail them out, but they couldn't possibly go ahead without telling him. I begged them not to sell up. I worried it was so they could afford to keep me in school, but looking back, I realise it enabled them to eat, too.

'Meanwhile, my dad told us they were after Mum's money now she was dead. Picking over what she'd left, like vultures. He chipped away at Kitty, convincing her that Granny and Gramps had hated our mother. He'd cut them off completely. But he "allowed" us to choose. That was the way he put it. I knew there'd be far-reaching consequences either way. The rest is history. Kitty opted to stay with him and he bathed her in his poisonous thoughts.'

'And you went back to school?'

He nodded. 'Granny and Gramps insisted. And in the holidays I made my home with them.'

'Your father cut you off too?' It must have been so hard, to lose his mother like that, then be forced to make such a choice. He'd only been twelve.

'Not entirely. I saw him a couple of times a year. It was like coming face to face with a polite but unimpressed stranger.'

'I'm sorry. It sounds painful. And what about Kitty?'

'We'd meet on neutral territory. I tried to change her mind about our grandparents, but Dad kept up his stories about them. How offhand they'd been, yet so controlling. He told her they'd hired a private detective to check on him. The awkward thing was, it was true. But only because they were crazy with worry.'

Eve tried to imagine how she'd feel if one of her adult twins cut her off. She couldn't imagine the agony. She wouldn't want to interfere – certainly wouldn't hire a detective. Heck, she hoped she wouldn't. But she could see it. She knew she'd be desperate to make sure they were okay.

'In the end, Kitty and I agreed not to discuss Granny and

Gramps. It was the one thing we rowed about. Even when my grandmother got cancer, Kitty wouldn't see her. She and my grandfather died within a couple of months of each other, without a reconciliation.'

'But Kitty regretted that eventually?'

He nodded. 'Dad didn't like it when *Soaring, Grounded* took off. He became almost as distant with her as he'd been with me.' He smiled, but his expression was bitter. 'His poetry's never made an impact. He's come to the conclusion that anything popular is crass and flawed. And he hates other people's success. He loathes my job in the City, of course, but I don't care. I've got past all that.'

His adrenaline was making her own shoot up.

'Very gradually, Kitty realised what she'd lost. It hit her hard. When I saw the chance to buy this place, she decided she needed to face it.'

It would make a statement to their father, too.

It was time to put the question she'd promised to ask. 'Are you planning to make it more open to the locals, like your grand-parents did?'

To Eve's surprise, Nate nodded instantly. 'In fact – and this is definitely off the record – I only plan to run this place as a luxury retreat for the first year or two. It'll get a lot of publicity while it's exclusive. After that, I want half the places subsidised by bursaries. I've created a fund and I'll add to it with the initial profits. Almost no one knows, and Julian certainly doesn't.' He sounded tired. 'He'd worry about his fee, but he needn't. I've told him I've got it all worked out and I've a trust fund coming from my mum's parents in a couple of years.' He sighed. 'I shouldn't need it, but it's an extra cushion. When I reminded Julian, it was enough to make him relax.'

'Reminded him?'

'Kitty already had hers, and the family wealth's never been much of a secret.'

Julian had known the added benefits of marrying Kitty, then, even after her career faded. So much for thinking he must have loved her for her own sake. The pig.

'As for inviting the locals to roam the grounds,' Nate went on, 'he'll accept it by the time it happens. I know him. With his feet under the table, he'll be too comfortable to rock the boat.'

'But do you need his buy-in? You've funded it all.'

He nodded. 'But people wouldn't come if it weren't for Julian. Between ourselves, when my plans for this place leaked, he got a rival offer from another retreat. Somewhere less exclusive, but they matched my pay and it was closer to London. It's the cachet of this place and Kitty's feelings that kept him on board. I want to keep it that way. I won't let this place fail.' That last sentence sounded final. Eve wondered how much of Nate's determination was down to his dad. He'd rescued the family home his father could have saved.

'You and Julian are good friends?' She needed to understand the dynamics.

'We hit it off when we met. He's supported my writing. He can be a lot of fun.'

The answer seemed evasive. She imagined Julian's contacts and good opinion had been tempting, though after four years, they hadn't yet made Nate's books popular. 'You were pleased when he and Kitty decided to marry? Their partnership seemed strong?'

'Yes, I think so.' There was a long pause. 'I'm sorry. The police asked me the same thing. It's made me wonder, when I hadn't before.'

Presumably the local force had followed up on the exchange she'd heard between Julian and Bonnie. Eve wondered how far to go. 'Bonnie's very beautiful.'

Nate shook his head quickly. 'I'm sure he wouldn't. He can't have. And besides, I've watched Julian since Kitty's death.

He's kept himself to himself, and he and Bonnie? They barely get on.'

He was plucking at his sleeve. Did he really believe that or was he frightened? Frightened that Julian had betrayed Kitty and that he was responsible. He'd brought him into Kitty's world, and now she was dead.

'Shall we walk around the garden as we talk?' Nate asked. 'I'm finding it hard to sit still.'

Eve followed him outside, with Gus at her heels. The CSIs had departed now, but she could still see them in her mind's eye. Nate must too.

She checked over her shoulder, then said: 'I imagine you and Kitty shared almost everything.'

He nodded. 'We did. And if we didn't tell voluntarily the other one would usually guess.'

'I hear Kitty was planning to ring-fence her trust-fund money to start up a drugs charity.' Her mother's troubled life must have influenced her. 'I suppose you knew about that?'

He looked surprised. 'The charity idea made it into the press, but not the stuff about the trust fund. Where did you hear it?'

'Luke says Kitty told him.'

His brow furrowed. 'That's odd. They hardly knew each other. But it's true about the trust fund. I didn't know about the ring-fencing, but it makes sense.'

'So you don't know if the arrangements were finalised?'

Nate gave her a sharp look. 'One of the villagers was talking about you yesterday. I know you've been involved in murder enquiries before.' At last, he sighed. 'I don't know about the paperwork.'

Their eyes met for a moment.

Eve found it easy to imagine Julian paying someone to kill Kitty. It was harder to see him getting his hands dirty, but if the trust-fund money was substantial and time was running out, he might. Independence for life would be quite a prize given his limited income and apparent love of luxury.

'Kitty only came into her money a couple of years ago,' Nate said, drawing Eve back to the conversation. 'Mum's parents put it in trust until she was thirty-five.' His jaw was set. 'I'd been wondering whether to go in with Kitty when I got mine. Support her charity.'

She'd been so focused on his story that she'd stopped noticing her surroundings. As she looked up, they walked through some trees and reached a sundial in a small clearing, the date 1640 chiselled into it. Eve got her bearings. The icehouse would be off to the right, beyond the trees.

'This is beautiful.'

Nate nodded. 'I love it. Kitty and I used to race each other here when we first arrived. It was a ritual.'

She watched as a tear slid down his cheek. She had the urge to comfort him but sensed he wouldn't want it.

'I was here when Bonnie screamed last night,' he said. 'I'd come for some peace and quiet. A sort of pilgrimage. It's where I go to mark anything that matters. Julian was celebrating hard, and everyone was focused on the retreat. I wanted to think about what's really important.'

He turned away as he spoke, and she wondered if he was telling a partial truth. Perhaps he'd decided an explanation was required, but she didn't doubt his love for Kitty, and she could see no motive for him.

Back inside the castle, Eve thanked him and they walked past the reception area.

It looked as though there'd been some kind of altercation between Julian and Freya. Eve watched as Freya turned her back on Julian and shot into the office, crashing down into a chair and hurling a pen onto the desk.

Julian turned towards Nate, his face red, and opened his mouth, only to snap it shut again.

Bonnie stood behind the reception desk, side on to Eve, scratching at her neck. She'd pulled the high collar of her dress down so she could get at the bit that was irritating her.

The sight pushed everything else from Eve's mind. Around her neck was an angry welt.

17

Eve went to the reception desk and Bonnie faced her, an eyebrow raised. So much for customer service.

'Could I have a quick word please?'

Bonnie shrugged. 'Of course.'

'In private might be best. I won't keep you a moment, but we could head outside?'

The PA's frown deepened. 'As you like.'

She walked off without bothering to explain her departure to Freya.

As soon as they were alone, Eve went for it.

'What really happened to your necklace last night?'

Bonnie turned sharply towards her. 'I told you.'

'You did, but it wasn't the truth.' Gus must have read Eve's tone. He was looking up accusingly at the PA. 'You've got a welt on your neck; I saw it just now when you rubbed at it. I think someone yanked the necklace off and it's odd to lie about it in the aftermath of a murder.'

Bonnie folded her arms, her eyes narrowed. Eve guessed she was deciding whether to lie again or not.

It was a moment before she spoke. 'All right. If you must know, it was all a stupid misunderstanding. The necklace looked like one which belonged to Julian's grandmother. He'd given it to Kitty and she thought Julian had passed it on to me, so it upset her. She followed me upstairs and tore it off me. I've no idea what she did with it, and I don't care. It was cheap costume jewellery and buying it was a mistake. It wasn't really my style.'

The story was hard to believe. Eve wondered if Bonnie had worn the actual necklace. She couldn't see Julian lending it to her – why would he stir up trouble? But Bonnie could have pinched it, aiming to upset Kitty and up the ante over her affair with Julian. Maybe she'd wanted to bring things to a head. Eve remembered her cruel smile as she'd twisted so Kitty could see the pendant. If Eve was right, Bonnie had known the necklace's history from the start. Julian must have told her. Maybe she'd spotted it in his bedroom and asked.

'If Kitty had explained what was troubling her, I could have cleared it up,' Bonnie said. 'It was such a stupid argument.' She paused. 'I hate that it was the last time we spoke.'

The regret sounded false. Eve wondered if it was really the last time Bonnie and Kitty had interacted. Or had that been in the icehouse?

'The very idea that Julian would let me wear a family heirloom is ludicrous. There's nothing between us. I'd rather sleep with a slug.'

Her voice shook with anger. Eve was starting to believe the affair might be over. She'd never imagined Julian wanted Bonnie for keeps and she bet he'd been livid about the upset with Kitty and the scene with Luke too. 'That's all very well, yet Julian told you about the necklace. How else could you have understood Kitty's anger?'

'There's nothing to read into that,' Bonnie said, after a pause which Eve guessed was thinking time. 'I asked Julian if he knew why my necklace had set Kitty off. When I reminded him what it looked like, he explained.'

'Why lie about how you lost it?' Though Eve could imagine.

'Are you crazy? The truth will make the police think Kitty and I were rivals. Her overreaction was ludicrous.'

'I suppose they will focus on you, given you found her body.'

Bonnie scoffed. 'It's not my fault Julian sent me to look for her.'

He could have been setting her up. 'The police still need to know about the argument. You'll tell them now?'

Bonnie didn't meet her eye. 'Oh, all right.'

Eve would too, just to make sure. 'You had a dramatic time last night, what with Kitty ripping off your necklace and the row with Luke Shipley. I'm sorry, but lots of people heard.'

That shrug again. 'He made a pass at me. He didn't like it when I gave him the brush-off.'

But Eve thought back to the exchange she'd heard. She'd reread her notes several times, knowing she'd need the information at her fingertips. The conversation didn't fit Bonnie's version of events. *I don't believe it. Is this your idea of a joke?* Luke had said. *I knew it! I knew there was something.* Then Bonnie had replied: *But you didn't though, did you? You had no idea. Not until now.* And finally, there'd been a chair scraping and a cry and a crash. What was it that Bonnie had added? Eve dug for the words. Something like, *Well done, but it won't do you any good. And you know that.*

Eve was sure Bonnie was lying, but she had no idea if the row related to Kitty's death.

'How did you get on with Kitty in general? I'm writing her obituary; it's useful to have as much input as possible.'

Bonnie sighed. 'Honestly? She could be difficult. And a bit

useless, half the time. She'd sit around mooning over old family albums. Droning on about the past.'

'Had you known her long? When did you start work for Julian?'

Bonnie looked at her fingernails. 'Around a year ago. I was part-time. I had work elsewhere too.'

Eve wondered if the PA job was simply cover for their affair.

'I went full-time when I came here. Before that, I rarely saw Kitty.'

So the strain of sharing the same space was new. Bonnie's determination to get Julian to end his marriage had probably escalated.

In her peripheral vision, Eve caught sight of Luke, emerging from the formal gardens. He was headed in the direction of the icehouse and thoughts of murderers revisiting the crime scene flitted through her head.

'You must see most things that go on here. Who do you think killed Kitty?'

Bonnie cocked her head. 'Maybe Ella Tyndall. She certainly hated her. You could see it in her eyes. She really wanted Farfield, but it was more than that. She wanted Kitty *not* to have it. She might have hoped the murder would put an end to the retreat. If so, I think she'll be out of luck. The people Freya and I have spoken to this morning are all keen to come as soon as the murder's solved.' She looked over her shoulder. 'But Freya's another possibility. She couldn't bear Kitty either, though she's offhand with Julian too. I don't know the background, but Kitty had a guilty conscience. You should have seen the size of the bouquet she sent Freya this morning.'

'This morning?' For a moment, Eve was nonplussed.

Bonnie nodded. 'She must have ordered it before she died, to coincide with Freya's first day. Freya dumped the flowers on the desk, then I saw her head off with them at lunchtime. When I walked to the beach, I found she'd thrown them into the sea. I could still see odd stems floating on the waves.' She shivered. 'It was like a memorial.'

It reminded Eve of the bouquet she'd seen, out in the fields.

18

Back in Eve's room, Gus lounged in a patch of sunlight on the warm wooden floorboards as she messaged Greg Boles to tell him what Bonnie had said about her necklace.

Afterwards, she turned her thoughts to that evening. Viv's summons to the Cross Keys could prove useful. Eve made a note to seek out Moira while she was in Saxford. She wanted to know if the isolated bouquet had been bought from the village store. She'd want to talk to Jo, too. Hearing from someone close to the Marchants could only help.

Eve stayed upstairs to write up her interview notes. It felt good to have her own space. She shuddered a little at the memory of Luke creeping up behind her.

On the back of her interview with Nate, she googled his books again and found a positive review dated just a week earlier. Someone who'd taken a second look at his output on the back of the news about the retreat. They hinted he might be the next big thing. Ten minutes later, she found a second article, reaching a similar conclusion. Perhaps that view would take hold.

Eve was jolted out of her thoughts by a knock at the door.

She closed her work and Gus scampered over but seemed subdued when he realised it was Bonnie. She wasn't the sort to indulge in tummy tickling.

'Julian's having a drink in the formal gardens and wonders if you'd like to join him. He's ready to talk to you about Kitty for the obituary.'

'That'd be great. Thanks.' She gathered up her notebook and pen and followed Bonnie down the stairs with Gus trotting after her. As she went, she reviewed her plans for the interview. She'd want all the usual details of course; the story of their first meeting, what Kitty was like on that very close, personal level that only a partner gets to see. Her joys and her demons. But privately, she wanted to know if Julian might have killed his wife for her money.

At the end of the long west-wing corridor, Eve stepped into the formal gardens, the box hedges neatly cut into balls and cones, the scent of roses and the sound of bees filling the air. Around the edge of the area was the yew hedge which had hidden Luke. She walked past the carp pond and glimpsed bronze-gold scales between the plate-like leaves of the water lilies.

Once again, Gus looked far too interested. Julian helped distract him by offering attention. He made up to everyone.

'Thanks so much for seeing me at such a terrible time.'

She watched as his expression changed subtly in response to her words, as though she'd reminded him he should be grieving.

He nodded slowly. 'Please, take a seat. What would you like to drink? Bonnie will fetch you something.'

There was an edge to his voice. The PA was still standing in the doorway and Eve glanced at her automatically. She was in time to see her features twitch. Fetching and carrying drinks was probably outside her job description but there was more to it than that. If she'd killed Kitty to get close to Julian, it seemed her plan had fallen flat. And looking at them now, Eve guessed neither of them would want a reconciliation. Maybe one of them was guilty and the other had been caught off guard.

'I'm fine, thanks. I need to drive to Saxford later.'

Julian had a whisky at his elbow. Eve hoped it might loosen his tongue.

As Bonnie withdrew, he smiled and sat back in a Lutyens-style chair. 'Please, ask me whatever you need to know.' Eve wondered that anyone could look that composed a day after losing their wife.

'How did you and Kitty meet?' Uncontroversial questions first. 'One of you mentioned it was through Nate, I think? It was him you knew first?'

Fisher smiled. 'That's right. Kitty and I locked eyes at a dinner party at his place. I'd always admired her on television. Such beauty. We got talking and hit it off. I was fascinated by her outlook on life. She'd come from a wealthy background on both sides of the family, but she turned down a private education and all this.' He gestured at the castle behind him. 'She made money of her own, of course, but lived modestly. She wasn't a bit materialistic. Just like me, in fact. I've never sold out. I could make much more money if I wrote commercial fiction, but that's not what motivates me.'

Eve wondered about the French villa and the smart London pad he and Kitty had occupied before they downsized. If the rumours about Julian's debts were true, he'd lived grandly off her. He might have been waiting eagerly for more of the same. Her trust fund must have hit her bank account just after they'd married. Only Kitty had had other plans.

'You moved around quite a lot during your marriage. Was it Kitty's decision to come back to Suffolk?' She thought of the two-up, two-down they'd occupied in Little Mill Marsh. Was that when Fisher had got restless and started his affair with Bonnie? Maybe life with his wife had lost its shine.

'She was keen to return to her roots.' Fisher looked irritable for a second but smoothed his features quickly. 'Of course, it suited me too. London's good for keeping up with publishing-world friends, but Suffolk's more peaceful. I can work here.'

'You found Little Mill Marsh a good base?' It would be a lot less peaceful than Farfield. It was the sort of place where youths hung out on street corners and made a racket.

'It showed me a different slice of life. For a writer, that's invaluable.'

Something he'd turned his back on now, obviously. 'Did you or Kitty have any input into Nate's plan to set up the writers' retreat? And to use Farfield?'

Fisher shrugged. 'It was all Nate's idea, though I bought into his vision, of course.'

Eve could imagine.

'It was Nate who ran with it,' Julian went on. 'It's his invest-ment.' He glanced over his shoulder and lowered his voice. 'When we talked about venues, the news of Freya Hardwicke's husband's wrongdoing was already coming out. I wonder if that drove Nate on. He must have guessed the castle would come on the market sooner or later. I imagine the local who was after it, Ella Tyndall, made the same calculation. From what I under-stand, a lot of the grant applications and fundraising she did were well advanced by the time this place went up for sale.

'But Nate was determined to get it, of course. It was his childhood home. And Kitty wanted to make peace with the past by coming here.' He shook his head. 'Farfield was hugely impor-tant to both of them.'

And for Fisher, moving to the castle from Little Mill Marsh would have been life-changing. It ought to be secure too. As a friend and brother-in-law, Nate was unlikely to chuck him out. Unless he found out he'd been cheating on Kitty. And Eve was pretty sure Kitty had suspected, even before the launch party. Might Julian have killed her to stop her telling her brother?

With the added temptation of her inheritance, it seemed more than possible.

Seeing Bonnie wear the necklace could have helped Kitty make up her mind to leave him... Eve needed to work the conversation around to that.

'Did you and Kitty ever talk about your writing?'

Fisher raised an eyebrow and seemed to withdraw slightly. 'What makes you ask?'

It seemed like an odd response to a perfectly ordinary question. 'I want to give *Icon*'s readers an impression of your relationship and your careers. It will make the article more rounded.'

He relaxed again. 'Of course. But I'm afraid rarely, is the answer. I'm very private about my work. I observe quietly, then pour my words straight onto the page. I don't feel the need to involve others.'

Eve saw her chance. 'Before things got so awful last night, I was doing a bit of people-watching. It made me think how much drama you can see whenever crowds congregate.'

'Of course.' His tone was rather sharp. 'I learn from real life too, but I don't simply report it.'

'Whereas I do, as faithfully as I can. And last night, I saw an unsettling interaction between Kitty and Bonnie.'

'Really?' He sounded nervous now.

'As it turns out, it had a perfectly innocent explanation.' *Like heck.* 'Bonnie explained it to me.' Eve relayed the story of the necklace Bonnie had worn, which had apparently looked exactly like one belonging to Julian's grandmother. 'It was such an unfortunate coincidence. I could tell how much Bonnie regretted it.'

As she said the PA's name, irritation flashed over Julian's face. 'Indeed. Very bad luck.'

'Funnily enough, my mother collects 1920s jewellery.' That was a total lie, but a harmless one in a good cause. 'It's made me interested too. I'd love to see the original necklace. I could send her a photograph if you wouldn't mind. She's got a huge collection.'

Julian turned his palms upwards in a gesture of helplessness. 'I'd have loved to oblige, but that pendant was lost in the move from France to London. A great shame. I was fond of my grandmother. It reminded me of her.'

Very convenient. Eve still believed Bonnie might have worn the original to force a row and reveal the affair. It might explain Julian's fury with her now. Gossip about an argument would be dangerous for them both. Especially if one of them had killed Kitty. They had the run of the castle. They could have taken the keys to the grille.

Eve switched tack. 'It's lovely that you helped Freya Hardwicke by giving her a job here, on top of Nate buying Farfield.' She was still intrigued by Freya's decision to accept the role, given her relationship with Kitty. Unless she'd taken it to get access to her.

Julian laughed. 'That's the Marchant social conscience coming to the fore. Nate's idea. He could see she had the right skills. He understood something of her background and invited her to apply.'

'I understand she had an awful time after her husband died.'

Julian nodded. 'He was a bad lot. But adopting lame ducks isn't always a good idea.' He sounded like Nate's dad. 'Of course, it's not just Nate's grandparents that influence his noble deeds. His wife, Rhoda, is a reporter – traipsing off to war zones and what have you. Nate's less showy about his good works, of course. I think that's better. More genuine.'

Eve was familiar with Rhoda Marchant's work. Julian implying she did it for show got her goat. She looked at him, sitting comfortably in his chair in the warm May sunshine, and seethed silently.

But she mustn't get distracted. 'I guess you're right – about it not always being good to adopt lame ducks, I mean.' She hated quoting him. 'I saw Freya and Kitty argue. And I had the impression you were finding her difficult too.' She waited for him to comment.

Julian took a deep breath. 'She doesn't have the bedside manner for a public-facing role. As for Kitty, they were good friends, but I believe she offended Freya in some way.' He shook his head. 'She seems very thin-skinned. Poor Kitty. She was so gentle. Wouldn't hurt a fly. Either way, I think Freya's put me in the same bracket. She's cold shouldering me too.'

'Didn't you warn Nate it could be problematic when he suggested hiring her?'

Julian shrugged and fiddled with his whisky glass. 'Farfield's his baby. It's his decision.'

Surely it was odd though, not to tell Nate that Freya had such a dislike of Kitty. Nate wouldn't want to make Kitty's life miserable. And Freya could have looked for work elsewhere. What was Eve missing?

'I gather Kitty was planning to set up a drugs charity with proceeds from a trust fund. It must have meant a lot to her, after what happened to her mum.'

She watched Julian's lip twitch before he controlled himself. 'That's right. She said she couldn't just spend it on herself. It had to mean something.'

'Will you set up the charity now, in her memory?'

Her question was met with the longest pause of the interview yet. 'I'd rather you didn't include any confirmation in the obituary. I'm still reeling from Kitty's death. She had big plans, but she already had experience of charity work. She knew what she was doing. Whereas I'm a novelist. I'm worried about biting off more than I can chew. I'm considering a donation to an existing charity instead.'

One that left most of the cash free for Julian to enjoy, perhaps.

'Of course. I understand.'

Whether he'd killed Kitty or not, Eve was sure he'd thought about what it would mean to inherit her money.

As she re-entered the castle, she glanced over her shoulder to call Gus away from the pond and saw a slight darkening in the yew hedge. She walked up the corridor, frowning. A moment later, she saw Luke Shipley striding across the grass towards the deer park.

19

Eve had got hot as she talked to Julian Fisher. Hot in the sun and hot under the collar. She went upstairs to change before heading to Saxford to meet Viv.

As she unlocked the door to her room, she heard a creak from the bedroom behind her, followed by silence. It must be Luke Shipley's quarters. Eve had yet to see him enter or exit, but she remembered Julian saying he was opposite her.

She felt a spike of adrenaline. There was no way it was Luke in there. She'd just seen him, striding towards the deer park.

She turned, undecided, then knocked. 'Luke?' Best to pretend she thought it was him.

There was no reply.

Her heart thudding, she tried the door. Locked. And still there was silence.

Eve ushered Gus into her room and fetched herself a glass of water. Old houses did creak. She wasn't *sure* someone had been in Luke's room, but again, the oddness of Nate and Julian asking them to stay filled her head. It would make far more sense to get them back when there were guests on site. They couldn't possibly get a proper impression of the retreat with it empty and the staff suspected of murder. There had to be another reason for wanting them there. Was Luke's room being searched? Eve wondered what had happened to Julian's laptop.

Her nerves were still on edge when Robin called, just before she was due to leave for Saxford.

'*Are you okay? How's today been?*'

She stood still so he wouldn't break up and filled him in on the interviews she'd conducted and the creak from Luke's room. 'There are still more questions than answers.'

'*It's early days. Please take care.*'

She asked after his day. He told her the preparations for his final appearance in court were going well and he'd had a meeting about another case too. He sounded less worried as he talked about it. Excited and alive. Engaged. It was bound to be more compelling than his life in Saxford. Doubt gnawed at her but she pushed it from her mind. She wanted Robin to be happy.

'Well done. They must value having you back on a more official basis.'

'*They seem to.*' She could hear the pleasure in his voice. '*Of course, it's only temporary.*' But if Eve were them, she'd want Robin for other projects too. '*I've got news from Greg. Have you got time to hear it?*'

'Of course.'

He filled her in, then she wished him luck for the following day, her insides knotting. By the time they cut the call she had plenty to share with Viv. And an email had come in from Portia Coldwell at *Icon*, promising to ask around about Luke Shipley. Eve hoped she did it quickly.

Forty-five minutes later, Eve was sitting in the Cross Keys' garden opposite Viv, while Gus scampered round on the grass with the pub schnauzer, Hetty. Eve and Viv each had a white wine, condensation trickling down the sides of the glasses. The lawn and tables with their white parasols stretched away towards the estuary in the distance, crowded with wading birds.

'Come on then, tell!' Viv sipped her drink.

The need to keep Greg Boles' habit of sharing information with Robin secret meant Eve had to put her information down to the village grapevine.

'Kitty's death must have been between 8.45 p.m. – which is when I last saw her, walking down the west wing corridor towards the gardens – and 10.15 p.m., when Bonnie Whitelaw found her. Julian had sent her to look for Kitty, she said.'

That was straightforward enough. Robin said the pathologist hadn't been able to pin the time down any further.

'Apparently, there were no fingerprints on the grille. It's quite rusty, so I guess that would be the case even if the killer didn't take precautions. The keys were clean too, and back on their hook in the kitchen when the police arrived. They're just where they were in Nate and Kitty's grandparents' day. Anyone could have known that, or spotted them if they were staying in the house.' It made Luke Shipley just as possible as Julian and Nate. And of course, Freya had lived there too, while Ella Tyndall was a regular visitor in the old days. 'People were in and out of the kitchen all day. Taking them would have been easy.'

Viv had her notebook out again. 'Do you know how the police decided the death was murder?'

'Rumour has it the injuries to Kitty's head weren't consistent with her fall. I guess the killer hoped they could make it look like an accident, but they couldn't control how she landed at the bottom of the well.'

'So she was hit with something?'

Eve nodded, shivering for a moment as she thought back to her conversation with Robin. 'There's talk of someone using a champagne bottle. The killing sounds brutal and intimate. Committed by someone who was very angry or very frightened, I guess.'

Viv shuddered too. 'Horrible to think of something celebratory like that being used.'

'I know. But the bottles were everywhere. After the waiting staff dashed off to check on the boy who fell from the tree, people helped themselves.'

'I remember. The killer was an opportunist, then.'

'Yes, but they must have planned, at least to a degree, because they unlocked the grille.'

Viv nodded.

'From what I hear, Kitty had no other marks on her, except those caused by the blow and the fall. I guess that means she wasn't manhandled. The killer must have caught her by surprise. Either she trusted them, or maybe she had no idea someone had come into the icehouse behind her.' She thought it through. 'They must have visited the icehouse before her to open the grille. Maybe they left the murder weapon handy too, or they could have walked in with it. Seeing someone carrying a champagne bottle wouldn't ring alarm bells. I doubt anyone would remember later.'

'Especially given the amount consumed. So, the killer set things up, and then?'

'Maybe they arranged to meet Kitty there. They could have come up with an excuse for wanting a private talk.' Her mind ran through the possibilities. Kitty had wanted to speak to Freya, but Freya was having none of it, and their argument was clearly an old one. Julian could have lured her there to discuss their marriage if things had come to a head mid-evening. Though convincing her to meet in the icehouse could have been a hard sell. Surely she would have wondered why he wanted to talk there, not in their suite in the castle? Still, he could have come up with an excuse. The others seemed possible too.

Bonnie, Ella or Luke could each have said they wanted to confide something in private.

One thing was clear. Kitty hadn't been worried for her safety, but then why would she be? It was such a horrific and unforeseeable crime. Take Bonnie, for instance. She might have been a threat to Kitty's marriage, but Eve doubted Kitty had imagined she'd kill over it.

'Any idea who the police are focused on?'

'I'm hearing it's Ella and Luke Shipley. Ella because she had such a public row with Kitty, and Luke because several people have said he had an unhealthy interest in her. Bonnie's up there too. The row over the necklace has probably made a difference, though she's sticking to her story about it all being a misunderstanding.'

'What about the scene you witnessed in the woods?'

'I'm not sure it's being treated seriously.'

'How come?'

'Both Bonnie and Julian deny being there. My case wasn't improved by the fact that it was early, dense with trees, and I'd never met them before. Maybe it would have helped if I'd heard them address each other by name.' But maybe not. Palmer never took her seriously. 'On top of that, Julian has an alibi for Kitty's death. Of sorts.'

Viv groaned. 'That's inconvenient.'

'He's cobbled together a group of recently charmed villagers who say he was either manning the exhibition stand, giving a speech or conducting tours during the time-of-death window. I'm sure he could have slipped away, though. It's hardly solid.' Her heart sank as she remembered Robin's dampening words. 'The upshot is, Palmer's all but written Julian off as a suspect. Bonnie's still in the running, but of course he'd prefer it to be an outsider. The powers that be don't want a high-value enterprise like the retreat threatened.'

Viv sipped her wine. 'Who's top of *your* list?'

'Julian's moved up since I discovered Kitty had money to leave. She was saving it for good works and planning to ring-fence it legally. He had a motive to kill her before she managed it – assuming he's her beneficiary. And I'm sure he imagines he is. He's clearly been thinking about how to cling on to as much of the cash as possible.' She explained his suggestion of donating to a charity in Kitty's memory instead of setting up a new one. 'If he donates fifty thousand it'll be great PR, but Kitty's trust fund was likely way more than that, if Nate's hints are anything to go by. And we know Julian lied. He told everyone he was going to be sick when he heard Kitty was dead, but Daphne says he went to his study, not the bathroom. I want to know what he was doing there. And why someone stole his laptop.'

Viv nodded. 'So Julian's right up there. Anyone else?'

'Bonnie still. I can imagine her killing to remove a rival. She's a cool customer. But I need to follow up on the others too. Nate was close to the crime scene, but any of them could have been, given the timing and the confusion of the party. It's a nightmare. None of them is out of the running.'

'So what's your plan?'

'Most immediately, I'm going to knock on Moira's door.' She explained about the bouquet of flowers she'd seen in the fields near the castle. 'It's probably too much to hope that they were bought in Saxford, but you never know.'

Viv nodded across the lawn. 'I can save you the trouble. She went and got a table down the garden five minutes ago.'

Eve had had no idea. She had her back to the pub door. 'And you didn't say hello?'

'She didn't see us. I thought it was our lucky day.'

'Cruel but fair.' Eve stood up and marched off to find her.

20

'Oh no, Eve.' Moira's frown was deep in response to her question. 'No one bought that sort of bouquet from me. Though I can't think why they chose to shop elsewhere.'

Eve could. If the buyer wanted anonymity, it made total sense.

'Perhaps you could try the florists in Blyworth?'

'Thanks, I'll do that.'

Moira invited Eve to sit down and provide her (and her dour husband Paul) with a full update, but Viv was waving to her.

'Our food's due any minute. I'll pop into the store and let you know what's going on when I've heard more myself.' She dashed back to their table and gave her update.

Viv nodded. 'Anything else on the agenda?'

'Watching Bonnie and Julian like a hawk. I need to know how Kitty left her money. Being on the spot, I might hear something.

'As regards the others, bizarrely, Ella Tyndall's coming to do a history tour at the castle tomorrow. Luke and I are down to attend, despite what's happened.' She sighed. 'It's so weird that they've asked us to stay. It feels kind of wrong, but the tour's good news. I want to quiz Ella and see more of Luke too. I'm hoping for extra background on him.' She explained the request she'd put in to Portia at *Icon*.

'I've contacted Benet Marchant too, to see if he'll talk to me. I want to hear his side of the rift with his parents. He ought to give more insights into Nate, and he'll probably have an opinion on Julian.'

Jo brought their food over. She stood by their table, hands on hips. For once, she looked distracted as they enthused over the smell wafting from their fish pies.

'I was hoping to talk to you, Jo,' Eve said. She waited for the cook to tell her that sleuthing and food didn't mix, and insist she concentrate on her meal.

But instead, Jo nodded. 'I thought you might. They've asked you to stay on at Farfield, I suppose.'

How would she know that? 'That's right. I was surprised.'

Jo nodded again. 'Naturally, but I'm not. I knew you'd look into this business, and you're needed. Last night, I made sure to say loudly how lucky it was that they'd got you on the spot. And how keen they must be to keep you there, what with you being most likely to solve the murder.'

Wait. What? Eve stopped feeling hungry. 'You said that? When?'

'When we were waiting to talk to the police. Didn't let DI Palmer hear me, of course, the great oaf. But word went round quick enough. If anyone tries to push you out now, they'll look like they've got something to hide. I reckon you'll be welcome for as long as you need. Though you're to take care and if you want to leave you've only to tell them so.'

'Ah. Right. Thanks.' *Probably.* Nate's invitation for her and Luke to remain at Farfield made a little more sense now. They wouldn't want to treat them differently. But she still suspected they had additional reasons of their own.

'I had reservations about the writers' retreat, as you know,' Jo continued, her eyes narrowing. 'The Marchants would have wanted whoever bought the place to welcome the locals, just like Ella planned. Tragic that their own grandchildren haven't taken that into account.'

Eve wished she could pass on what Nate had said, earlier that day. 'We don't know the long-term plan yet. I suspect Nate might come good in the end.' If only he would publicise his ideas and to heck with Julian Fisher. But he wasn't leaving anything to chance when it came to the retreat, and Julian had had that rival job offer.

Jo folded her arms. 'Seeing is believing. But Sophie and Daniel Marchant were dear to me. Kitty hurt them badly when she sided with her dad. I find it hard to forgive her, but she was just a kid, led by Benet. Sophie and Daniel would want us to work day and night to find out who did this.' She looked Eve in the eye. 'Are you up for it?'

Eve nodded. 'We can't possibly stand by. And I suspect you're right – that Benet was to blame.' She told Jo what Nate had said.

The cook's eyes were damp when Eve had finished. 'That man has a lot to answer for. He ruined multiple lives.' She patted her on the shoulder. 'All the best with the investigation then. Eat your fish while it's hot.'

'You normally get snippy if someone tries to organise you,' Viv said after Jo had left. 'How come she gets away with it?'

'Mainly because she's right. I wanted to stay anyway.'

'Mainly?'

'Partly because she's terrifying, obviously.'

Eve reflected on the turn of events. She was left in control, with a free pass to stay on at Farfield. But it had also alerted the entire household to the way she might meddle in their affairs.

She might as well have been wandering around in a deerstalker hat with a magnifying glass.

It was ten minutes later when Moira arrived, breathless, at their table.

'Excuse me. I must just sit with you a minute.'

'Must you?' said Viv.

Eve glared at her. 'Of course.' She pulled out a spare chair. 'Is everything all right?'

'I'm afraid not. Or at least, I've just heard something rather startling.' In fact, she looked excited.

'It's to do with Kitty's death?'

'Poor dear, yes, it is. Deidre Lennox stopped at our table with an extraordinary story.' She lowered her voice to a dramatic whisper. 'Is Nate Marchant on your list of suspects?'

Eve thought of his sudden appearance near the icehouse just after Kitty's body was found. But she wasn't going to share that with Moira. 'You think he should be?'

The storekeeper leaned forward eagerly. 'I'm afraid so. I wrote down exactly what Deidre said.' She pulled a shopping-list pad from her bag and peered at it. 'She'd gone to explore the castle and nipped upstairs. Just for a moment. I'm sure we can't blame her. Nowhere seemed to be off-limits.'

Not in Deidre's view, clearly.

'And as she was tiptoeing— I mean, walking along the east corridor, she heard voices. A man and a woman. "You read me like a book," the man was saying, "but that's quick, even for you."' Her eyes met Eve's then her gaze was back on her notepad. 'Then she heard a woman laughing, but she says she sounded emotional. Full of sadness, anxiety and fondness, Deidre says. She's always overacting in the amateur dramatic society of course, but all the same, she insists she's not exaggerating. The woman said, "I overheard. Sorry. I was curious." And then she added: "I'm just worried for you, Nate. You're playing a dangerous game. And it's not just you who's at risk." And he said, "I know."'

Moira looked triumphantly at Eve. 'Deidre made herself scarce, but she peered to see who came out of the room and it was Kitty that Nate had been talking to! He was keeping a secret and she'd discovered it. What do you say to that?'

21

The castle seemed deserted by the time Eve returned and let herself in with the key she'd been given.

The police had reopened the east wing. Julian, Nate, Freya and Bonnie had access to their rooms again. She glanced at her watch. Half past ten. After the horror of the day before, she wasn't surprised people had turned in early. She'd want privacy and time to mourn if she was them. But which of them was really grieving?

Eve found herself creeping upstairs as quietly as she could, as though making too much noise might wake something more than just a sleeping inhabitant. But try as she might, the old wooden stairs creaked, and just behind her Gus's name tag chinked against his collar.

Eve was relieved to get inside her room and lock the door. She stood still for a moment, thoughts of the creaking she'd heard in Luke's room filling her head. She wondered if anyone had entered her quarters in her absence. Nothing seemed out of place. There was no unfamiliar smell.

Suddenly, she longed for the calm familiarity of her own home. That and Robin – his arms around her. She imagined him in London. Wondered what he was doing. Poring over the case against his old enemies, she suspected.

Checking her emails, she found she had one from Benet Marchant agreeing to see her in London, late the following afternoon. She contacted the twins and arranged to meet them for a drink afterwards. And then she messaged Robin, explaining her plans. He ought to have finished in court by the time she'd seen the twins. She wondered whether to suggest a meet-up, but she didn't want to seem clingy. He was due back the day after in any case.

His reply came quickly.

Good luck with Benet. Have a wonderful time with the twins. x

He'd need the evening to take stock after testifying for the final time. It wasn't surprising he hadn't suggested meeting either.

She and Gus settled down. After a short time, she heard the dachshund's soft snores, but Eve's mind was still whirring. Thoughts of Robin vied with questions about Kitty's murder. Why had Freya chosen to work at Farfield when she hated Kitty? Why had Luke been so obsessed with her if they'd never met before? What had Kitty and Bonnie said to each other during their row over the pendant? And how much money did Julian think he'd inherit?

She turned over as her thoughts shifted to Ella. How far would she go to get revenge?

And what was Nate's secret? She and Viv had discussed Deidre Lennox's story after Moira left them. Eve had gone to talk to Deidre herself too, once she'd finished her food. She'd repeated the tale, word-for-word. It confirmed what Eve and Viv had been thinking: Nate's secret was interesting, but Kitty hadn't sounded like a threat to him. She'd been concerned, not set on giving him away. *A dangerous game...* What had Kitty meant? An affair with a married woman? She'd said it wasn't just risky for Nate. Or perhaps it was something financial, which might affect him and his wife.

It was no good. If she couldn't sleep, she might as well do something useful. She settled on downloading the audio version of Julian's latest novel. She'd been intending to listen to it ever since he'd got tetchy with Luke as they'd discussed his work. Eve remembered him flushing as Luke described his output as hit and miss. But the critics had raved over certain scenes in his latest book. It had been well received. Unlike his second, as Luke had pointed out. She was still wondering if Julian had smashed his glass deliberately to halt the conversation. A moment later, she was lying down again with her earphones in.

An hour and a half after that, she gave up for the night as her concentration waned. She'd carry on tomorrow. But still she wasn't sleepy.

She was starting to drift at last when she heard a thump. It had sounded distant. Downstairs perhaps. She propped herself up on one elbow and listened intently but there was nothing more.

Someone must be up and about. In general, they were being quiet, but they'd slipped up. Dropped or knocked something to make that thump.

She told herself to be calm. She could already feel adrenaline-induced breathlessness, which wouldn't help if she was going to investigate.

She hesitated, the sheet and blanket half flung back. It could be totally innocent, but she had to find out. She pushed the covers off fully and eased herself out of bed. Gus twitched but didn't wake.

A moment later she'd pulled on a dressing gown and was at the bedroom door, unlocking it, then easing the metal latch upwards, holding it so it didn't rattle against its moorings. She looked to left and right. No sign of anyone in the corridor. She closed her door after her and crept over the carpet, quiet, but not silent.

Eve was halfway down the stairs, moving slowly, when she saw Bonnie Whitelaw, fully dressed. She'd just tiptoed from the sitting room into one of the writing rooms.

What was she up to?

Eve couldn't see from where she stood, but if she went all the way down she'd have to cross the hall to reach a safe position from which to watch. She hovered, poised on her toes, undecided. But if Bonnie caught her, she could tell the truth. She'd heard a noise and come to investigate. So she went for it. Descending the remaining stairs, rounding the corner and slipping into the bathroom. The door was ajar. She'd peer from there. It ought to be all right. So long as Bonnie didn't go there next...

Eve stood still, willing herself to calm down. At last, she risked a look. The writing room door was open and through it, Eve saw Bonnie crouch down low on the floor. What on earth? A moment later she got lower still and reached under a deep bookcase. She swept her hand back and forth, then stood again, on tiptoe this time, feeling along the tops of the books. Going from shelf to shelf. Methodically. Moving from the top to the bottom.

Searching.

For the pendant?

Eve bet that was it. She imagined Bonnie and Julian arguing. Him asking why the heck she'd decided to pinch his grandmother's necklace and flaunt it in front of Kitty. And if it was valuable, of course, Julian would want it back. He'd probably told her to find it. Bonnie must suspect Kitty had hidden it once she'd yanked it off. She'd have seen her dash downstairs.

It was just a theory, but it fitted the facts. If Eve was right, it seemed Bonnie had no idea where to find it. She'd gone from one room to another. Of course, Eve knew Kitty had headed straight for the grounds. It would be like looking for the proverbial needle.

Eve was so focused on Bonnie that the appearance of another figure almost made her gasp out loud. *Calm, calm.* But repeating her mantra couldn't work miracles.

Freya Hardwicke was now standing in the hall between her and the writing room. She stopped suddenly. It was clear Bonnie had taken her by surprise. The PA was facing away from Freya, still searching the room, and the manager turned quickly. She was making for the bathroom.

Eve dashed into one of the cubicles, not closing the door but standing behind it. If only Freya didn't pick that particular stall.

But she didn't make for the loos at all. She took up a position in the exact same place Eve had used, and watched. She must be wondering what the PA was up to as well. Eve could see her through the chink in the door above the hinges. After what felt like an eternity, Eve watched Freya disappear into the lobby again.

She waited another five minutes before risking any manoeuvres herself.

Stiff and chilly, she crept out of the bathroom and back up the stairs, seeing no one.

In bed, Eve imagined the row between Bonnie and Kitty. Maybe Julian had had lovers before. He seemed the sort. Kitty might have told Bonnie about them, and how Julian would never leave her. Then yanked the necklace off. And Bonnie, livid after the physical attack, could have decided on her next plan of action.

To lure Kitty to the icehouse.

But how would she have got her there after such an acrimonious scene? At the Cross Keys, Eve had airily decided she could have found an excuse, but could she? What would have made Kitty meet her there?

But on consideration, Eve could imagine it. Bonnie could have rushed up to her later. Told her she'd seen Julian with yet another woman. Pretended they'd both been wronged. Asked to meet to decide how to pay him back.

It was just one idea, but Eve could see it working.

22

The following morning, Eve could smell bacon frying as she approached the dining room. She knew the evening meals were provided by the outside cook, but glancing through the hatch she saw it was Freya who was at work now. Eve watched as she put the slice she'd been using down and stood back from the frying pan, her clenched fists to her eyes. A moment later, she stood up straight and picked up the implement again.

Eve knew from years of obituary interviews that it was hard to lose a close connection, even if you'd argued. Harder sometimes. Reconciliation was out of reach. Freya was well down her list of suspects, given the apparent age of her and Kitty's falling-out, but she couldn't be discounted. Emotions were complicated things.

Eve scraped a chair so Freya would know she'd entered the adjacent room.

The manager appeared almost immediately, her face slightly red, her eyes unnaturally bright. It looked like the result of emotion, though it could be the cooking.

'How are you?' Freya asked. 'You and Luke must be in

shock, just like the rest of us. Please have a seat and I'll bring you some food.'

She was pulling out all the stops. Once again Eve could see why Nate had hired her. The lack of bedside manner Julian mentioned was baloney. It must be specific to him and Kitty. Eve had hoped to ask Freya why she'd accepted the post at Farfield, but Luke arrived at that moment. It would be better to wait for some privacy.

A minute later, they both had bacon, eggs, sausages, beans and mushrooms in front of them. The breakfast was expertly cooked, the coffee and freshly squeezed orange juice the perfect accompaniment.

'This is wonderful,' Luke said.

He sounded keen and grateful. Much as he had at Kitty's exercise class. Eve couldn't reconcile that innocent almost boyish aspect of his character with the way he'd spied on Kitty.

But as Luke ate, he seemed increasingly nervy, tapping the side of his coffee cup and eating quickly. Jo would not approve. 'I was surprised Julian and Nate asked us to stay on,' he said suddenly, fixing Freya with his gaze. 'It must have put an even greater strain on everyone.' He was probably wondering what their motivation was, just like Eve. Jo's interference would have had a bearing, but she was still uneasy.

Freya coloured slightly. Maybe they'd discussed their reasons in front of her.

'It was Nate who was adamant,' she said. 'He's in pieces over Kitty's death. I've seen him. They were so close.' She took a deep breath. 'But he knows you've both set aside a week for this. He said it would be wrong to send you away, then expect you to come back again. And although we've rejigged people over the next three weeks, the castle's booked solid after that.'

They'd want the publicity before long, then. You'd imagine they'd be worried about appearances, if nothing else, but Eve had seen the determination in Nate's eyes. He wanted this to work. She thought again of his relationship with his father. The way he'd talked to Kitty about him. *He's a fraud. Not worth a second thought. I assumed you'd realised that by now.* Nate was on a mission. Benet had abandoned his parents in their time of need. Now, Nate was picking up the pieces a generation on. Starting again.

'Please,' Freya went on, 'let's make the rest of your stay as comfortable and normal as we can. We have toast and marmalade to follow. Let me top up your coffee and orange juice.'

As they ate, Eve explained her plans to head to London after lunch to interview Benet Marchant.

'Of course. If you'd like a late supper, please let me know. That can easily be arranged.'

But Eve shook her head. 'Thanks, but I'll make my own arrangements.'

After that, Freya talked them through the programme for the day: the history tour with Ella Tyndall that morning, then free time in the afternoon with an optional tour around local attractions for Luke, if he felt like it.

As she described the history tour, Luke started tapping his cup again, his look intent. Eve was keen to get started too. Bonnie and Julian were her top priority, but she couldn't ignore Ella. She wanted to know why she'd agreed to work with Nate, and more about her relationship with Kitty. Kitty had barely been seventeen when Benet refused to help his parents. Just a child. Why was Ella's hatred for her still so strong? And would she have killed over it?

Eve went to fetch Gus, then met Ella and Luke by the Farfield sundial at ten o'clock. Ella looked tired, with dark shadows under her eyes, and winced slightly in the bright sunshine. She smiled at them both, though her brow wrinkled as her gaze fell on Luke. It looked like curiosity, mixed with concern. Of course, the pair of them were the police's top suspects, along with Bonnie. If Ella knew *she* wasn't guilty, she might be wondering about Luke.

Her shoulders relaxed when she turned to Eve. They were only passing acquaintances, but Eve had always found her friendly. Treating her as a suspect felt uncomfortable.

A moment later, Ella was bending to pet Gus. How could this down-to-earth, community-spirited teacher be a killer?

'I feel there's an elephant in the room,' Ella said, 'or rather in the grounds.' Her hand shook slightly as she raised it to her face. 'I lost my temper with Kitty less than a week before she died. I feel awful about my behaviour. It's no excuse, but I was exhausted. I'd spent so many months fundraising, applying for grants, jumping through hoops, knocking on doors – you know. And it seemed it would all pay off until Nate came along with his bid. He and Kitty were so insistent that Farfield *had* to be the venue for the retreat. It made me especially cross with Kitty, after she abandoned her grandparents.' She sighed. 'I was very close to Mr and Mrs Marchant. My grandparents worked for them. My mother was brought up here and they treated me like an extra grandchild. I used to play with Kitty and Nate. I saw Sophie and Daniel's pain when she wouldn't visit. And their reaction when they heard she and her dad had watched the removal firms emptying this place.' She wiped the back of her hand across her eyes. 'They were devastated. It was hard to get past that.'

It was good to have it out in the open, but her voice had become less and less controlled as she'd talked. Eve could hear the shake in it. She hadn't forgiven Kitty, even now she was dead. As for her exhaustion, it had been months since she'd fought to get the cash to buy Farfield.

Eve had been curious to see Luke's reaction to Ella's words, given his apparent liking for Kitty. He'd bristled at first, but now he appeared to be ruminating, a frown furrowing his brow. It was a measured response for an obsessive, and not what Eve had expected. Once again, she wondered if he'd been making up to Kitty with an ulterior motive. If so, to get at Nate and Julian was still her top theory. He must have liked her though, hence the initial bristling.

Eve felt Kitty's actions needed putting in context. 'It must have been a crushing disappointment not to get Farfield. You worked so hard, and I know the village appreciated it. But I guess Kitty would have been in a fragile state when she sided with her dad. Being forced to take sides so soon after her mother's death would have been harrowing. And it sounds as though Benet put the worst possible spin on Sophie and Daniel's motives. Made Kitty believe they'd hated her mum. I realise I've got this second hand from Nate. I'm probably missing the subtleties.' But Eve thought the extenuating circumstances were compelling.

She watched as Ella dug her nails into the palm of her hand. 'Did she need to stay away for so long? She wasn't a child by the time her grandparents died. And to come back now? Should her need for closure trump the village's desire for a local history museum and community centre?'

'What made you agree to do the tours?' Luke asked. His tone was gentle, his eyes kind.

It would have been Eve's next question too.

'I was hoping to persuade the three of them to open the grounds to the public. I'll keep working on Julian and Nate. They must see what needs to happen.'

She wouldn't know of Nate's plans to do just that and more, and Eve couldn't tell her. The balance of power between him and Julian was so weird. 'I get the impression Nate might be receptive once they're bedded in here.' She wanted to give her hope.

Ella gave her a stiff smile, then put her shoulders back. 'Let me tell you all I know about the castle. Stories told to me by Nate and Kitty's grandparents – learned as I toddled round the grounds after them.' Her eyes were damp.

Eve wondered how the heck she'd write her article. Could she honestly recommend a venue seething with painful memories and resentment? She tried to focus on Ella's words and forget the baggage.

Ella told them about the castle being given to a powerful family in the Middle Ages as part of a bride's dowry. She gave them both fact and fairy story, family history and legend. And to Eve's relief she did it brilliantly. Eve really did forget the background tensions for a precious hour. Ella's passion for the place shone through.

The spell was broken when they left the castle gatehouse for the Tudor parts of the building. Ella pointed out Nate and Kitty's old bedrooms and the rooms on the other side of the castle where their grandparents had slept. It brought home the reality.

'You should have seen the place they moved to,' she said, drawing a juddery breath. 'It was damp, dark and tiny. Almost all their possessions had to be sold. And after everything they'd done for other people.'

Luke was shaking his head. He seemed caught up in her emotion.

The tour ended outside. The place was free of police now, but Ella didn't approach the icehouse as she related its history. Eve found the details fascinating, but thoughts of Kitty's death invaded her mind.

Before Ella left, Eve asked if she could talk to her about Kitty for the obituary.

The teacher looked uncomfortable. 'You really want my input?'

'It's good to get a balanced view.'

'I'll leave you to it.' Luke made for the castle, but when Eve glanced over her shoulder, she caught him staring back at them.

Eve and Ella walked around the grounds again, Gus just behind them, the sun on their backs and the smell of warm grass filling the air.

'It's useful to find someone who knew Kitty as a child. Did you always dislike her so much?'

Ella gave her a sharp look. 'I didn't just take against her for no reason. It was her behaviour that put me off.'

'The way she treated her grandparents? Or was there more?'

Ella hesitated. 'She behaved selfishly. She was selfish!' Her fists were clenched again. 'We got on when we were younger. Ran around together. Thick as thieves. Kitty was daring. She ran wild.'

But she'd changed. Lost confidence. She'd been through so much, it wasn't unnatural.

'Have you met her dad?' Ella asked.

'I'm due to, this afternoon. The impression I have of him so far is down to Nate.'

Ella nodded. 'Benet paints himself as a rebel. Passionate and uncompromising. A dangerous combination. People find his disregard for convention compelling. Kitty followed in Benet's wake, then very belatedly, guilt set in. It made her want to come back here. Talk about closing the stable door after the horse has bolted. She could have fought for her grandparents at the time, and dissuaded Nate from bidding against me now. She didn't seem to realise her actions had consequences. You might excuse it in a seventeen-year-old, it's rather different in a woman of thirty-seven.'

Ella had been running her hand through her hair distractedly. Now, she stilled, catching her breath.

'What about Nate? He stood up to his father and sided with his grandparents, I gather.'

'Yes,' Ella sighed, 'even though he was four years younger. I always admired him for that. Yet his dad saw him as the weak one.' She shook her head. 'Nate still minds what Benet thinks, whatever he says.'

That mirrored Eve's thoughts. She wondered how many of his actions were driven by his dad. It didn't seem healthy.

They were returning to the west side of the castle when Eve glanced up at a window and saw Luke, watching them again.

She turned away but couldn't quell the creeping sensation that ran over her.

Back upstairs with Gus, she sat down to write up her notes. After a while she felt stiff and got up to walk around the room. When she neared the window, she saw Luke was back outside with Ella. He must have caught her before she left. She assumed he wanted his own private word. But why? He wasn't writing an obituary.

Ella was gesticulating and Luke kept his distance. It seemed they were arguing. Then suddenly, Ella faced Luke and they both stopped, stock-still, on the lawn. Ella approached him and there was a long pause. Then she patted his arm and his shoulders went down. After a minute, they walked off, heads close together. Whatever they were talking about, they carried on for another ten minutes. Eve glanced at her watch. If Luke had caught Ella just after her interview, they must have been chatting for over half an hour.

'Very interesting, Gus,' Eve said, as she watched them part. 'Very interesting indeed.'

23

The sight of Luke Shipley talking so intimately with Ella Tyndall had Eve checking her emails, hoping for news from Portia Coldwell. Any gossip about him would be useful, but there was nothing yet. She hoped Portia hadn't forgotten. She'd chase if she hadn't heard by the following day.

'Time for some lunch, I think,' she said to Gus. 'I'll be back very soon, yes I will. And then I'll take you for a walk on the beach before I go to London.'

He leaped up and did a funny sideways skip at the word beach. She was going to leave him at home in Saxford during her trip. Tammy would drop in to make a fuss of him after her shift at Monty's.

As Eve reached the bottom of the stairs she saw a man in a smart charcoal-grey suit cross the lobby. There was something in his eyes and the speed of his step that told her he was happy to be leaving. A moment later, she heard Julian's raised voice.

'This is rank foolishness!' Then came a crash, as though he was thumping his desk. Up above, Gus let out a short, sharp bark.

She heard someone – Bonnie she thought – reply in tart

tones, which clearly incensed Julian further. He swore at high volume. 'That's not the point and it's none of your business. How could I expect you to understand? This wretched charity. She hadn't thought it through. The whole thing is nonsense.'

Eve took refuge in the bathroom where she'd hidden the night before. It felt undignified, but she suspected Julian or Bonnie would come storming out of the office at any minute. She didn't fancy coming face to face with them.

The departing man must have been a solicitor, she guessed, come to discuss the contents of Kitty's will. From Julian's reaction, she must have got round to ring-fencing her trust-fund money after all. And he hadn't known. He could certainly have killed her hoping to stop her making the change. He was living at Farfield in the lap of luxury, but he was entirely dependent on Nate's goodwill. Kitty's money would have given him independence. For life, probably.

And Bonnie might have hoped he'd get his hands on it too, and that she could get her hands on him. But not any more, by the look of it. Eve hadn't seen them address a civil word to each other since Kitty's murder. The idea seemed dead in the water.

Eve could still hear raised voices and disappeared into a cubicle.

A moment later she heard someone come into the bathroom and sniff. She wondered if Julian had reduced Bonnie to tears. Angry ones, Eve imagined. She wasn't the sort to lapse into misery.

But a moment later Eve heard a gasp and a gulp from someone who sounded desolate.

She flushed the loo, then opened the door to see Freya's retreating back. She was hurrying, a sticky note clasped in her hand. Perhaps she hadn't realised she had company until Eve made her presence known.

The raised voices from the office had died down, and Eve decided to follow Freya. She wondered if Julian had been yelling at her too, or if she was simply upset by the way her new job was panning out. A murder and open warfare would be enough to throw anyone. Farfield must already be bound up with painful memories. And now this.

Up ahead, Freya turned down the east wing corridor. Eve saw her wipe her eyes with a tissue.

By the time Eve entered the corridor, Freya had disappeared, but she could hear her voice.

'I just spoke to Rhoda. She'll be back in the UK on Friday. She should get here around lunchtime.' She sounded as if she was still reining in tears.

'Friday? That's unexpected. But I doubt she'll be here long.' That was Nate, of course. There was a pause. 'Are you all right? It's been a stressful morning.'

'Yes. It doesn't matter.'

'Did Rhoda pass on any message?'

'She wanted to know how you're bearing up. And when the funeral might be.'

'Ah.'

Nate's wife must be between reporting jobs. Eve wondered how often they managed to snatch time together.

'I'm sorry about Julian.' That was Nate. 'I could hear him all the way down here. His behaviour's unforgivable.' His voice shook.

Nate was right. Eve wondered if he would tell him to leave.

'Are you still happy to have him here?' Freya clearly had the same thought.

There was another pause. 'Happy is overstating it, but I don't want to boot him out now. He's just lost my sister. I might have to ask you and Bonnie to put up with him.'

'We'll cope.' Eve heard the strain in her voice, then her footsteps as she moved towards the door.

Eve ducked into a side room but Freya didn't pass. She must

have gone down towards the dining room. Maybe to sort out lunch.

Eve headed in the same direction. She'd like to talk to her privately. But as she followed, her mind was distracted. Julian wasn't behaving like a grieving husband, yet Nate was determined to keep him on.

Was it just because he needed Julian to make a success of Farfield? Or did Julian have a hold over him? Because Nate had been very close to the icehouse when Kitty's body was found. Eve still had no adequate explanation for that. But she did know Kitty had discovered a secret he was keeping.

From Deidre's account, she hadn't sounded like a threat, but it might depend how much Nate stood to lose.

If only some of the suspects had proper alibis for Kitty's death, but it had been chaos at the party. People here, there and everywhere. Drink flowing. She'd just have to keep watching and digging. And being as careful as she could about it. Her continued presence at the castle wasn't just an advantage to her. It would play into the hands of the killer if they suspected she was onto them.

24

Eve waited outside the dining room door; she didn't want Freya to guess she'd overheard her conversation with Nate.

She could hear the clatter of plates and cutlery and pictured Freya laying the table, bringing the utensils through from the kitchen beyond. Eve wanted to give her time to calm down, but not too long. Catching her in a moment of weakness was mean, but she might get more out of her that way. Eve wanted to know what she and Kitty had argued about and if it would give Freya a motive. She still had her doubts, given it was an old disagreement, but she needed to be sure.

After a minute, she followed Freya in.

'Oh!' Freya almost dropped a plate of salad on the table. She must have been deep in thought. To be fair, there was a lot to distract her.

'Can I help?'

Freya smiled now, despite her red eyes. 'Definitely not. You're our guest. And in any case, our caterer's still bringing in food for lunch and supper. But thank you.'

It was so weird, to continue this charade with Julian yelling in the background and a murder investigation under way. Eve was acutely conscious of what Jo had told everyone about her past involvement with the police. Was that why Freya seemed so nervous?

'How are you?' Eve sat at the table, wondering if Luke might appear. 'It must be so hard to carry on as normal after what's happened.'

Freya straightened her back for a moment. 'We're bearing up.' But then her shoulders drooped. 'I must admit, it's peculiar that it's all happening in what still feels like my home. My husband owned Farfield for ten years. This life is superimposed on top of our old one.'

Eve felt for her. 'Was it a difficult decision, accepting the job here?'

'I wondered if it was wise at first. But it's a great role, and Farfield's beautiful. Turning my back would be like sticking my head in the sand. This way I can work through everything.' She blushed. 'I'm not planning on using our clients for talking therapy, though. I'm sorry. Once we're up and running, we want everyone to feel relaxed. Guests should leave refreshed and invigorated after a complete break from their everyday lives.'

There was passion in her voice and Eve realised she'd misread the situation. This wasn't just a way for Freya to cling on to her memories, or merely a practical move to keep a roof over her head. She'd found something of her own out of the ashes of what had gone before. She sounded driven.

'I'm sure they will. My visit's terrible timing. Luke and I aren't seeing Farfield at its best, but we both understand why. And I can see what it could be like.'

Freya sighed. 'That's good to know. I did wonder about Nate's decision to ask you to stay on. It must be hard to see beyond what's happened. But we heard you'd be a useful person to have around, of course.'

'I don't know about that.' She must be referring to Jo's speech.

Freya was moving towards the door, but Eve hadn't finished yet.

'Will you have some lunch with me?' She gave an apologetic smile. 'I have to write Kitty's obituary and I know you were friends once.'

Freya hovered in the doorway, uncertain.

Eve was acutely aware of Jo's comments now. Freya would assume she wanted to grill her, and of course, she'd be right. How could Eve put her at her ease? 'I gather you and Kitty fell out, and you're not the only ones. I've already spoken to Ella Tyndall. I know your own quarrel was an old one. I doubt it's relevant now, but it's useful to get everyone's views. I don't have to quote you if you'd rather I didn't. We can even talk off the record. It will just inform what I write.'

Freya glanced up and down the corridor, then came back into the room.

'Okay.' She took a plate and helped herself to tomato, basil and mozzarella, and a second salad with red cabbage, walnuts and apple. 'How did you know I'd fallen out with Kitty?'

'I overheard you arguing during the preparations for the launch party.'

'Ah.'

'I wondered how you'd met.'

Freya leaned on the table a moment and rested her head in her hands. 'She came and knocked on the door around five years ago and explained her connection to Farfield. I knew her by sight of course – she was still a famous face – and I'd heard about her link with the house via Moira in the village store.' She gave a wry smile. 'She got very excited when she heard Kitty had been to visit.' Then her face fell. 'I expect she's found my recent woes just as juicy. Of course, most of it's been reported in the papers. That must have made her job a lot easier.'

Eve refrained from commenting but her mind flitted over the details Moira had dished up.

'Anyway, I offered to let Kitty look round the house, and we became friends. She wasn't in Suffolk often, but she always dropped in if she was in the area.'

'How would you describe her?'

'At the time she seemed kind. Dedicated. She was back to running clubs for charity as well as evening classes to keep her head above water.'

'You say "seemed"?'

Freya took a deep breath, then shook her head. 'That's right. And I found her sympathetic too.' There was a pause. 'Things were already getting shaky back then. I confided in her about Craig. Not about the criminal stuff, of course; I didn't know about that until later. But about our relationship. Just odds and bits. She made it easier because I could see she was hurting too. She never went into details about her estrangement from her grandparents. I suppose she was worried I'd be indiscreet.' Freya gripped her napkin and blinked. Eve could see the anger in her eyes.

It was a moment before Freya managed to continue. 'But although she didn't share the details, it gave us a sort of bond. I honestly thought of her as one of my best friends at that point. I'd only see her every six months or so, but we clicked.'

Eve understood that. It had been the same with her and Viv. She'd never met someone so open and easy to get on with. For a second, she imagined them falling out and how crushing it would be.

'It was just after Kitty married Julian that the scales fell from my eyes. I'd rather you didn't quote me. She came here before she left for France. It was ridiculous, but I felt upset. It wasn't just her impending move, perhaps, but her new bond with Julian. She seemed less forthcoming suddenly, tenser. I had the feeling that our friendship would never be quite the same. Selfish, I know.'

But Eve understood that too. She'd been harbouring secret selfish thoughts about Robin, now that he had his freedom at last. She wondered how he was getting on in court.

'And then while she was visiting, she disappeared into the bathroom, and she took a long time. I ended up following her and found her snooping about the place. Nipping into her old bedroom. And I suddenly realised, she didn't come to Farfield to see me. She came because she missed the house. And now she knew she'd be around less often, she wanted one last look, to remind her of her childhood, back when she'd been happy.'

Freya's reaction seemed extreme. 'Couldn't she have minded about both you and the house?'

Freya looked down. 'At the time, I told myself that. But afterwards it became plain to me.' She got up suddenly and picked up her plate, her salad still uneaten. 'Excuse me. If that's enough for you, I ought to be getting on.'

All her formality was back. She looked deeply uncomfortable. Eve felt for her. She hated laying her feelings bare too. It usually took her at least a day to recover.

On her way back to her bedroom to prepare for her London trip, Eve bumped into Nate. He glanced at her briefly.

'I'm sorry if you heard the row earlier.'

'There's no need to apologise.' But she waited, her eyes on his, hoping he'd say more.

'Julian doesn't see things the same way Kitty did.'

That had been abundantly clear. 'What about you?'

'I'm glad the charity will go ahead.'

'Who will run it, now Kitty's dead?'

Nate's look turned dark. 'My father.' He closed his eyes for a moment. 'I can't believe she nominated him after all he's done. She wrote to me explaining. The letter was with her will.'

That was interesting. Kitty must have anticipated Nate's

reaction. She'd been sufficiently worried about it to write that explanation, though she couldn't have expected to die. It showed how much she'd minded about her brother and his good opinion. And the same applied to her dad.

Nate took a deep breath. 'Kitty's note says it's because of what happened to Mum. She knows he'll make sure the charity works because he loved her. She says he's not a bad man. That he never understood Granny and Gramps, which was tragic, and that she failed them too.' He shook his head. 'She can't see how he twisted things. How selfish and manipulative he was. And how is a poet qualified to administer a multimillion-pound charity? Kitty's recommended some trustees in her will, but whether he takes any notice is another matter. She was still in Dad's thrall. She just couldn't see it.'

Eve remembered their previous conversation. 'You said you might contribute some of your trust fund to Kitty's charity. Will you go ahead, when it comes in?'

Nate's eyes met hers. 'I would have, if he wasn't involved. I shan't now. But it'll spur me on to do my own thing. Put even more into this venture, perhaps.'

As Eve walked towards her bedroom, she reflected on what he'd said. He might do his 'own thing', but he'd be doing it because of his dad. If it weren't for Benet, he'd have supported his sister's project.

Over in Saxford, Eve let herself into Elizabeth's Cottage and wished that her time at Farfield was over. Being on the spot was working well in practical terms, but not emotionally. The atmosphere was miserable and claustrophobic.

A moment later, Viv appeared at the door.

'The customers?' Eve knew the schedule she'd created for Monty's off by heart. It was only Viv and Lars on that afternoon, until three, when Tammy would join them for the busiest period.

'Lovely to see you too.' Viv's rose-pink hair glinted in the sunshine. 'I only slipped out for a moment to check up on you. The quicker you give me your news, the quicker I'll be back at Monty's. But Lars is fine. You know how capable he is.'

'He hasn't got two pairs of hands. All right, come in quickly then. I've got a train to catch.'

'Not terribly welcoming.'

'Sorry.' Eve gave her a hug. She was thinking of Freya and Kitty's falling-out. It made her emotional.

'You're forgiven.' Viv gave her a strange look. 'Are you all right? I'm not used to you displaying moments of vulnerability. It's disturbing.'

Eve explained what Freya had told her. 'That's in the strictest confidence.'

Viv waved aside her worries. 'I won't go and quote you at Moira's.' She put her head on one side. 'It's sweet that it made you think of us, but you don't need to worry. I can't imagine going off you when you're so useful at the teashop.'

'Thanks.'

'So, go on then,' Viv said. 'What do you think about what she said?'

'It's an extreme reaction.'

Viv nodded. 'Though I suppose Kitty's behaviour does sound a bit sneaky. Why not just ask for one last look round?'

'To avoid what happened, I suppose – Kitty was probably worried Freya would think she'd only befriended her to get back inside the house.'

'Maybe...'

'Either way, I'm sure Freya's holding something back. I keep thinking of the discussion I overheard. Kitty was trying to build bridges but Freya said it was too late. And then that she thought they were friends. And that she'd never have guessed Kitty "had such a hateful ulterior motive". It's way too strong a reaction to Kitty sneaking into her childhood bedroom.

'Freya said her opinion of Kitty was confirmed later. And Ella called her selfish. Neither description matches the woman I saw.' But Eve had hardly known her. 'Let's see what Benet says, and what he thought of Julian too.'

25

Eve arrived in London by four. She'd left Gus happily anticipating Tammy's visit. She seemed to rank as several degrees more entertaining than Eve.

Fine.

As she sat on the tube, she tried to focus on her questions for Benet, though thoughts of Robin giving evidence were hard to quash. It felt weird to know he was so close, but she wouldn't see him. Anticipation of her meet-up with the twins cheered her up, giving her a warm glow.

Eve met Benet Marchant in a community café in a disused railway arch in Southwark. The curved ceiling was plastered with posters, a lot of them political. The tables were rough boards scrubbed clean. It was definitely beat-poet territory, but Eve couldn't help thinking of all the money Benet had inherited from his wife.

She walked in with clear ideas in her head. She needed to understand how his parenting had affected Kitty, because of the obituary, and Nate, because he was a suspect. And she wanted his thoughts on Julian.

Eve guessed Benet was in his seventies. She'd found the odd

photo of him online and identified him that way. He was dressed in black jeans and a T-shirt, looking rugged with a five o'clock shadow. His untidy, tufty hair was grey and he looked at Eve judgingly, without smiling. She was making her mind up about him, too.

She offered him a coffee and he accepted. Even that felt like a minor triumph. He looked determined not to give an inch.

'Thank you for seeing me.' She sat down and put the coffee in front of him. 'I'm so sorry for your loss. I got to know Kitty briefly before she was killed. I liked her.'

He gave a slight nod.

'I wondered if you could tell me about her – both growing up, and as an adult. It sounds like you were close.'

'When she was a child, we thought very much alike.'

'That tends to be the case, perhaps. Children normally start to lock horns with their parents when they enter adolescence.'

'It happened even earlier with Nate, but not with Kitty. She, her mother and I were thick as thieves. United. We'd knock around together, hang out with the same friends. Play music, talk about art and literature. It knocked me sideways when she sold out.'

Eve had been jotting in her notepad. 'Sold out?'

'Followed the money. Allowed herself to be flattered into book deals and TV. But at least she was better than Nate. He couldn't cut the apron strings with my parents. Accepted them paying for his education, then went into banking, of all things.'

Said the man who must stay afloat thanks to his wife's money. 'He writes too, of course.'

Benet shrugged. 'No one recognises his work except Julian Fisher and that hardly counts, given Nate cultivated the friendship. He's a follower, that's the trouble. He's never been brave enough to forge his own path. If your work's unoriginal, then it's just self-indulgence.'

'He's had some interest recently.'

'On the back of this new venture, from reviewers who can't think for themselves.'

He must have followed the coverage as carefully as she had, and it clearly wasn't out of fondness. Eve sensed Nate would have to be a very particular sort of writer to gain his approval. Acclaimed as groundbreaking, but not financially successful, or Benet would say he'd 'sold out'.

'I read some great reviews of your poetry.' She wanted to test him. 'It must be frustrating that your collections don't sell more copies.'

He twitched. 'Not at all. There just aren't enough people who're able to understand my work. I knew that would be the case. If people opened their eyes – looked up from their phones – they'd see it. But they won't. It's just a fact of life. I'm happy to be breaking new ground. That's what Nate needs to do.'

She was starting to understand why Nate still kicked against his dad.

'As for the retreat!' Benet snorted.

'I gather Kitty hoped you might attend the launch party.'

He put his mug on the table. 'At the moment it's an exclusive bolthole for the rich. Nothing to do with talent. Kitty came to me with some plan for giving out bursaries but it was all talk, not action. If Nate does it, perhaps I'll visit then.'

Big of him. But Nate wouldn't want him there, and it was too late for Kitty. Eve waited for him to express regret, but he didn't.

She'd found it hard to imagine Benet watching his parents' furniture being carried out of Farfield. Carted off to a salesroom as Sophie and Daniel gathered their remaining belongings and locked the door for the last time. It was deeply cruel. But now, it didn't seem so impossible.

He might have been in pieces at the time, still stunned by his wife's death, but he seemed vindictive and uncompromising by nature.

'What mystifies me is Nate's marriage to Rhoda.' Benet leaned back in his chair. 'And her love for him. She devotes her life to uncovering the truth. Reporting on some of the worst regimes in the world. Yet he... he plays around with other people's money.'

Just as Benet was. Not as a job, but in his private life as he spent his wife's. Eve's heart rate ramped up. She almost said something, but it wouldn't help the rest of the interview. She needed more on Julian. He was a top suspect.

'What was your reaction when Kitty decided to marry?'

His expression got harder. 'I hated it. Julian's a fraud.'

Eve couldn't disagree with him there.

'And controlling.'

'In what way?'

'Recently, Kitty told me she felt watched. Once, she'd come back to their house in Suffolk for a quiet talk with a friend. Julian said he'd be out, but when the friend left she found him sitting in the dark, listening.'

Eve shivered. It was creepy. 'You and Kitty must still have been close, if she confided in you.'

He shrugged. 'She wanted to know what I thought. Julian talked his way out of it. Said he'd come home unexpectedly. Didn't want to interrupt. She said she was inclined to believe him, but why ask for a second opinion if she was convinced?'

'But we didn't meet to talk about that. She got in touch to say she planned to use her trust fund to set up a drugs charity in memory of her mum. In the end, I agreed to work with her. The plan had some merit.'

Praise indeed. Eve imagined Kitty trying to close the gap between them. A gap that had opened when she got successful. She had to agree with Nate. He wasn't worth it. But when you'd been brought up by someone, she guessed it wasn't easy to recover when they cast you aside.

'We met here, as a matter of fact,' Benet went on. 'Kitty told me about her plans to ring-fence the inheritance so Julian couldn't get at it. She was still indulging him, but she was starting to wake up to reality. She said he was hopeless with money.'

'This was recently?'

'Three weeks ago. Until that point, I imagine Julian thought he'd talk her into spending her cash on him. I suspect he knew he was marrying into money when he proposed. He's far too wily not to have looked into it. He'd have made himself as pleasant as possible. Wooed her quite deliberately.'

It was a nasty thought, but it made sense. A deliberate effort on Julian's part to disguise his true character would explain Kitty marrying him.

'Thankfully, Kitty got the legalities sewn up before she died. I've had a call from her solicitor. The money's in trust and Kitty names me as a trustee. I'll be putting her plans into action.'

He spoke as if the charity was more important than his daughter's life. The thought of anything happening to Eve's children filled her with the deepest, most unbearable pain. She couldn't imagine when, if ever, she'd be able to focus on anything else again. What kind of a man was Benet? He'd probably say he was unconventional. Able to rise above the feelings of mere mortals.

'Kitty was careful about her plans for the charity,' he went on. 'Told no one but me about her intention to ring-fence the money. She didn't want any interference. She knew Julian was greedy, yet she stayed with him.' He sounded disgusted.

Eve had a feeling that might not have lasted much longer. Another reason for Julian to act quickly and kill her if he hoped to get the cash.

Then suddenly the import of Benet's words struck her. 'Wait a minute. You say she only told you?'

He nodded. 'That's what she said.'

Yet Luke had known. How? Would Kitty really have

confided in him? Once again, Eve wondered if they'd known each other better than they'd admitted.

On impulse, she took out her phone. 'Can I ask you if you recognise this man?' She found Luke's photo on *Cascade*'s website.

Benet's eyebrows went up when she showed him. 'A reporter? So that's who he was.'

'Excuse me?'

'He was here. On another table, the day Kitty came to see me. I know the regulars and he's not one of them. Besides, he's not the sort who usually comes here, any more than you are.'

Eve glanced at the other clientele, who looked perfectly normal, and felt faintly irritated.

'It's funny.' Benet closed his eyes for a moment. 'I had the impression he was paying us too much attention. I got a wild idea Julian had employed an investigator to tail Kitty to see what we talked about. But then he left, and I decided I was being fanciful.'

The interview with Benet Marchant filled Eve's mind with questions, but after she'd been through them, she was left feeling depressed. What would it be like to have a dad like him? Her thoughts drifted to her own father all the way over in Seattle. His gentle encouragement and his pride in her achievements, whatever they were, had always felt unconditional.

In a haze of sorrow for Kitty, she texted Robin to say she hoped his day had gone well. She had no idea when he'd be finished. She guessed there'd be debriefs with lawyers and colleagues before he was free.

Seeing the twins was restorative. She spent a happy hour with them in a bar in Camden, eating, drinking and meeting her daughter Ellen's new boyfriend. As they talked, she noticed the pair exchange secret glances and smiles with her son Nick and his girlfriend. For a moment Eve felt left out, but then Nick disappeared, returning with a bottle of champagne. And then, the news was out. It brought tears to her eyes. Happy ones. Nick and his girlfriend, Fiona, were engaged. They'd been savouring the news, wanting to announce it with ceremony, but not wanting to steal Ellen's thunder.

There was much whooping, a lot of hugging, then more tears.

Eve spent the train journey home feeling ridiculously sentimental. Her hazy, happy thoughts turned to Robin, who'd texted to say the day in court had gone smoothly. He was still tied up with colleagues but he'd be back in Suffolk the following day. Regret at not seeing him that evening seemed ridiculous now. She was on the home straight. His presence was like a warm glow in front of her.

It was dark by the time she collected Gus from Elizabeth's Cottage. She was tempted to go inside. Spend time in familiar surroundings. But it would make returning to Farfield even more difficult. She closed the door regretfully and headed back to her car.

She was daydreaming about Robin, and nearing the turn to the castle, when she saw the patrol car. She felt her skin prick. 'Worrying,' she said aloud, looking at Gus in her rear-view mirror. 'Especially at this time of night.'

Gus looked back at her sleepily.

The patrol car turned towards the coast instead of the castle. In the distance, she saw its headlights pick out the reeds by the creek where Farfield's rowing boat was moored. She couldn't see the boat itself.

The patrol car's lights went out and Eve took the turn up the long castle drive. Wondering. Watching in her rear-view mirror.

And then another vehicle turned up, following the first towards the creek.

She got out of her car and released Gus from his harness, all the while on high alert. What had happened? And who to?

Who had called the police?

Inside, the castle was deserted.

'Bed soon, I promise, Gus.'

She started walking across the lawns towards the old deer park and the quickest route to the creek.

26

Eve walked over the grass, smooth in the castle gardens, then rougher in the old deer park. The scene in front of her clarified as she crossed the scrubby path towards the creek, marshes ahead of her.

She could see a couple of uniformed officers taking notes, another on his radio. Nate stood with his hand in his hair, tugging at it. Bonnie was shaking her head and Freya was walking up to the water, then crouching down to examine something.

Julian stamped his foot, petulantly. 'He's clearly guilty.'

The only person Eve couldn't see was Luke.

Bonnie raised her eyes to Eve's, her expression unfriendly, and now they all turned to look at her.

'I saw the patrol cars. What's happened?'

It was Nate who spoke. 'Luke's disappeared.'

'He turned down our offer for a guided tour of local attractions this afternoon,' Bonnie said. 'Then, at around half past three, I saw him head in this direction, carrying the oars for the boat.'

'I wasn't sure if he'd want supper,' Freya added, 'so I went to look for him at around six. There was no answer when I knocked on his door, so I wandered out here, and saw he wasn't back.'

'Freya waited for a bit, then let me know,' Nate put in. 'I called his mobile, but he didn't pick up. I wouldn't have worried normally, but with what happened to Kitty...' He let the sentence hang. 'I gave him a little longer, then called the police.'

'He did it!' Julian said again. 'And he got the wind up. Now he's gone off in our boat and we'll never hear from him again.'

'But if he's guilty, why would he have hung around until now?' Eve said.

Julian gave her an exasperated look. 'It took a while for him to feel the pressure. The police were onto him. He had their full focus. He must have realised the game was up. He thought he could make himself seem innocent by hanging around, but in the end, he knew the plan wasn't working. This is my wife's murderer we're talking about. I'm not waiting while everyone argues, and he gets away.' His fists were bunched as he strode back towards the castle.

Freya had been looking out to sea as though Luke might still be there, bobbing around in the boat. She turned back in response to Julian's words, a worried look in her eyes, her face pinched.

'Sir! Sir!' one of the officers called after Julian, to no avail. The man turned to Nate. 'You both have our deepest sympathy, but we can't have Mr Fisher taking matters into his own hands. DI Palmer will be here in a minute, and he'll want to interview everyone. We've alerted the coastguard.'

Eve glanced at her watch. Past eleven already. If Luke had been gone since half past three, he might be anywhere by now. If he'd really left. He had plenty of questions to answer, but if anyone was after a scapegoat, he'd be an ideal candidate. He'd been the police's top suspect, like Julian said, jointly with Ella. And Bonnie, officially, but Palmer would far prefer Luke to her

as the killer. It would be much less damaging to the area's reputation if an outsider was to blame.

'I'll talk to Julian.' Nate walked around, presumably
searching for a signal, then made the call. He got through all
right. Maybe he'd dialled the house phone. Eve heard him beg
Julian to stay put. Assure him that the authorities had it
covered. He was cut off abruptly, partway through a sentence.

Eve imagined one of them following Luke into the deserted
marshy area where the reeds were high and hid the creek from
view. They could have hit him over the head, just like Kitty,
then rowed him out to sea to dump the body. She needed to
know where everyone had been that afternoon. But maybe
Julian was right. Luke could have done a runner.

'I suggest you all go back to the house.' It was the
uniformed officer who'd asked Nate to remonstrate with Julian.
'I expect you'd like hot drinks or something of the sort. PC
Dashwood will come with you. DI Palmer will follow on in due
course.'

Nate nodded and they traipsed back across the grass.

Gus had decided it was well past his bedtime. He glanced
up at Eve briefly, a look of censure in his eyes, then dashed
towards the castle with all due speed.

Eve, Gus and Freya were ahead of the others.

'So you didn't see Luke at all this afternoon?' Eve asked. 'I
guess you were inside? I know how busy you've been.'

Freya grimaced. 'I was in the library, indexing books. I'm
afraid I left Bonnie to field calls. They're thinning out, and I've
done the honours up until now. I just needed some space. I had
my head down. I didn't even look out of the window.'

Not exactly gold standard, as alibis went, but she sounded
honest.

They reached the door before the rest of the group. Just
inside, Eve could hear scrabbling upstairs.

Her and Freya's eyes met. In unspoken agreement, they

climbed to the upper floor – just in time to see Julian emerge from Luke's bedroom.

The author looked at them defiantly. 'I thought he might have left a note. Or some clue as to his true relationship with Kitty. It's useless to rely on the police! They'll never get this sorted out.'

PC Dashwood had appeared at the top of the stairs now. 'I strongly advise that you leave the case to us, sir. Interfering and contaminating evidence will only hold up proceedings.' Eve saw her scan Fisher closely. She was doing the same thing. He held nothing in his hands, and his pockets looked empty.

She didn't think he'd taken anything from Luke's room. And it had sounded like he'd been searching it. But, of course, that could be what he hoped they'd think. He might have planted something, if he wanted Luke to look guilty.

27

The atmosphere the following morning was tense. Eve was still reliving her interview with DI Palmer, who'd pushed and probed. He seemed to think she and Luke might be in cahoots because they were both journalists. Or at least that Luke might have confided in her. He ended the interview by warning her off any amateur sleuthing. Eve thought of the request she'd put to Portia Coldwell for information on Luke, and said nothing. She'd mastered the art of nodding and smiling at Palmer. However hard she had to clench her fists while doing it.

Now, she, Nate, Freya, Bonnie and Julian were in the dining room eating breakfast. The latest development had laid their true situation bare. Eve couldn't be expected to write a decent review of Farfield any more. Not with Luke missing and a fresh batch of reporters gathered outside the castle gates. Julian had let rip in front of her more than once. Now, Nate was doing his best to stop him saying too much to the press.

'I believe you're right.' He had his work cut out, trying to hold Julian's attention. 'Luke might be guilty. But think about what you're doing! I'm no lawyer, but what happens when he's caught if you've spoken against him publicly? What if his representatives say we prejudiced the trial or something?'

Julian thumped the table. 'The press are already talking about him as a "person of interest" without my input.'

It was true. Eve had seen the first online reports of Luke's disappearance at around eight that morning. Someone had leaked the information. Maybe the reporter had a contact on the force. Or maybe Julian had done it.

'We have to find him,' Julian said. 'I'm going to hire a boat. Go and look myself. We can't wait.'

He was red-faced and twitched in his seat.

'How did he look when he wandered towards the creek, Bonnie?' Eve lifted her coffee cup. 'Were you close enough to see his face?' She wanted to know where she'd been.

'No. I was stuck in blasted reception all afternoon.' She shot a look at Freya. 'I happened to see him through the window. And thinking back, he looked furtive. I suppose that's why I carried on watching. He skirted the edge of the gardens before he cut towards the creek.'

'There you are then!' Julian said.

But if they wanted to pin the blame on Luke it was in all their interests to tell that story.

'I wish I'd seen him,' Julian growled. 'The muse picked the wrong moment to seize me. I wrote a thousand words yesterday afternoon, but I'd sacrifice every one to have stopped my wife's killer.'

What dedication. Eve saw the pain in Nate's eyes. 'You didn't see him?' she asked.

The financier shook his head. 'I was on the phone to my office in London all afternoon. It feels horrible now. The wrong priorities. But one of the juniors on my team needed support.'

Eve thought of Julian's talk of the Marchant social conscience. Nate came across as a decent man. But what was he hiding? It could have made him do something desperate.

When she glanced up, she met Julian's furious gaze.

'I imagine you'll want to go home now,' he said, his voice gravelly with suppressed anger. 'We can't possibly function normally with Kitty's killer on the run.'

Nate turned towards her. 'I'd been thinking the same thing. It was wrong of me to suggest you stay.'

It must have been Luke they'd wanted to keep around then. Now he was gone, they were happy for her to leave. And Julian's tone had been threatening. But they couldn't force her to go. Not without looking guilty, thanks to Jo's performance. And despite the quivering in her stomach, Eve was determined to stay. The party and the afternoon of Luke's disappearance were similar. No one had an adequate alibi. No one could be ruled out. All she could do was watch and eliminate people as each relationship became clear. She couldn't do that from Saxford.

She took a deep breath. 'It's very thoughtful of you, and it's true, of course. It wouldn't be fair to write a review of Farfield now.'

She watched their relief.

'But I'm still composing Kitty's obituary. I really mind about it, having met her. Being here's helping me feel connected with her. So unless you object, I'd love to see out my stay. I'll try to keep out of your way as much as possible.'

Julian reddened, but after a brief pause, Nate nodded. 'Of course. We understand.'

Eve felt a tight knot of awkwardness, but it would be worth it.

'Well, I can't waste time sitting around talking about the media!' Julian rose, slamming his coffee cup down on the table. 'I've got other priorities.'

'Catching a killer?' Bonnie sounded irritable. 'Luke might be at the bottom of the sea by now. That boat was for rowing up and down the creek, not for open water.'

Her boss stormed out of the room without replying.

An hour later, Eve was with Viv in the kitchens at Monty's, having left Gus at Elizabeth's Cottage. She wasn't working that day, but it seemed efficient to muck in while she passed on the news.

As she sifted flour, she told Viv about the scene at breakfast, then filled her in on her meeting with Benet.

'He sounds like a right charmer.' Viv glanced over her shoulder as she broke eggs into a bowl. 'What do you make of it all?'

Eve was just opening her mouth to tell her when Lars appeared in the doorway.

'Moira's here. She seems very excitable. I'm going to fetch her a camomile tea but she says she'd like to talk to you, Eve.'

Viv dashed forward. 'I'm coming too.'

'What about the cakes?'

'What about them? She's obviously got news. I refuse to be kept in the dark.'

Eve sighed. 'Please could you tell Moira we'll be with her in five minutes, Lars?'

He grinned. 'Sure.'

Viv huffed. 'How did you get to be so good at this delayed gratification thing? It's unnatural.'

'It'll give us time to chew things over before we get fresh information.'

'All right then.'

Five minutes later, Eve and Viv joined Moira at her seat in the window.

'Ah, Eve dear.' Moira let out a relieved sigh. 'I thought you'd never come. I've left Paul minding the shop.' Always a grave decision. He was a past master at repelling the regulars. 'I was so shocked to hear about Luke Shipley's disappearance. Though of course, we were all wondering if he was guilty. He sounds very unsavoury.'

'What makes you say that?'

The storekeeper leaned forward importantly. 'I've been given to understand that he'd been spying on Kitty through her bedroom window. He's clearly a peeping Tom. It's one of the reasons I wanted to see you. People were in and out all day yesterday with news.'

Eve needed all the information she could get, of course, but only if it was accurate. 'Who said that?'

'Let me see. An awful lot of people have been in.' She hesitated. 'I believe it was Gwen Harris.'

Viv and Eve's eyes met and Viv raised an eyebrow. 'She's not terribly reliable, is she?' she said, turning to Moira.

She'd once told DI Palmer that Eve had been having a fling with a murder victim. Eve had never quite forgiven her. 'The thing is, Moira, the only time Gwen could have seen him do that was on the night of the launch party, when Kitty was fully clothed and mainly downstairs.' When she wasn't having a stand-up row with Bonnie Whitelaw, obviously.

Moira put her head on one side. 'She did seem very sure about it, Eve.'

Lars arrived with more tea and some chocolate heart cakes. As soon as they'd thanked him, Eve cast her thoughts back to Gwen.

Perhaps she was the boy who'd cried wolf. Maybe Luke had watched the row between Kitty and Bonnie. Looking for information. Gwen might have assumed Kitty was in her bedroom because she was upstairs.

The thought of Luke monitoring Kitty made the hairs on Eve's arms lift. He might have had the same goal down in London, when he'd listened to her and her dad talking. Why had he wanted details of her private dealings? One interaction had been about money, one a row about emotional matters.

How did it fit together? Benet said he'd wondered if Julian had sent Luke to spy on Kitty. Did that make any sense? Julian seemed to despise Luke and now he was making a big noise about his possible guilt. He certainly seemed panicked about his disappearance. But what if it wasn't out of a desire for revenge but from fear? What if he and Luke had collaborated and Luke was no longer following their agreed plan? Or might Luke be innocent, but know something damaging about Julian?

For a moment, Eve wondered about Julian's missing laptop and the fact that Luke's room could have been searched twice, once before and once after his disappearance. Was that what Julian had been looking for? Had Luke run to escape him? But if the laptop had anything damning on it, why wouldn't Luke take it to the police?

'Anyway,' Moira went on, 'Gwen's just one person who came to see me. There have been plenty more. I feel I must be here for them. It's something of a duty.' She paused and shook her head. 'Until we heard Luke Shipley had disappeared, I'm afraid several people thought Ella Tyndall was just as likely to be guilty as him.'

'Why's that? Apart from what we already know, I mean?'

'Well.' Moira leaned over the table and lowered her voice conspiratorially. 'April saw her sitting in the churchyard for two hours yesterday. She was there when she left for Blyworth, and still there when she returned.' April was Moira's sister. 'It suggested a guilty conscience to us.'

Eve bit into a chocolate heart cake for strength. She'd need to unpick that. Ella could have gone away while April was in town, then come back again. But why would she? The location seemed irrelevant to Eve, but sitting anywhere for that long suggested the need to think things through.

'Anything else?'

Moira nodded eagerly and Eve knew she should expect an especially juicy morsel. The storekeeper tended to save them up. 'Ella came in earlier this morning when a group of us were discussing the news about Luke Shipley and defended him, if you please! And now I hear, from Pam Crockett, that he was outside Ella's house, late lunchtime yesterday.'

Shortly before he returned to Farfield and disappeared, assuming Bonnie's report was correct. That was interesting. 'You mean right outside? In her front garden?'

Moira nodded. 'As if he was on his way out. Pam watched him walk off.'

Eve thought back to the way Ella had patted Luke's arm after their one-to-one chat following the history tour. And then he'd gone to visit.

At that moment, the bell over the teashop door jangled and Molly Walker, Moira's most level-headed friend, came in.

She greeted them, her eyes anxious. 'Do you mind if I join you?'

Lars was already bringing her a chair.

Molly thanked him, but her brow was furrowed, and she chewed her lip uneasily. 'The village is full of the news about Luke Shipley.'

Eve nodded and poured tea and milk into the extra cup Lars had provided. 'Are you all right, Molly?'

She blinked. 'Hearing his name on everyone's lips has jogged my memory. And now I'm worried I saw something I should have mentioned to the police.'

Moira put a hand on her arm. Eve wasn't sure if she was offering comfort or restraining her from leaping back up again before she'd shared her thoughts.

'I'm sure you're not to blame,' Moira said. 'Maybe you can tell me, or rather,' she cast a regretful look at Eve and Viv, 'us, all about it. Get it off your chest. And then you can pop along to the police station if talking it over makes you think it's important.' She pushed the chocolate heart cakes in Molly's direction.

Molly took one without looking at it and nodded. 'It was

just an odd thing after that row we overheard at the launch party. You know the one Luke Shipley had with Julian Fisher's PA?'

Moira nodded. 'Yes.' She sounded breathless.

'Well, when they appeared, I was standing nearby and I happened to notice Luke Shipley had blood on his hand. I half expected the PA to emerge with a bloody nose or something, but when I saw she looked normal I forgot all about it, especially after what happened later. I should have remembered. Told the police. And now Kitty's killer has got away.'

28

Eve's mind was full of Molly's news, but it didn't alter her plan. She wanted to talk to Ella, who seemed to have a secret link with Luke. She hoped she might find her in, given it was half-term. She wanted to know what had made the pair of them pal up, and why Ella had hung around in the churchyard.

She went to fetch Gus, then walked along the estuary path to reach Ferry Lane, where the teacher lived.

Thoughts of the blood on Luke's hand filled her head. It could have been his, not Bonnie's, but it suggested a violent altercation, just as Molly had said. What had gone on between them? She remembered Luke's words again. *I don't believe it. Is this your idea of a joke? I knew it! I knew there was something.*

There'd been that crash too. Perhaps Luke had thrown something. Smashed a glass? Julian had been angry about the rumpus. Bonnie could have cleared up the mess before anyone saw it.

Eve had arrived in Ella's road, Ferry Lane, a pretty route between the estuary and the village green. She'd been to her cottage before, for neighbours' drinks. The scent of wisteria filled the air.

Eve knocked on the door and Gus looked up eagerly, preparing for the attention Ella always gave him.

'I wouldn't get overexcited,' she said. 'I don't think she's in.' There were no windows open, despite the warm day.

Eve knocked a second time, to be sure, but the place remained dark and quiet. She stood back, looking up at the windows and wondering. Gus, on his extendable leash, was sniffing around the base of the cottage and now he looked round at Eve.

'What have you found?' She went to join him. A pair of wellington boots, sitting in the shade. Dry, but with a small damp patch just underneath. 'It's a good clue.' She bent to stroke him. 'But it only tells us she was here earlier, I'm afraid.' She must have walked near the estuary or the sea. There'd been no rain.

Gus put his head on one side.

'I know, let's stop off at the Cross Keys.'

The dachshund sprang to attention and dashed down the garden path. The Cross Keys to him meant Hetty, the pub's schnauzer and the love of Gus's life. To Eve it meant the chance to catch up with her friends behind the bar, and grab lunch before she headed to Blyworth. She wanted to visit the florists and see if she could find out who'd left the mysterious bouquet near the deer park.

Toby Falconer, Jo's brother-in-law and a co-owner of the Cross Keys, greeted her like a long-lost friend. 'I know you've only been gone since Saturday, but a lot's happened since then. What can I get you?'

As Gus scampered over to Hetty and Eve asked for a Coke, Jo and her husband Matt appeared.

'What news?' Jo said. 'You're not taking risks, I hope. I'd feel responsible.'

'If Luke Shipley's guilty like everyone's saying then I ought to be safer now he's gone.'

Jo peered at Eve narrowly. 'You think the gossip's off the mark?'

'I'm still not sure, to be honest.' Eve ran through everything she'd discovered so far in a low voice.

Jo tutted. 'You'll get there. Just you watch your step. I want you back here in one piece to sample our new dish next week. Rigatoni with globe artichokes and smoked bacon.'

She stalked off to the kitchen to laughter from Matt and a wry smile from Toby.

As Matt went to serve another customer, Toby took Eve's order for a ploughman's lunch. As she paid, he leaned in, frowning. 'I've got some information for you. I didn't like to say too much in front of Jo. She's so invested, and this might mean nothing.'

'What is it?'

'I saw Ella this morning.'

Eve raised an eyebrow.

'Hetty woke early. One of the B and B guests made a racket and that was that, so I took her for a walk ahead of time. I spotted Ella mooring her boat.'

Eve thought of the drying wellington boots. What the heck had Ella been doing out on the water at that hour? 'Did you talk to her?'

'No.' Toby looked even more uneasy now. 'I was walking through the woods when I saw her. And—' He stopped abruptly and sighed.

'You don't have to tell me if you don't want to.' She fervently hoped he'd feel obliged.

Toby shook his head. 'Sorry. It's just that I feel bad saying it, but I had the impression she didn't want to be seen. She was looking over her shoulder, as though she was checking for onlookers. Hetty stayed quiet, thankfully, and I hung back.'

'So Ella was out in her boat, less than twenty-four hours

after Luke disappeared in his. And before the news hit the online sites.'

Toby's sober eyes met hers. 'That about sums it up.'

Eve's mind was full of Toby's news as she drove to Blyworth with Gus in the back seat.

'I can't help feeling Ella's boat trip is connected with Luke's.' Her dachshund's eyes met hers in the rear-view mirror. 'And what was he doing, going to see her yesterday lunchtime?'

He could have told her he was planning to run, but would anyone confess their guilt to someone they'd only just met? And why would Ella feel any sympathy? She'd disliked Kitty – hated her even. But that didn't mean she'd protect her murderer, if that's what Luke was. Most people had lines they wouldn't cross.

Either way, the idea of him confiding in her, then Ella heading out in her boat hours later, made no sense. Why would she?

'The more I discover, the more confused I get,' she said to Gus. 'There's an explanation that will make everything fall into place but I sure as heck can't see it.'

She parked her Clubman in a back street and walked to the florists, which occupied the ground floor of a timber-framed house. Pushing the door open she was greeted with the smell of stock, early freesias and roses. She noticed the change in humidity too. It reminded her a little of the flower stalls in Pike Place Market back in Seattle. She felt a sharp stab of homesickness that took her by surprise. The case was unsettling. If only her parents weren't so far away.

The woman behind the counter finished wrapping a bouquet in patterned paper, took the money for the flowers and turned to Eve. 'How can I help?'

She was prepared for some playacting. 'Some friends

bought a lovely bouquet from you. Gypsophila, white roses and stocks. There were some other flowers too. I can't quite remember... I'd love to have one made up exactly the same.' She didn't mention the sea thistles. They were too distinctive. The florist might recall the bouquet and reproduce it without giving Eve the information she needed.

The woman's brow wrinkled. 'We can certainly try to recreate it for you. Or something very similar if that will do.'

'I'd love to have one just like it if possible. Might you have the details written down if I give you my friend's name?'

The woman brightened. 'Yes, if it was a special order, rather than a pre-prepared bouquet.'

Eve hoped it was. She hadn't seen anything to match it in the green buckets around the shop. 'That's wonderful.' Then she bit her lip. Talk about ham acting. It felt transparent. 'I've just realised, I'm not sure which of my friends put the order in.' She could leave out Nate and Julian. They had no reason to keep a floral tribute secret. 'It might have been Luke. Luke Shipley?'

If she recognised his name, the florist gave no sign of it. She tapped the details into her computer. 'Sorry, no. Nothing's coming up.'

As another customer joined the queue behind her and Gus sniffed at a bucket at floor level with a little too much interest, Eve tried again. 'Then perhaps it was Freya Hardwicke?'

Another shake of the head.

'I'm sorry to be such a nuisance, but that narrows it down. It had to be Ella Tyndall or Bonnie Whitelaw then.'

The man standing behind her was tapping his watch.

But the florist smiled. 'Got it! Ella Tyndall. With the white roses, gypsophila, stocks and sea thistles.'

Ella? Heck. 'That's the one. Thank you.'

The florist happily took her payment of thirty pounds and

agreed to deliver the flowers to Elizabeth's Cottage the following week.

'Thirty pounds, Gus!' Eve fastened him back into his safety harness. 'Still, the information's useful. But what does it mean? Why would Ella leave flowers after Kitty's death when she hated her? And why keep it secret by putting them out in the fields instead of at the castle gates like everyone else?'

Whatever the truth, it made speaking to Ella even more urgent. Eve drove straight back to the village green in Saxford, parked, and returned to Ferry Lane.

But there was still no reply at her cottage. A moment later, one of her neighbours appeared in their front garden.

'You don't know when to expect Ella back, do you?' Eve asked.

The neighbour bent to pat Gus, who was shamelessly revelling in the attention. 'I'm afraid not. I haven't seen her today, which is unusual. The place looks shut up, doesn't it? Only she normally leaves a hopper window open unless she's gone away.'

Eve slowed her car to a crawl as she re-entered Farfield's grounds. Palmer's vehicle was parked on the gravel. There must be news.

She released Gus and let herself into the castle quietly. She'd need to be subtle if she wanted to listen in. She'd told Nate she'd try to keep out of the way, and Palmer wouldn't welcome her either.

She crouched down to look Gus in the eye and put her finger to her lips. They walked cautiously through the lobby and Eve listened for voices. As she reached the other side and the east corridor which led to the dining room, she heard a low rumble. Gus stiffened. He didn't like Palmer either and his cadence was recognisable.

Eve turned down the corridor and spotted Freya, who

jumped. Eve couldn't help but smile. She was listening in too. They shared a look of understanding, and Eve crept along to join her, signalling for Gus to wait at the lobby end. His paws would be too audible on the tiles.

'And where exactly is Mr Fisher?' Eve heard Palmer say.

There was a pause. 'He had to go to London, I believe.' That was Nate's hesitant reply. 'To see his agent.'

A likely tale. He'd probably gone off in search of Luke, as he'd threatened. Once again, she wondered if Luke had run to escape Julian, but the way he'd waited several days, then bolted, was still odd.

'So long as he's not taking matters into his own hands,' Eve heard Palmer say.

There was a long pause.

'We found blood smeared on the boat,' Palmer said at last.

They'd recovered it, then.

'Not a huge amount, but significant. We can't say for sure whether it's Luke Shipley's. We can't match the prints found in his room with the ones on the oars, but he could still have left under his own steam if he wore gloves.'

'And there's no indication what happened to him?' Nate's voice was urgent.

'No. The boat was stuck amongst some reeds on marshy ground. Some of the vegetation further up the beach shows signs of disturbance. It's possible he left the boat, waded through shallow water, then went ashore.'

'What do you think happened?'

Palmer sighed. 'I'm working on the assumption that Luke Shipley set this up to disguise his guilt. Abandoned the boat, hoping we'd believe he was attacked. Shipley's a key suspect and an attempt to put us off the scent would fit.'

The solution would make Palmer happy. He'd be allergic to investigating Nate or Julian too closely. The local powers that be were determined the Farfield enterprise should succeed.

Palmer was winding up. Eve raised an eyebrow at Freya and they crept back up the corridor to the lobby.

A moment later they'd darted into Freya and Bonnie's office. Bonnie was nowhere to be seen.

'Probably listening outside the window,' Freya said, when Eve asked, but she sounded tense, not jokey. 'And that was rubbish about Julian and his agent. He's gone out looking for Luke, supposedly.'

'Supposedly?'

Freya shook her head. 'It doesn't matter. I'm just jumpy. Ignore me.'

Eve wondered if Freya thought Luke was dead, and that Julian knew it.

29

Eve's happiness at receiving Robin's text, ten minutes after Palmer left, telling her he was back in Suffolk, left her feeling ridiculous. She was behaving like a teenager. She bent down to tell Gus they were going to meet him in the woods.

Gus looked wildly excited too, which made Eve feel better.

An hour later, they were walking with Robin through the trees, a flock of long-tailed tits flitting about in the hawthorn. Gus had dashed off and Robin and Eve walked arm in arm. Robin told her about his final session in court. It was painful to imagine him standing in the witness box, relaying what he'd been through. The betrayal and the danger. It made her happiness and relief at seeing him even more intense. She must have conveyed the feeling somehow. He looked down at her and drew her in tight. Eve's mind turned to the verdict and her stomach clenched. But there was more wrapping up to come first. They wouldn't hear anything yet.

'I've brought scones from Monty's,' he said. 'Shall we find somewhere to sit? We can carry on catching up as we eat.'

'That sounds perfect.'

There was silence for a moment, then he spoke again. 'I was able to help with a new case while I was down in London. They wanted a second eye on something.'

Eve had wondered if that might happen. The thin end of the wedge. 'It must be exciting to be involved openly in police work again.' She kept her voice even.

He smiled. 'It was; they've asked me if I can spare some more time soon.'

She took a deep breath. 'That's great. And you're all set for Friday evening?' He was due in the capital again, to give a talk at a gathering of trainee police officers. Eve knew how pleased he was to be asked.

He nodded. 'But it's not my top priority right now. I've been in touch with Greg. I heard about the blood on the missing boat, but no Luke Shipley. I gather Palmer thinks he staged the whole thing. What's your hunch?'

Eve reviewed everything she knew. 'It's true that the set-up seemed stagey from the start. But it's possible someone made it look that way to misdirect us all.'

They'd reached an even patch of grass in the shade of a tree. Robin threw his jacket down and they sat on it and made themselves comfortable.

'None of the key players has an alibi, according to Greg.' He handed her a scone from the paper bag he was carrying. It was filled with cream and jam. After that he told her what Bonnie, Freya, Julian and Nate had told the police about their movements the afternoon before. They matched with what she'd heard. 'Greg's been pushing for permission to follow up. He wants to contact Marchant's firm but Palmer's insisting on a kid-glove approach.'

'Figures.'

Robin gave a low laugh.

'It's frustrating. Any of them could have been involved in

Luke's disappearance on the face of it. It's just like Kitty's murder. I keep thinking back to who was where in the grounds, but the time of death is too broad and the scene too muddled. I can't rule anyone out. Does Luke have a record?'

He shook his head. 'So let's imagine for a moment that he's innocent. Who do you think might want him dead and why?'

Eve spooled through what she knew. 'It could be anyone who felt threatened by him. Maybe he was onto Kitty's killer but didn't have enough evidence to go to the police. There's no way he'd get into a boat with someone he suspected, but they could have killed him on dry land then manhandled him aboard. Or they could have gone out together for another reason and Luke could have twigged while they were on the water.'

'After which the killer panicked and finished him off with whatever came to hand. That would fit.' He nodded.

'The killer could have set the boat up to look staged, hoping to convince the police Luke had run for it. He'd be the ideal scapegoat. As for who, well, I hate to say it, but Luke's interactions with Ella in the run-up to his death make me wonder. That and her actions afterwards.' She told him about Luke's private chat with the teacher at the castle, his visit to her cottage and her boat trip, the morning after Luke disappeared.

'Before the news broke?'

Eve's heart sank. 'I'm afraid so. If she's guilty, maybe she was worried about where she'd left the body or how she'd staged the boat. She could have gone to check. I want to talk to her about it but she's nowhere to be found.'

'Which is worrying in itself.'

Eve nodded. 'Another possibility is that Luke's guilty and staged the boat scene, just as Palmer says. He was certainly trailing after Kitty with a motive I can't fathom.' She explained his appearance at the café where Kitty met her dad. 'I'm still not sure if he was stalking her or if he had a practical goal. The weird thing is, he seemed interested in her financial dealings, but also in her personally.'

'Any alternative scenarios?'

'That Shipley's innocent and staged the boat scene himself, because he felt the need to disappear. Either because he feared he'd be arrested, or because he felt threatened by the killer.'

'Why not just go to the police, if he knew their identity?'

'Lack of trust? He's been a prime suspect all this time. Or lack of evidence perhaps. Maybe he's sure he knows the culprit and they've been dancing round each other. The pressure could have got too much.'

'Could be. And if the guilty party's not Ella?'

'Julian's my other focus. He could have killed Luke or caused him to run. He claims he's mighty keen to find him; he's passing it off as a desire for justice but that doesn't fit with his reaction to Kitty's death, which was distinctly lukewarm.'

'You've got a theory?'

She nodded 'That Luke has or had something he wants. Julian was scrabbling about Luke's bedroom yesterday and came out empty-handed.' She stretched to ease her tense shoulders. 'What's more, I think it might be the second go he's had.' She explained about the creak she'd heard from Luke's room, when he'd definitely been out.

'If Julian killed him, my bet is he didn't find what he was looking for on his body or in his room, and he's dashed off to extend the search. We still don't know what happened to Julian's laptop.'

'You think Luke might have taken it?'

'It's possible. The police seem to have written it off as a random theft when the castle's security was lax, but I don't buy that. Maybe there are emails on it that refer to wanting Kitty out of the way. Or to Julian's plans to use her inheritance. Luke could have made off with it if he thought Julian was a danger to him.'

'Why would he choose to leave by boat?'

'I wondered about that. If he was frightened of Julian then a car would be faster. And the timing's odd too. If he took the laptop on Sunday evening, why wait until Tuesday night to make off with it?'

'And again, if it holds evidence that might convict Julian, why not take it to the police?'

'Like I said, because it's only circumstantial and he doesn't trust Palmer.'

'Could be.' Robin looked unconvinced.

'Either way, it doesn't explain why Luke waited to run. I keep wondering if he was mixed up in a plot to kill Kitty. If there was any way he could get his hands on her money, that could give him a motive, but I can't see how he could.'

'Unless he and Julian are in league.'

Eve considered it as she ate some more of her scone. 'I suppose Julian might have agreed to cut Luke in on the inheritance if Luke had a hold over him. Luke knew Kitty was planning to put the funds beyond Julian's reach. He could have told him about that and bargained with him, using whatever leverage he had. Julian and Nate noticed a change in Luke's behaviour when he arrived at Farfield. He'd become confrontational. Nate suggested it was because they'd been badmouthing him. But if Luke had a new-found hold over Julian that would be an alternative explanation. He'd got the upper hand.' She sighed. 'But it doesn't fit. If he already had a hold over Julian when he arrived, why would he need to steal the laptop?'

'We don't know that he did.' A text came in on Robin's phone. He glanced at it briefly, tapped in a reply, then put the mobile next to him on top of his jacket.

'I take it you've got no problem seeing Julian as a killer?'

'None whatsoever. I could see him paying someone to do it, or managing it himself if he was desperate. And he has a huge financial motive for Kitty's murder. He clearly had no idea she'd already ring-fenced her money.'

'And what about Ella?'

The question demanded a much longer pause. 'Her hatred towards Kitty seems powerful.' She thought of what she knew. 'I wish she'd heard what Benet and Nate had to say. Maybe she'd forgive Kitty for hurting her grandparents if she understood what she'd been up against. But what with that, and the row over the retreat, I could see her losing control in the heat of the moment.' She shook her head. 'But that's not what happened. The killer had to go and find the key to the safety grille, unlock it and lure Kitty there. I believe the decision to kill her was triggered that evening, and that the killer had a sense of urgency, but it still involved planning. It's harder to imagine Ella committing premeditated murder. But even if she's not guilty, I'd swear she's keeping a secret. The flowers, the boat trip and the conversations with Luke have to mean something.'

Robin looked thoughtful. 'That all makes sense. As for the killer's sense of urgency, that could have been driven by either emotional or practical reasons.'

'Yes.' She sighed. 'Any of the others could have killed Luke too. Bonnie had a prime motive for Kitty. She was jealous and they'd had a row that turned physical.' She'd already described the welt on Bonnie's neck. 'Freya had a falling-out with Kitty, supposedly over Kitty minding more about Farfield than her, which seems far-fetched. It's definitely not a motive for murder, but I'm sure I don't know the full story yet. And Nate has a secret which Kitty had discovered. If any of them are guilty, Luke was one of the most likely people to see something significant. He was keeping such a close eye on Kitty.

'The liars I've identified so far are Julian, Bonnie and Luke. We know Julian went to his study instead of rushing to the bathroom to be sick. Bonnie came out with a load of baloney about losing her necklace and Luke claimed Kitty told him about her charity plans, when in fact I'm sure he got that information by eavesdropping.'

'If someone went off with Luke, who d'you think's most capable of either killing him onboard or finishing him off on land and manhandling him into the boat?'

'Ella, because of her expertise on the water, and Julian, because of his heft. He wouldn't have a problem lifting a body. It's harder to see Bonnie doing it. I've never seen her wear anything but high heels and pencil-skirts or dresses. But you never know.'

'If someone's frightened or desperate enough, they'll pull out all the stops.' Robin pulled her into a comforting hug as Gus stuck his nose excitedly into some leaf matter. 'So, what's next?'

'Portia Coldwell at *Icon*'s come through. Not just with gossip, she's gone one better and put me onto a colleague of Luke's.' Her email had arrived when Eve was on her way to meet Robin. 'I'm hoping he'll talk to me. Give me more background on Luke's connection with Julian and Nate. I'm going to go through all my notes again too. See if I've missed anything. There are lots of mini mysteries. If I work to solve them, the mist might clear. But most immediately I need to work out how I can find out more about Julian. He's one of my top suspects but he's been on the back-burner, what with the Ella Tyndall developments.'

Gus had got bored and appeared at Eve's side. She'd brought his ball and threw it for him from a sitting position.

Gus seemed to roll his eyes before turning to fetch it.

Robin laughed and stood up to make better job of it second time around. The dachshund bounded off, in seventh heaven, with Robin chasing after him.

Within a minute, Robin's phone sounded another text alert. It was automatic to glance at the screen and inevitable that she saw the message flash up.

Why don't you move back to London then? It's clear you miss it. It's your home, mate.

When Robin and Gus re-joined her five minutes later, she'd already practised her brightest smile.

30

As Eve re-entered the castle, she found Freya talking to Nate.

'It was your father on the phone.' She sounded nervous.

Nate's shoulders tensed. 'What did he say?'

As Eve walked slowly upstairs, she heard Freya answer. 'He's coming to Suffolk tomorrow. For a meeting about the charity Kitty wanted to set up. He said he'll call in.'

And then Nate's voice, fainter: 'An inspection visit. I ought to refuse him entry.'

Eve could understand his bitterness. It might have been nice if Benet Marchant could have come to support his son. Been there so they could share their grief. But Benet clearly wasn't the sort and she guessed Nate would reject him anyway.

Back in her room with Gus, Eve tried not to think about Robin's possible move to London. If he went, they could still visit each other. If that's what he wanted. Either way, there was nothing she could do. She tried to ignore the sinking feeling in her chest and turned to work instead as Gus drank from his water bowl.

She began with Julian Fisher, browsing him and his family, wondering about their background. The research was broad, but you could miss things by homing in on a subject too narrowly.

There was plenty online, of course, what with his fame. His father had been a lawyer, his mother a teacher. There was nothing about the grandmother who'd owned the necklace, but Julian did have a sister, Roberta, who ran a gallery in Cambridge. Eve remembered him mentioning her to Bonnie. He'd said they didn't get on.

It was interesting that the necklace had ended up with Julian, not Roberta. Was that a sign of another family rift? It probably wasn't relevant, but Eve had the urge to talk to her. If there were tensions, she might have interesting things to say about her brother and possibly about his relationship with Kitty. She called the gallery to check Roberta would be in the following day. She claimed she was a buyer who wanted to catch her personally.

'It might be a wild goose chase,' she said to Gus. But it might not. Researching the heck out of a subject often paid dividends.

Next, she reread her notes as she'd planned, looking for connections and what they might mean.

After an hour's solid work, she'd come up with tiny details that were probably irrelevant.

Freya had fallen out with Kitty, but she wasn't just antagonistic towards her. She'd had a run-in with Julian too. Eve hadn't heard her quarrel with anyone else. It was specific to them.

And Bonnie hadn't just been ignoring Kitty, the night of the murder. She'd blanked Freya, too. Was there a reason she'd marched off when each woman called? Had she been avoiding people in general? But how could you hope to do that, when there was a party going on? She'd turned around in the end, of course, when Kitty refused to give up.

At that moment a WhatsApp message sounded on her phone. The work contact of Luke's could see her that evening.

She replied to confirm, then spent what time she had spare walking around Farfield's grounds with Gus. What had Julian been searching for in Luke's bedroom? If it was his laptop, had Luke taken it with him on the boat? Certainly not, if Julian had been on the boat with him. Possibly not, even if he'd gone alone. He might have worried it would be lost or damaged. So he'd likely hidden it somewhere he could come back to later. Somewhere he was sure it would be safe.

But where?

Eve went to the icehouse, steeling herself to look inside, though she doubted it had any suitable hiding places.

The police cordons had gone, but no one at Farfield would forget Kitty's body in the well. It was weird to think of future visitors, people who hadn't been personally touched by what happened. For whom Kitty's death would become a sort of legend. Ghouls who might visit the icehouse as a dare late at night. Guests who might hear the story over mugs of cocoa, years later.

Luke had visited the icehouse before Kitty died and stayed an oddly long time. Much as Ella had sat too long in the churchyard.

Eve used her torch to examine the rough walls, the smell of dusty earth rising up to meet her. The icehouse dome was thick, and there were small gaps between the bricks. Eve even spotted a crevice low down with dust just below, as though something had been disturbed. But it was nowhere near deep enough for a laptop. She checked inside anyway, thinking of the pendant. After all, Kitty had been there too. But she found nothing.

On her way back across the lawn, she bumped into Bonnie. 'Any news?'

The PA shook her head.

'How's it going with Freya?'

Bonnie shrugged. 'She's settling in okay. Why do you ask?'

'I was thinking back to the night of the launch party. I

remember you blanked her when she called you. I thought there might be some tension there.'

Bonnie widened her eyes. A look of surprise, but to Eve it seemed acted. 'I don't even remember that. I was very busy. There were so many people calling me. I couldn't see to everyone all at once. When was this?'

'Early in the evening. It doesn't matter.'

Eve walked back indoors with Gus at her heels and Bonnie occupying her thoughts. Her response seemed overly defensive and that was interesting. It had been busy. Eve could imagine her forgetting, especially after what happened later. But her prickly reaction led Eve to guess she remembered it clearly. It must have meant something. Was there anything odd about Freya's relationship with Bonnie, as well as with Kitty and Julian?

Or was there any chance that Bonnie had failed to turn around for the same reason she'd initially failed to turn for Kitty? That Freya might recognise the necklace she was wearing?

Eve shook her head as she entered her bedroom, ready to pick up her bag for London. 'What possible relevance could Julian's granny's necklace have for Freya?' she said to Gus.

She dropped him at Robin's, then drove to the station, still pondering the necklace and why Freya might recognise it. Could she have had an affair with Julian, just like Bonnie? Got to know him somehow when Kitty first contacted her? Could that have come between her and Kitty?

But it didn't fit. Freya hadn't seemed jealous when she'd talked about Kitty. She'd sounded bitter and hurt – wronged. The way she acted around Julian wasn't right either. And she didn't seem jealous of Bonnie.

Maybe Bonnie blanking Freya was nothing to do with the jewellery she was wearing. But if so, Eve had no idea why it had happened, and why it might be significant.

31

Eve was sitting opposite Luke Shipley's colleague, Brad Salthouse, a guy with thick dark hair and brown eyes who Eve guessed might be in his forties. They were in a pub called the Drop Anchor.

'Thanks for seeing me,' Eve said. 'I was so glad when Portia put us in touch.'

He nodded. 'We were at a press do last night and she quizzed me about Luke. When I heard he was missing this morning, I called her to ask why she'd wanted information. It seemed like a weird coincidence. She told me about you.'

Eve wasn't surprised his radar had gone off. Hers would have too. Instinct told her it was best to be upfront now.

She explained why she'd been staying at Farfield with Luke and how her commission for *Icon* had expanded to include Kitty's obituary.

'I googled you,' Brad said. 'I know you've written about murder victims before. And helped with police investigations.'

Once again, Eve wished she was more anonymous. 'It happened by accident the first time. I was interviewing the exact same people as the police, delving into their relationships with the deceased. I ended up with more information than I bargained for.'

'Talking about Luke is problematic for me. He's an old friend. The police have been in touch this afternoon, and the press too. I'm not happy about going behind his back. I'm seeing you because any chance to find out the truth is important. Luke's a good guy.'

'Not the sort to kill?' She might as well be blunt.

There was a very slight pause. 'I'm sure not.'

Not quite the easy, firm reply he might have given.

He leaned forward. 'Why are you interested?'

Eve took a deep breath. 'I want to understand all Kitty's relationships, and to be honest, the way Luke behaved around her was odd. I had the impression they'd never met before.'

Brad nodded. 'I don't believe they had.'

'But he followed her around. I saw him secretly watching her in the gardens at Farfield. He even trailed after her here in London. He seemed eager to be around her. It made me wonder.'

Brad flushed.

'What is it?'

He looked down into the beer she'd bought him. 'Nothing.'

'Please tell me. I promise I won't write about it. What do you know? Has Luke behaved like this with other women?'

'No, not at all.' He'd answered quickly.

'So what is it then?' He was definitely uncomfortable. 'He might not have met her before he went to Farfield, but he'd talked about her?'

'No.'

But Brad knew something. She could see his relief each time she asked a question he could answer honestly. She needed to go broader.

'You knew he was interested in her?' She waited for him to look up. 'If you tell me, I swear I won't splash it all over *Icon's* pages. I just want to understand what's going on. I think it might be important.'

When he didn't reply, she added: 'Kitty's father says Luke followed her to a café where they met.'

Brad put his head in his hands. At last, he spoke: 'I found a couple of press cuttings about Kitty recently. I was fishing in one of Luke's desk drawers.' He shook his head. 'I shouldn't have done it, but I had a cracking headache and I wondered if he had any aspirin.'

'Did you tell the police about the cuttings?'

He shook his head slowly. 'I should have, I know that. They asked me if he'd been back in touch, if I knew where he was, and if I knew of any reason he'd have to harm Kitty. The answer to each of those questions was no. Luke's not a killer. I'd swear to it.'

But he'd hesitated when Eve asked if he thought he might be. The press cuttings had worried him. They had the same effect on Eve.

Brad leaned forward. 'The fact is, Luke never trusted the police. And when they asked me about him they sounded aggressive. Like they'd already made up their minds.'

'Why didn't Luke trust them?' Eve felt the same when it came to Palmer, of course, but she was willing to keep an open mind in general. Greg Boles and Olivia Dawkins were excellent.

'His mother was killed in a hit-and-run. He always said they'd bungled the investigation, then given up. No one was ever caught. It took him a long time to come to terms with it. It was just the two of them and they were close.'

That explained it. Poor Luke. If it had been Eve, she was sure she'd feel the same. Some things couldn't be forgiven.

'You've been on the spot,' Brad said. 'What do you think happened to him?'

'I'm honestly not sure. At first, I wondered if Luke was

obsessed with Kitty and might have killed her. And if he had a problem with women in general.' She told him about Luke's argument with Bonnie, how he'd apparently emerged with blood on his hands.

'But I overheard the row and it didn't quite fit with that.' She remembered his and Bonnie's exchange again. *I don't believe it*, he'd said. *Is this your idea of a joke? I knew it! I knew there was something.* And she'd replied: *But you didn't though, did you? You had no idea. Not until now.* Then she'd congratulated him, sarcastically. *Oh, very well done, but it won't do you any good. And you know that.* And she'd laughed.

'And on top of that not fitting, other things make me feel I'm missing the bigger picture.'

Brad raised his glass to his lips. 'Go on.'

'He established some kind of connection with a Suffolk local, Ella Tyndall, who had hoped to buy Farfield. I saw them chatting and she put a hand on his arm. It was almost motherly, though she's not so much older than he is. She's another suspect for Kitty's murder.'

She watched his eyes, wondering if Luke had mentioned Ella before he left for Suffolk. But she couldn't detect any reaction other than a look of worried concentration.

'And I gather his behaviour towards Nate Marchant and Julian Fisher changed recently.'

He glanced at her quickly. 'Really? In what way?'

'When he arrived, Julian was patronising towards him. I had the feeling he and Nate were used to being top dogs in their relationship, but Luke was antagonistic and irritable in response. It seemed to surprise them.'

'I can imagine.'

Eve frowned. 'How do you mean?'

He sighed. 'I'd begun to think Luke was obsessed with them, never mind Kitty. I'd organised a night out for my girl-friend's birthday and Luke bailed on us when Nate Marchant invited him along to some posh banking do. It was frustrating. I could see he only wanted Luke there for publicity. Julian was the same. He and Nate seem to come as a pair. Julian's given Nate some glowing reviews. Perhaps that's the appeal there. And Nate's generous with his money. He threw Julian a very glamorous book launch from what I hear. And whenever they want Luke, he comes running.'

That was interesting. 'Well, something must have changed Luke's mind.'

'I'm glad.'

As Eve travelled home, she remembered Nate and Julian talking about the way they'd badmouthed Luke. They thought he'd overheard. The reason they'd been insulting him in the first place was his cloying behaviour. What had led to that?

Had he been sucking up to them because he was after something? And if he hadn't got it from them, had he hoped to get it from Kitty instead?

32

It was late when Eve got back to Farfield. She spotted Freya along the west wing's ground-floor corridor, holding a tray of tumblers with what might be brandy in them. She'd paused outside a room, the tray balanced on one arm, hand outstretched to open the door, when Julian appeared from inside, almost knocking into her.

'I'm going to bed.' He took one of the drinks without saying thank you.

Then Freya said quietly but quite distinctly, 'I hate you.'

Eve didn't want to be seen and the chances of discovery were high, especially given Gus was with her. She should go, but she was compelled to carry on watching.

Julian stood, stock-still, staring at Freya. 'I don't know what you mean,' he said at last.

Eve turned and crept towards the stairs, but she was only halfway up when she heard Julian enter the lobby. He must know someone had heard, thanks to the creaking. He probably realised who too, if Nate and Bonnie were in the room he'd just left. Judging by the number of brandies on Freya's tray, that was the case.

Inside her room, Eve sat thinking.

'Freya saying I hate you is clear enough,' she murmured to Gus. 'Yet Julian said he didn't know what she meant. What's to misunderstand? It was as if he was answering a different comment. An accusation.'

Gus didn't appear to be listening. He went over to his travel bed and settled down. Fair enough, really. She went and gave him a cuddle to make sure he knew she loved him for his own sake, not just as a sounding board.

After that, she got ready for bed, still nonplussed at what she'd witnessed. It wasn't just a question of why Freya hated Julian (and had hated Kitty too). It was why she'd come to work at Farfield under the circumstances. And why she'd express her feelings like that. Eve could sympathise. The way Julian had snatched a drink without a word of thanks was enough to make anyone cross. But Freya was an employee.

Not that Julian could sack her, probably. It was Nate who paid the bills. But Julian could ask Nate to let her go. Did that mean there was something odd about the balance of power between Julian and Freya? Might she have a hold over him? Could he have had an affair with her after all, while he was married to Kitty, or engaged to her? He'd be in trouble if she told Nate. But that still didn't fit with Freya's attitude towards Kitty: the sense that Kitty had betrayed her, not the other way about.

As she settled down under the crisp linen sheets, her mind was a jumble of conflicting ideas.

There was no chance of switching off. She decided to get back to the audiobook of Julian's latest novel. She'd forgotten about it the night before, what with Luke's disappearance. She put in her earphones. Why had Julian been so touchy when Luke commented on his work? Was it pure neediness, or something more? She visualised his smashed glass on the dining room floor. A distraction that had seemed like panic.

Once again, she got involved in Julian's writing. She found his book an uneasy listen. Everyone always said how marvellous he was at capturing relationships and – irritating though it was – she had to agree. This part of the story featured a couple who had money troubles. The man was controlling, twisting everything the woman said, jealous of anyone whose company she enjoyed. The tension built and built until the woman discovered the man at home with his lover, brazenly goading her in front of a friend, telling her how much money he'd spent on her rival. Money she'd helped earn.

A violent row ensued, each of them throwing crockery, the lover hiding, the man running through to the couple's kitchen, sweeping equipment off the worktops, emptying drawers of cutlery, throwing stuff around, then picking up a knife.

There was a vivid description of the woman fleeing the kitchen. Looking through a hatch at her husband. Him spouting vitriol, and in the background, a window beyond him, framing a dead tree, dark against the blue sky.

Eve paused the recording. Felt prickles crawl over her skin.

She was thinking of the dining room at Farfield. The hatch that gave a view into the kitchen. The window beyond, framing the dead tree.

She navigated to information about the audiobook. When had it been published? Eighteen months earlier, she saw, after Julian and Kitty had left France, during the year they spent in London. Well before they'd come to live at Farfield. There was no way Julian could have used personal experience to describe that room. Was it coincidence? Eve couldn't believe it. Kitty had known the house, of course. She could have described the view through the hatch and Julian might have remembered it. The sight of the tree had struck Eve and it made the scene in his book even more dramatic.

Eve lay back in bed again, wondering. But then a new suspicion sparked inside her. She was back to fiddling with her phone, navigating to an earlier point in the book. The bit where the husband goaded his wife over how much money he'd spent on his lover.

She found it. One hundred thousand on a convertible Porsche.

The prickles were back. Eve had heard the story at least three times, thanks to Moira. Freya's late husband, Craig, had spent a hundred thousand on a sports car for his lover. Moira hadn't mentioned the make. Eve googled for articles about the Craig Hardwicke scandal. The papers had been full of it after his death. At the time, Eve hadn't read them on principle. She'd glimpsed photos of Freya being doorstepped and that was enough. Journalists like that gave the rest of them a bad name, and she'd imagined being in Freya's shoes. The shock and grief she must have felt at Craig's death, followed by the revelations that had ensued.

Googling Craig's name and 'Porsche' brought the details up immediately. He'd spent just shy of one hundred thousand pounds on a Porsche Carrera Cabriolet. According to the article, Freya had known nothing about it until after his death, just under a year ago.

Yet details that seemed too close to be coincidental had appeared in Julian's book, published eighteen months ago and written before that. Written, in fact – Eve checked her notes – in the aftermath of Kitty's final visit to Farfield.

Somehow, Julian had known certain details about Craig well before they became public knowledge. And he'd either invented a horrific scene involving Freya, Craig and Craig's lover or the scene had been real.

Eve had been wondering if Freya might have been Julian's lover, and now, for a split second, she wondered if Kitty could have been Craig's.

She shook her head almost instantly. That wasn't the answer. The recipient of the Porsche had been named. And in any case, there was no way she'd have chatted about it to Julian if she'd been unfaithful. It seemed likely the information had got to him via Kitty, though. If so, it was no wonder Freya loathed them both. Kitty had gossiped about something horrific and deeply private, and Julian had used the tragedy to hook his readers. It would explain Julian's reply when Freya said *I hate you*. He'd said, *I don't know what you mean*. He'd been answering an accusation only he could hear, not the words themselves. He was still pretending he hadn't cherrypicked bits of Freya's life to put into his book. But how much of it had he pinched?

If Eve was right, Kitty had known about Freya's husband's betrayal well before he died. It probably meant Freya had known too, if she and Kitty witnessed that episode together. The scene Julian described sounded appalling. Harrowing. Yet Freya had stuck with him. Perhaps she'd had no idea how to get out. Or she'd lost belief in herself. It must have been hard to hang on to it in the face of such behaviour.

Poor Freya. Eve liked her, but with hurt so deep from so many sides, the idea of her killing Kitty seemed more believable. If Kitty had passed the story on to Julian it was yet another betrayal, and from someone she'd thought of as a friend. Maybe Kitty had witnessed more than one altercation. Gathering material for Julian could definitely be the hateful ulterior motive Freya had referred to. The thought of Kitty doing it seemed incredible, but the transfer of information had taken place somehow. The proof was right there in Julian's novel. Eve needed to talk to Freya again.

33

The following morning, Eve sought out Freya after breakfast and asked if they could talk. They ended up walking over the fields in the direction of the old hunting lodge. Gus was off the leash and dashing ahead, trotting happily with the occasional glance over his shoulder. He liked to make sure Eve was keeping up.

'He's sweet,' Freya said. 'I love dogs. So much more straight-forward than humans.'

Eve had thought exactly the same when her husband walked out, but bought her Gus as a present. She'd been infuri-ated by his presumption. (He hadn't asked if she'd be happy to look after a pet, just assumed she'd need company after his departure.) But, of course, she'd adored Gus on sight. He was a very superior upgrade.

'You said it,' Eve replied. 'It must be hard, to come into your new role at a time like this. But that aside, how do you find Julian, Nate and Bonnie?'

'I like Nate.' She was quiet for a moment. 'And Bonnie's all right really. I know people think she's hard-nosed, but you know where you are with her.' She gave a half smile. 'She bought a packet of posh chocolate biscuits for us to share yesterday. I suddenly felt almost close to her.'

Chocolate biscuits could do that.

'I'm not sure she'll stay, though,' Freya went on.

'Really?'

'I caught her looking for another job. I don't think she finds Julian easy to work for.'

That answered the question about their affair then. It really was over. Eve wasn't surprised. 'And how about you?'

She didn't reply.

'Freya, I was listening to Julian's latest book last night.' Eve heard her catch her breath. 'I couldn't mistake the description of the dining room and kitchen here at Farfield. And then there was the couple who feature in the story. The sports car the husband buys for his lover...'

Freya flushed and put her hands to her face.

'How did he get the information? You said you'd fallen out with Kitty because she visited you to see Farfield, not out of friendship, but that wasn't the whole truth, was it? Kitty passed on what she saw to Julian, and he wrote about it.' It was still an educated guess, but it fitted.

Freya gasped and Gus turned to look at her, pausing uncertainly, eyes anxious.

It took her a while to speak. 'It was Farfield that drew Kitty here, not me.' Her eyes were full of tears. 'But yes, she clearly told Julian what she'd seen, and he made use of it.' She was white-faced. 'I couldn't believe it. It was many months before it was published, of course. But I remembered what happened that day clearly and he'd used it, scene by scene, in precise detail. I'd gone over it hundreds of times myself. Playing and replaying it my head. The words and actions. The humiliation in front of Kitty. And then there it was, laid bare on the page.' She closed her eyes and stopped walking.

'The newspapers said you only found out about Craig's lover after he died.'

'I couldn't tell the truth. No one would understand why I stayed. But the money we had was all in his name. I had nowhere to go. I'd always worked for him. He said he'd tell any future employer how lousy I was – how miserable to have around. Boring, difficult, mopey.'

'I'm so sorry.'

Gus came up to Eve and she bent to pat him. To let him know it was okay. But it was far from okay for Freya. And if she'd killed Kitty because of it, it never would be again.

After a moment, Freya took a hesitant step forward and Eve felt able to ask another question. 'What about the details of Craig's financial mismanagement? Is the book accurate on that?'

She shook her head. 'I didn't know anything about that before Craig died. I assumed he was relying on loans. I knew the business was in debt, and we were too, yet he carried on spending. But Kitty knew I was worried about money. She must have passed my anxieties on to Julian who dreamed up the rest. When I finally asked Craig about it, he got angry, of course. Told me I was being paranoid and he could pay everything back. He had a plan...' Her shoulders sagged.

'So Julian mixed truth with invention?'

Freya nodded. 'But all the personal stuff and the horrendous scene in the kitchen was one hundred per cent accurate. I can still remember the day I found out what Julian had done. And what Kitty did.'

'So it was later on that you cut Kitty out of your life? Not immediately after her visit here, just before she left for France?'

Freya nodded. 'We were kept apart anyway, of course, because she was abroad. When she got back to London she didn't call. I suppose she was pulling back. Anticipating my reaction if I found out. And six months later I did. By that stage I hadn't even got the stamina to contact her. I thought I was already at my lowest ebb, and then I was faced with that. How could she?'

How indeed? It was what Eve had been wondering, because Kitty hadn't seemed the sort to be so unutterably cruel. Maybe she'd been sufficiently shocked by what she'd seen that she'd blurted it out to Julian the moment she saw him – offloading her feelings without thinking.

But if that was the case, the description of the kitchen hatch with the dramatic tree in the background was odd. If you were venting, you didn't normally bother with scene-setting. It made no sense, unless she'd settled down to tell it to Julian like a story. Eve just couldn't imagine her doing it.

'Julian wasn't with Kitty on that last visit?' Eve hadn't got that impression, but it would explain everything.

'When Craig went berserk in the kitchen? No, of course not!' She sounded genuinely incredulous.

Eve could only conclude that there was more to Kitty then had met the eye. Of course, that was usually the case. She'd been surprised by her obituary subjects plenty of times before. But it still beggared belief.

'Freya...' She walked slowly alongside her and spoke gently. 'If you hated Kitty so much, why did you come to work with her? You must have known what a strain it would be.'

Freya looked at the ground and paused. 'It gave me a roof over my head, back in the house I loved, and an income. People associate me with Craig's mess now – I doubt many places would have me.'

Was that really true? Eve would have thought most people would be more clear-sighted. But it was what Freya thought that counted. If she was too afraid to put it to the test, accepting the job at Farfield made sense.

When Eve stayed quiet, Freya added: 'I'd have sold Farfield to Nate anyway. I had to. He offered significantly more than Ella and I was left with so much debt. But I did ask if they might have any work going. Nate had got to know me; I expect he just felt sorry for me. That'll be why he took me on.'

'You seem to be doing a good job.'

Freya shrugged. 'I'm preparing to be judged all over again now. Nate's dad's visiting at lunchtime, and his wife's home for a flying visit tomorrow.' She shook her head. 'Rhoda Marchant. Can you imagine? Talk about high-powered.'

'You're each expert in your area.'

'I don't think being an administrator quite compares with being a renowned news correspondent, do you?'

'Freya, what happened the night Kitty died? She wanted to talk to you. Clear the air.' Eve had to ask. Freya was a top candidate for murderer.

'You think I killed her in revenge?' She'd gone white again. 'That would be crazy. Julian's still here. I hate him just as much. More, if anything.' She paused and faced Eve. 'I swear to you I didn't.'

She sounded honest, but the point about Julian wasn't convincing. He was a big, hefty guy. Attacking him would be a lot harder. And Freya had been badly hurt. Killing Kitty with so many people around wouldn't have been straightforward, but she might still have gone for it. Chosen an occasion when alternative suspects were on site.

Killing during the party had certainly muddied the waters. Any of the key players could be guilty. They all had motives, and each of them had opportunity.

Eve closed her eyes for a moment. She desperately needed a breakthrough.

34

It was ten minutes after Eve re-entered the castle that she realised she'd missed a call. She must have been out of coverage. Moira had left a voicemail asking Eve to get in touch urgently. She sounded breathless and full of self-importance.

Eve pressed to return the call.

'*Ah, Eve, at last. Ella Tyndall's back in the village. I know you wanted to speak to her.*'

'That's really useful. Thanks so much, Moira.'

'*You know me, Eve. I'm always keen to help. And if you'd like to pop in afterwards, perhaps we can put our heads together and work out what's going on.*'

Eve ought to have known there'd be a pay-off. 'Of course. I'll see what I can do. Though it might not be straight away. I've got another appointment this afternoon.' That was an exaggeration. Julian's sister Roberta Fisher wasn't expecting her, but Eve *had* been told she'd be at her gallery. That counted. She was determined to make the trip to Cambridge.

Moira sighed. '*Of course.*'

Eve was sure the wait for details would be agony, and Moira

was bound to be disappointed. Whatever Eve found out, she wasn't intending full disclosure.

After a moment's thought, Eve picked up her bag and called Gus, ready to leave for Saxford immediately. She should have time to find Ella then come back to Farfield for lunch before she left Suffolk. She was hoping to be around when Benet visited. It would break her promise to keep a low profile but watching him with Nate would be informative.

In the meantime, she needed to know why Ella had gone out in her boat the morning after Luke went missing. What was the extra connection between them? Why had they formed a bond, and did Ella have any reason to want Luke dead? Could he have guessed she'd killed Kitty? But if so, why hadn't he told the police? Would his lack of trust in them be enough to stop him when things were so desperate? Eve imagined he'd have gone to them if he'd had proof.

She was just getting into her car, Gus behind her in his travel harness, when her phone rang again.

Viv. Bubbly and excited.

'*Ella Tyndall's back.*'

'So I hear. I'm on my way to find her now.'

'*Seriously? Did Moira beat me to it? Huh! I might have guessed.*' She sounded dejected.

'She wants me to give her a debrief afterwards.'

'*I'll bet she does. Not before me!*'

'Deal. And you'll get the real goods, but not immediately. I'm due in Cambridge this afternoon and I need to come back to Farfield before I leave.'

'*Party pooper. Right, dinner at the Cross Keys tonight then. And no wriggling out of it.*'

'Yes, ma'am.' Eve would be glad of a sounding board. Her mind was milling with questions. She'd probably have more by then.

. . .

Ella Tyndall came to the door in a pale green linen dress, her red hair tied back but escaping. She was fully made-up but beneath it she looked pale. The sunlight made her hair glow but there were shadows under her eyes.

'Eve!' She sounded bright and brittle. Eve knew she'd be used to putting on her best front, even if she felt fragile. As a teacher, she'd have no choice. 'What can I do for you?'

'I felt the urge to talk to you after Luke went missing.'

The tension in her face increased a fraction. 'It's terrible. It sounds as though he was attacked, I gather.' She shook her head quickly, not meeting Eve's eyes. 'But why did you want to speak to me?'

'I noticed you had a long chat with him at Farfield on Tuesday, then someone saw him drop in on you a short while after that.' The day he'd disappeared.

Ella shook her head quickly. 'I must have been out.'

'I heard you were out in your boat too, the morning after he went missing. I wondered if you were worried about him. Especially worried, I mean.' She held her breath as she waited for Ella to respond. She shouldn't have known Luke was missing by then. Unless she was involved. But Eve doubted she'd walk into the trap and felt mean setting it.

She was still standing on the doorstep and a neighbour had appeared at a window.

'You'd better come in.' Ella stood back in the shadows.

For just a second, Eve hesitated. Every part of her rejected the idea of Ella as a killer, but she needed to be realistic. She had a motive for Kitty and a weird connection with a man who'd disappeared. But even if she was dangerous, the cottages on Ferry Lane were terraced and the neighbours were home. Eve could shout if she ran into trouble. So she followed her to a cool, shady kitchen with thin curtains that fluttered in the breeze.

They sat at a scrubbed wooden table. Behind Ella, Eve

could see a pile of exercise books, no doubt waiting to be marked.

'Of course I'm worried about Luke, just like everybody else,' Ella said, 'but that's not why I was out in my boat. I didn't even know he was missing by then.' She was looking Eve straight in the eye and it felt unnatural. 'It's half-term. I always get out on the water when I can. Sailing was my thing. I used to have a boat at the yacht club, but it was a faff, having to use my inflatable tender. I've got a little dinghy with an outboard now, moored just up the lane. I love to go out and watch the sun rise.'

'Ah, I see. I just wondered. I wasn't sure when you'd gone and what time the news of Luke's disappearance broke. I came to ask you yesterday, but you were out.' She knew she was being intrusive.

'I took myself off for the night. It's good to ring the changes.'

She was smiling, but again, as if she was on stage, putting her best foot forward. Eve imagined being a child in Ella's class. Whatever was happening in her private life she'd keep the show rolling.

'Had you met Luke before he came to Suffolk? I hadn't.'

Ella shook her head. 'No, but we'd spoken. He was interested in the history of Farfield and my bid for it. How I came to be so devoted to the place. He said he'd be writing about it and wanted to understand the background.'

He took the same approach as Eve, by the sound of it, paying attention to every detail.

'By the time he turned up, I almost felt I knew him, so I was horrified to hear he'd disappeared.' She was twisting the sleeve of her dress. Her anxiety seemed genuine.

'What do you think's happened to him?'

She cast her eyes down. 'I think he must have been attacked, don't you?'

'People are saying he was obsessed with Kitty. That he

followed her around. Not just here in Suffolk, but down in London.'

Ella's direct gaze met hers again. 'People will spread tittle-tattle, won't they?'

'To be honest, I saw him watching her myself.'

She sighed. 'All I know is, I talked to him at some length, and I simply can't imagine him harming her. Or anyone for that matter.'

Conversation closed, that much was clear. Ella got up and fetched herself a glass of water, swigging it down. She hadn't offered Eve a drink.

Eve thought of the floral tribute Ella had left, far from the main piles of bouquets outside the castle gates. She still wondered if they, and Ella's long sit in the churchyard, were down to guilt.

'I noticed a beautiful bouquet, out in the fields near Farfield,' Eve said, watching Ella's eyes. 'I was curious about it. There was no card or note. When I asked around, someone mentioned seeing you leave them.'

Ella flushed. 'I didn't see—' Then she pulled up short. A moment later she gave a quick, sharp sigh. 'Yes, it was me. I didn't want to lay them at the front gate.' She shook her head. 'Kitty and I were friends once.'

She was moving towards the hall. 'If you'll excuse me.' Her voice cracked.

Eve got up and followed her to the front door.

As she walked away with Gus, it was the emotion in Ella's voice that filled her head. That and the number of tissues she'd seen in her bin. And yet she'd still been properly angry with Kitty when she'd given Eve and Luke the history tour. So was all this down to guilt? Or upset over Luke? And if the latter, why were her feelings so intense when they'd only just met?

Eve shook her head as she walked Gus to the car. There were too many unanswered questions.

35

Eve drove back to Farfield with Ella's words floating in her mind, but as she entered the castle grounds she switched her attention to Benet's visit. Her interview with him had been useful, but seeing father and son together would be even more enlightening. The next best thing to seeing him with Kitty. The only problem might be observing them – Eve didn't imagine they'd want her hanging around while they talked.

In the end, she needn't have worried. Benet, Nate and Julian were chatting in the formal gardens, and Freya asked Eve to join them.

'Benet wants to tell you more about the charity Kitty was going to set up. He thought you might like to mention it in the obituary. He'll be one of the trustees now.' Freya walked ahead of her, down the west wing corridor. Something about her speed and the sound of her shoes tapping on the tiles made her seem tense. Eve could understand it. Benet had no role at Farfield, but he'd be an exacting person to have around.

Freya opened the door to the garden and Eve followed her out.

None of the men looked up as they appeared. Benet was in

mid-flow. '... actually well thought out. One of the experts I spoke to was impressed. Clients of the charity will be involved in decision-making from the start. I'm glad Kitty found a way to help people without inviting them into her own home. Families suffer when that happens.'

Eve remembered Nate saying how jealous he'd been of the people his parents had helped. And then they'd lost their money to that one bad apple. She bet Benet had held on to that.

Julian was scowling after Benet's speech, but he'd probably had very different plans for Kitty's money.

Nate's face was immobile; he looked an inch away from letting rip. Of course, he'd considered putting funds into the charity too, until his father had taken control.

As they talked, Freya asked if Eve would like a drink and a sandwich and she accepted. It still felt odd, being waited on, but she could do with some lunch before her drive to Cambridge.

As Freya disappeared, Benet turned to Eve.

'I thought you'd want to include details of the charity in Kitty's obituary.'

Hello to you too. Gus gave Benet a hard stare.

'Nice to see you again. And yes, I'd love to. I can include the fundraising information if you'd like.'

'Naturally.'

Hopefully the charity would speak for itself and not rely on Benet's charisma.

By the time he'd filled her in, Eve was sure it would benefit lots of people. Kitty would change lives in memory of her mum. It was such a shame she wouldn't be there to see it.

A moment later, the talk turned to domestic arrangements.

'You can stay here if you want.' Nate spoke stiffly, his hands gripping the arms of his chair. 'It's your family home, in case you'd forgotten. Though you'll have company and I know you hate to share. Rhoda's due in tomorrow.'

Benet shook his head. 'I'd never stay here. Please tell Rhoda how much I admired her report from Tajikistan. She has an original mind.' He frowned. 'I'm glad you're still together, but in all honesty, surprised. You're not natural soulmates. You have such different goals in life. I always saw you with some- one... very different.' His tone was full of distaste.

Eve imagined he'd be happy to see them break up. It would prove him right.

Freya had just reappeared with Eve's refreshments. She seemed to flinch as Eve turned to thank her. Perhaps she was reliving their conversation from earlier. Thinking again of Kitty's betrayal and Julian's base behaviour.

Eve was distracted by Benet, addressing her again.

'By the way, that man you asked me about when we spoke in London.'

'The one in the photo I showed you?'

'That's right. Who is he?'

Eve realised she'd never told Benet his name. 'The journal- ist, Luke Shipley. The one who's disappeared.'

'Disappeared?' Benet looked mystified.

Surely he'd been following the coverage of his daughter's murder. 'Yes, he was staying here at the castle, but it seems he went off in a boat on Tuesday afternoon. He hasn't been seen since.'

'You didn't see the news?' Nate's tone was low and dangerous.

Benet waved his question aside. 'No. I've been writing. But I saw him. This morning.'

'You saw Luke Shipley?' Julian was standing up and Bonnie had appeared behind Freya now.

Eve looked around the group. Everyone seemed shocked and mystified, except Benet, who looked confused and annoyed.

'Yes,' he said. 'Here in Suffolk. I was just leaving the pub where I'm staying. He was outside in the street.'

'What was he doing?' Nate's tone was urgent.

'Standing behind a tree. I had the impression he was watching me.' He frowned. 'I caught his eye for a moment, and he took a step forward. But then my phone rang and I saw a passer-by, pointing at him. The next thing I knew he'd gone.'

'Probably got the wind up,' Julian said. 'He's only the top suspect for my wife's murder. *Your daughter*. If you'd been reading the papers you'd know.'

Despite his words, Eve suspected it was Benet's vagueness that had made Julian angry, rather than his failure to raise the alarm. Julian's expression was thoughtful, as if he was reassessing matters, and if anything, his shoulders relaxed a fraction. 'So, he's back in Suffolk, is he? What the devil is he playing at?'

Nate walked towards the door. 'I'll call DI Palmer.'

Like that would solve anything.

36

Eve left Gus at Elizabeth's Cottage rather than taking him to Cambridge. She wasn't sure dogs would be welcome at a craft gallery. ('Even ones as adorable as you,' she'd said to him.) Allie, the newest recruit at Monty's, was free that afternoon; she'd drop in to give him some company.

As Eve navigated the A14 westwards, she considered again what she needed to find out. In particular, she wanted to know why Roberta and Julian didn't get on, and what she thought of him and Kitty, as a couple and individually. But she was curious about Julian's grandmother's necklace too, and why she'd left it to him. In her experience it was more common for granddaughters to come in for that kind of thing.

Roberta Fisher's gallery was on King's Parade. Eve parked her car along the Backs, looking across the River Cam to the rear of a series of ancient colleges, then walked through to the city centre. She'd chosen her blue shift dress with the purple trim and hoped she looked wealthy enough to afford the gallery's wares.

Inside the shop, an assistant greeted her and let her browse for a couple of minutes before discreetly offering help.

'I wondered if Roberta Fisher might be around?'

The assistant smiled. She was no doubt wondering what Eve wanted, but she didn't let it show. 'I'll check for you. What name should I give?'

'Eve Mallow. I've been staying at Farfield Castle with her brother. I'm writing her sister-in-law's obituary for *Icon*.'

'One moment.'

As Eve waited, she examined a beautiful lustreware vase. It was on sale for £4,000. She tried to look nonchalant.

A moment later the assistant reappeared. 'Please, come this way.'

Eve followed her through a door marked 'staff', down a whitewashed corridor and into an office.

Roberta Fisher leaped up and shook Eve's hand. She had glossy dark-brown hair and a ready smile, though she shook her head ruefully as she motioned Eve to a wooden chair on the opposite side of her desk.

'Such a beastly shame about Kitty. Still can't believe it. Coffee?'

'Thank you.'

The assistant, who'd been lingering in the doorway, nodded and retreated.

'So you've been staying at Farfield and you're writing about Kitty?'

'That's right.' Eve explained the background, and how things had panned out.

'How awful for you. I can't believe they made you stay on after something so dreadful. It seems extraordinary.'

Eve decided not to share Jo's part in the proceedings nor her decision to dig her heels in and remain after Luke's disappearance. 'Julian and Nate told me and the other journalist they didn't want to muck up our schedules. Maybe they were worried we might be guilty and wanted to keep an eye on us.' She might as well raise the idea head on.

'You!' Roberta raised her eyebrows. 'You're not, are you?'

It was clear she was joking, though there was no reason why she should be. She didn't know Eve.

'No. Definitely not.'

'But they might have been right about the other journalist, from what I've read in the papers. He's disappeared, hasn't he?'

Eve nodded. She didn't tell her about his reported reappearance. 'The boat he left in had blood smeared on it. No one's sure quite what happened.'

But it looked increasingly likely that Luke had faked an attack on himself. Maybe because the police were homing in on him and he wanted to escape. Possibly because he was guilty.

'Did Julian send you to me?' Roberta sounded surprised. 'I liked Kitty, but I don't know how much I can—'

'No, it wasn't Julian. I found you myself when I was researching Kitty's connections. I like to make my articles as rounded as possible.'

Roberta smiled and thanked her colleague as she brought in their coffees. After she'd gone, she leaned forward.

'Cards on the table, I didn't see a lot of Kitty. The honest truth is, Julian and I don't get on. We're civil when family occasions bring us together – or mostly, anyway.' She laughed. 'But we don't hold our hands out for cosy get-togethers. I think he's a jumped-up oaf, and he thinks I'm a prissy idiot. We're both quite happy feeling superior, so that's fine, but I regretted not getting to know Kitty better. As I say, I liked her, and I couldn't help feeling she'd have trouble with Julian sooner or later. He got used to an awful lot of adoration from an early age. He's addicted to it, and I don't think one person will ever be enough for him. You'd better not quote me on that.' She sounded regretful.

'I won't, don't worry. But it's useful to understand the background. I must admit, I'd picked up on the extra women myself.'

'Ah.' Roberta sounded sad. 'I'd so hoped I was wrong. Julian was a child prodigy and I'm afraid that didn't help. He excelled at school and that horribly autobiographical first novel – the one which was shortlisted for the Booker – was published when he was nineteen. He got used to awestruck interviewers. You should have heard the fuss he made when his second book was panned. We all breathed a sigh of relief when he found his form again with the third. His career's never made him rich but he's dined out on it, all this time. He can put on an excellent act, but underneath it all, he's an outsize toddler who still gets cross unless he's everyone's top priority.' She grimaced, then sipped her coffee. 'You'd better not quote me on that, either, but I'm enjoying the vent.'

'He seems to have a firm friend in Nate Marchant, Kitty's brother.'

'Ah, yes – they've been thick as thieves since they met at that awards do. Given how rarely I see Julian, it's noticeable that Nate's often there. It makes sense since Julian's marriage to Kitty, of course. Before that, I imagined it was self-interest on both their parts. Nate's lapped up Julian's praise for his writing, and Julian's enjoyed Nate treating him like a god. Nate's generous with his money too. Loans of smart holiday apartments and fancy meals for free would be quite enough to keep my brother onside. Take no notice. I'm just crotchety and embittered!'

Roberta's assistant knocked on the door to ask a question. It gave Eve the chance to gather her thoughts. Julian's support for Nate's work hadn't made a difference initially but Nate had nurtured the relationship. To the extent that Julian had married his sister and gone into business with him. A puff quote from a famous author was one thing. Appearing alongside them on TV documentaries about your new writers' retreat was another. It would put Nate in the public eye. Even now, speculation about the venture was working in his favour. She thought of the complimentary reviews she'd seen since the retreat had been announced. The tide might turn. It would be a triumph after his father had claimed his work was worthless. And Benet, as a fellow writer, would be jealous. Nate said Benet hated other people's success. She thought of Nate's bleak expression as she'd asked about the strength of Julian and Kitty's marriage. She wondered if he was seeing things with fresh eyes now. Acknowledging the effect his desire to score points off Benet might have had on his sister. Eve would be consumed with guilt if she were him.

The assistant left the room again.

'I'm so sorry.' Roberta leaned forward. 'Where were we?'

Eve glanced at her notes. She hadn't mentioned the pendant yet. 'I wonder if I could ask you about something that happened, the night Kitty died. I'd like your opinion in confidence, if you don't mind.' Eve didn't think she'd run to Julian to report their conversation, but you never knew.

'You're making me nervous,' Roberta said, 'but of course, for what it's worth.' Eve couldn't help wondering how long she'd spent since Kitty's death speculating if Julian had been involved. She knew Luke was a person of interest in the enquiry, but Eve imagined she'd considered her brother as a possible perpetrator too.

'Two things went missing that night. Julian's laptop, and a necklace bearing a striking resemblance to the one your grandmother passed down to him.'

'The what?'

'The art deco pendant.' Eve described it as best she could remember. 'Rectangular with silver filigree on a black onyx background.'

Roberta still looked confused.

Eve explained what Bonnie had told her, and how she and Julian had claimed her pendant was almost identical to the one belonging to Julian and Roberta's grandmother. And how Julian said it had been lost when Eve asked to see it.

'To be honest, I came to the conclusion the necklace Bonnie wore probably was your grandmother's, and the pair of them were trying to cover it up.'

'This makes no sense.' Roberta shook her head. 'We had one surviving grandmother as children, on my mother's side. She was the only person who saw through Julian. She told my parents he was spoiled, which went down like a bucket of cold sick, as you can imagine. When she died, although she left us both money, and my parents got the house, I got her jewellery. Julian was quite cross because it was valuable.'

'So the art deco pendant went to you?'

Roberta's frown deepened. 'No. She never had anything like you're describing and I'm sure I'd know. We were close.'

'What about your other grandmother? Is there any way her belongings might have been passed on to Julian?'

But Roberta shook her head again. 'Our paternal grand-mother had a daughter. The jewellery went to her. I have no idea why, but I'd say Julian and this Bonnie woman are lying. You need to watch out for that when you talk to my brother. He has no regard for the truth. He's decided the rules don't apply to him.'

37

That evening, Eve reported to the Cross Keys as planned, to provide Viv with her update. She'd already dropped in on Robin and been over the most recent developments. It had helped get things clear in her head. His main news related to the police's hunt for Luke Shipley. After Benet's revelation, a statement had been put out and now there were tens of sightings coming in, but from all corners of Suffolk, as well as Norfolk and London. A lot of them were probably cases of mistaken identity. She'd hoped Robin might join her and Viv at the pub, but he was busy preparing his talk for the following evening.

Jo darted over to Eve and Viv's table with their food. 'All right? I can't stop – the place is packed – but I'd like to know what's going on.'

Eve thanked her. 'I'll call you with an update when it's a better time.'

She and Viv had chosen fishcakes and salads. The saffron sauce was perfect with the haddock; it was just the meal for another warm late-May day.

Gus and Hetty were over by the window. Eve could hear Gus's tail thumping on the floor from where she sat.

Viv raised her glass of Pinot Grigio. 'Cheers. So, what's new?'

Eve got her notes out. 'Lots.' She filled Viv in on Benet's visit and the news about Luke.

'Blimey.' Viv got her pad out too, and started scribbling. 'I mean, everyone thought he might have staged the boat to look as though he'd been attacked, but if he's guilty, why show his face in Suffolk? You think he came back out of remorse? To face up to Kitty's dad, maybe?'

Eve frowned. 'I'm not sure. Perhaps he's innocent and has information but doesn't know who to trust. In the normal way he might go to the police, but Palmer's convinced he's the killer. Plus, Luke doesn't trust the authorities.' She explained about the bungled investigation into his mother's death.

'I guess that would colour his view.'

'I imagine he'd contact them if he could prove who killed Kitty, though. Even Palmer can't ignore hard evidence. I was thinking Luke might have Julian's laptop, but if so, I'd guess whatever's on it is suggestive but not conclusive.'

'Perhaps not. So if Luke's innocent, you think he bolted because he was frightened for his safety?'

'It seems possible. Either that or he was scared of being arrested. Maybe he thought creating the impression he'd been attacked would make the police consider other killers. He'd want his name cleared, and to feel safe. He still displayed an intense interest in Kitty. His behaviour's odd – following her around London, peering at her at Farfield. But that's not proof he killed her.'

'I see that. But he might have.'

Eve thought it through. 'True, but my hunch is he's inno- cent. If he was guilty, why make all that effort with the boat and blood in the first place, only to come back? It's hard to believe he'd follow Benet around at that point, with a sudden urge to confess. The way he reappeared makes me feel he's got unfinished business and an uneasy mind. Maybe he felt he could trust Benet because he's Kitty's dad, but he lost confidence when someone spotted him. He probably thought he'd been recognised.'

'He probably was.' Viv was adding more notes to her pad between mouthfuls of fishcake. 'His photo's been all over the papers. So it's not impossible he's the killer, but perhaps less likely?'

'I think so. Though everything I feel about Kitty's death is as tentative as heck.' Eve glanced around the Cross Keys, and lowered her voice. 'Following on from Luke and the boat, it's Ella Tyndall who comes to mind next.'

Viv sighed. 'I know we have to include her. How was she when you talked this morning?'

Eve reported back on the visit. 'She claims it was coincidence that she was out in her boat the morning after he disappeared.'

'You don't believe her?'

Eve still wasn't certain. She shrugged. 'She sounded overly bright and breezy as she told me. It felt like an act. I noticed a lot of tissues in her bin. Either she's been crying over Kitty – whom she seemed to hate – or I'd guess she's upset at Luke's disappearance. She was keen to tell me he must have been attacked; that he'd never have hurt Kitty, nor anyone else for that matter, But how could she be sure if she'd only just met him?'

'Very interesting.' Viv underlined something. 'So you think she might have gone to look for him out of worry?'

'Maybe. But if it was innocent concern, how did she know he'd disappeared? The news hadn't broken by the time she left. He'd visited her the day before, though she claims she was out. It would fit if he'd shared his plans with her then, but why would he? Either way, Ella going after him, hours later, makes no sense.

'She admits to buying the flowers I found in the field, by the way. She said her childhood friendship with Kitty still meant something and her voice cracked as she talked, but part of me wonders whether it was Luke's disappearance that made her emotional.' Eve ate some more fishcake. 'Then again, the death of someone you fought with can leave massive scars too.

'Either way, I'm sure she knows more than she's saying. If I'm wrong and Luke *is* guilty, they could be in cahoots. And I'm still confused by the force of Ella's feelings towards Kitty. I get that Kitty hurt her grandparents and that Ella loved them, but Kitty must have been knocked sideways by her mother's death at the time. Besides, Benet started brainwashing her when she was a young teen. It's him I blame.'

Viv nodded and took another forkful of food. 'I'm glad you've put me in the picture. Benet sounds like an unfeeling pig.'

'Perfectly put.'

'So there's still some work to do on Ella, but she's looking more like an accessory,' Viv gave a satisfied smile as she used the word, 'than the perpetrator.'

'Maybe. It's all maybe.'

Eve told Viv the true reason for Freya and Kitty's falling-out.

'Blimey. That's quite a betrayal.'

'It is. She must have been devastated when she read Julian's book. She says she's just as mad at Julian, which I'm sure is true. She told him she hated him. I guess he daren't retaliate, in case she tells everyone what he did. I know authors use real-life inspiration to spark their creativity, but the direct reporting of a personal, private scene without permission is pretty low.'

Viv frowned. 'So has that discovery moved Freya up the suspect list?'

'Initially I thought so, but on reflection, perhaps not. It's an old hurt. I could see it festering, and even imagine Freya killing Kitty in the heat of the moment. Perhaps if Kitty tried to justify herself, and Freya saw red. But the murder involved fore-thought, not just instantaneous fury. I can't prove I'm right and rule her out, though. It's the case with all of them, and it's driving me crazy.'

'So we're on to Julian, Nate and Bonnie.'

Eve nodded. 'And where Julian and Bonnie are concerned, I have perplexing new information.' Eve filled Viv in on that afternoon's visit to Roberta Fisher.

'Blimey. So they made up the story about the necklace?'

'It seems so.'

'But why?'

'I wish I knew.' The question had circled in Eve's head all the way back to Suffolk. 'Kitty was definitely upset when Bonnie turned round.'

'Maybe it was a new necklace which Julian had bought Bonnie. But then how would Kitty know that, just by looking?'

'Exactly. I can't think of any way she would. So, back to the facts. The necklace definitely went missing. And Bonnie had a mark on her neck consistent with it being ripped off. I saw Bonnie secretly searching the castle for something and I assume that was the necklace.' It made her think of Julian, also search-ing, but in that case it had been in Luke's room. Perhaps for his laptop. But then another possibility struck her. 'Wait a minute.' She paused, closed her eyes and took a deep breath, thoughts coalescing.

'What is it?'

'I'm just wondering if I've been taken for a fool.'

'Surely not! That would make you mortal like the rest of us.'

'Hah-de-hah. But seriously, what if it wasn't Kitty who tore the necklace off? She was certainly upset by it, but Bonnie had a second row that evening.'

'With Luke?'

'Exactly. And Molly Walker said Luke had blood on his hand. He could have cut himself yanking the necklace free.' She imagined the chain, cord or whatever it had been cutting into his skin. 'I haven't heard of any injury to Kitty's hand.' Surely a violent yank like that, which had marked Bonnie's neck, would have made a mark on the yanker as well as the yankee? Yet Robin had told her Kitty had no marks on her except for those caused by the fall and the blow to her head. She should have thought of that sooner. 'Heck, that would make a difference. If Luke had the necklace, maybe that's what Julian was looking for in his room. Or that *and* the laptop.'

The necklace would have fitted into the crevice she'd found between the icehouse bricks too, where she'd noticed the recently dislodged mortar dust. Was it possible Luke had hidden it there, then moved it somewhere later? Eve wondered if the CSIs would have found it when they'd combed the place after Kitty's murder. But perhaps they wouldn't, if it was pushed back into a recess. 'But why would Luke take it? And does he have Julian's laptop too?'

'And why would Bonnie and Julian make up that bizarre story about the pendant?' Viv added.

Why indeed. 'I'll need to talk to Bonnie again.'

'Be careful, won't you?'

Eve nodded. 'As for Nate, there's this matter of the secret he was keeping – which Kitty knew about. And the fact that he was mighty close to where she was found when Bonnie raised the alarm. The other thing that fascinates me is his relationship with his dad. He thinks he's distanced himself from Benet, but I'd say Benet affects every decision he makes.'

'Right. So, conclusions?'

'Bonnie and Julian are still top for me.' But she had so many questions left to answer it was driving her nuts. She couldn't wait to get back to it.

At that moment, Viv pulled a face like a cat bringing up a furball. 'Moira, at your six o'clock.'

Eve turned and saw the storekeeper had entered the pub with Molly Walker. The pair went straight to the bar.

'I'd better give her my update.' Eve hadn't been spotted yet, but it seemed wisest to take control.

She made for the bar and thanked Moira again for alerting her when Ella reappeared. 'She was out when Luke called on her. And her boat trip the next day was coincidental.' She was sure Moira would have heard about it. 'It was a half-term adventure, just like the overnight stay afterwards. I should have guessed.'

It was worth giving her Ella's version of events. Moira was bound to pass them on. If anyone knew otherwise, she'd find out. And so, in turn, would Eve.

'Ah, of course.' Moira looked disappointed. 'I never believed the gossip about her, naturally. Though I do hear that Luke Shipley's been spotted locally now and she *was* defending him. If he's alive, he must surely be the killer.'

'I'm not certain, to be honest. Anyway, I'd better get back to Viv. I hope you both enjoy your evening.'

It was two puddings and forty-five minutes later when Sylvia and Daphne entered the pub. A very different kettle of fish to Moira. Eve waved them over, and before long they were all seated together, Eve and Viv with coffees, Sylvia and Daphne with a glass of brandy each.

'We've been following the news,' Daphne said.

'Lapping it up,' Sylvia added.

'I wouldn't put it like that.'

'I was speaking generally. I'd say most of the villagers are. Especially this latest information on Luke Shipley. I suppose you've just told Viv everything you know.'

Viv laughed. 'One up on you there.'

Eve lowered her voice and provided a brief recap of developments. When she got to the bit about the bouquet Ella admitted buying, Daphne's forehead wrinkled.

'What is it?'

She sighed. 'I'm just remembering another time when there were flowers laid there. At least twenty years ago now. Don't you remember, Sylvia? The riding accident?'

Her partner frowned. 'It does ring a bell.'

Daphne shook her head. 'The funny thing is, Kitty was involved then too.'

Eve's skin prickled. 'Excuse me? How do you mean?'

'She was riding across country with a friend. I'm afraid I can't remember his name. They were young, being daredevils, as young people do, neither of them wearing riding hats. And the young man fell and broke his neck.' She closed her eyes for a moment. 'Awful. There were lots of flowers.'

'Where exactly was this? Can you remember?'

Daphne looked taken aback. 'I'm afraid I can't. Not precisely.'

Eve took out her phone and called up Farfield on Google Maps. 'Would you mind taking a look, in case it jogs your memory?'

Daphne took the phone from her, frowning. A moment later she pointed. 'It must have been around there. Close to the old hunting lodge.'

She was pointing to the exact spot where Ella had laid the bouquet.

'Thanks, Daphne. I think this might mean something.'

38

If anyone was likely to know more about the riding accident, it was Jo. She'd been close to Sophie Marchant, after all, and anything that affected Kitty would have touched Sophie closely. But when Eve went up to the bar to ask for a word, Toby said she'd gone off to bed with a headache. In desperation, Eve looked around for Moira. Any whiff of drama or tragedy would surely have reached her ears.

'I saw her leave an hour ago,' Viv said. 'Typical Moira, never there on those rare occasions when you actually want her.'

Sylvia laughed as Eve glanced at her watch. It was gone ten. She couldn't go knocking on her door now.

Instead, she said her goodbyes, called Gus and drove back to the castle. The internet would probably have the answer. She'd go straight upstairs and google. But on her arrival, she found an extra car in the drive. She might need to change plan.

'What the heck's Palmer doing here?'

Gus gave a light whine at the name and Eve's chest tightened. The police must have news. She undid her dachshund's harness, locked the car and made her way across the drive. Maybe Luke had been found.

She listened for voices, then walked down the west wing corridor, following the sound. She was planning to eavesdrop as she had before, but this time she found an open door and Palmer, Julian, Nate, Bonnie and Freya in the sitting room with the white sofas.

'Ah, Ms Mallow.' Palmer's piggy eyes narrowed at the sight of her. 'Here for the latest gossip, I see.'

Eve counted to ten. She didn't bother to reply; he didn't deserve it.

'I'm pleased to say that the investigation into Kitty Marchant's death is closed, bar tying up some lose ends. I'm sure it'll be a great disappointment to you, but you can put your magnifying glass down now.'

She saw Julian smirk and felt a fresh shot of adrenaline pump round her body.

'I was just informing Mr Fisher and Mr Marchant that Luke Shipley's body's been found.'

The breath went out of her.

'He jumped from the church tower at Wessingham and we believe he was killed instantly.'

Eve felt a heavy, dragging sensation in her chest. She knew Luke had been hiding something, but increasingly, she'd felt sure it wasn't his guilt. And now, she was almost convinced it was he who'd pulled Bonnie's necklace off and hidden it. A necklace Bonnie and Julian seemed to want very badly. Had he really taken his own life?

'Our theory is that he staged the boat to look as if he'd been attacked. That's borne out by his reappearance in Suffolk. I suspect he was obsessed with Ms Marchant but she was, of course, happily married. I've no doubt she tried to let him down gently on Sunday evening, but Mr Shipley was unbalanced. Couldn't take the rejection and killed her. He couldn't cope with his guilt either, and returned to Suffolk in spite of himself, with the intention of confessing to Ms Marchant's father. That plan failed and, in the end, he took another way out.'

Eve thought of the press cuttings about Kitty which Brad Salthouse had seen. And the way Luke had watched her without her knowledge. Him following her around London. It all seemed to back Palmer's theory. But if he was guilty, why wait until Tuesday evening to run? And why was the necklace he'd potentially stolen so important to Julian and Bonnie? And finally, if he'd been clear-sighted and cool enough to stage the boat scene, would remorse really drive him back to Suffolk?

As for Kitty being 'happily married' and Julian sitting there smugly, thinking everyone believed it... It was more than Eve could bear. She felt a kinship with Kitty. She'd find out the truth and get her justice if it was the last thing she did.

As Palmer got up to go, other questions filled Eve's head. Was Luke's change in behaviour towards Nate and Julian relevant? What had he done with the necklace? If Julian or Bonnie had pushed him from the church tower, did they have it now? And where did the laptop fit in?

Bonnie escorted Palmer from the room. She was looking up at him, nodding, appearing solemn and grateful. Palmer was lapping up her appreciation. *Eww.*

A moment later, Bonnie returned and Freya poured everyone a nightcap.

No one spoke.

'At least it's over, I suppose,' Bonnie said at last.

Julian nodded but Nate looked hollow.

Freya glanced at him. 'You'll be glad to have Rhoda home.' Her eyes were on his, but he barely responded. She finished her drink. 'If you'll excuse me, I think I'll go to bed.' Her voice sounded tight. Eve noticed her give Nate one last searching look as she left the room.

'I'd better go too.' Eve wanted some space to let the latest news settle. 'I must carry on writing the obituary. It shouldn't take much longer now.' She wanted to remind them she had an official reason for being there. It would be terrible to be booted out at this crucial stage.

The image of Luke, talking earnestly to Ella, following Kitty, waiting for Benet, filled her mind, a mix of memories and imagined scenes. The shock of his death had left her numb.

She arrived in Farfield's lobby, just in time to see Freya by the coat stand, her hand on one of the jackets. For a second, she thought she was about to take something from one of the pockets. Either that or slip something in. But then, as Eve watched, Freya stroked the sleeve and sighed.

Eve recognised the jacket. It was the blue one Nate had worn the night Kitty died. Nate with his attractive high cheekbones and blue eyes.

Suddenly, several memories merged. The way Freya had flinched just after Benet had sung Nate's wife's praises. The day she'd passed on the message about Rhoda's impending visit. Her voice had sounded tight then, just like tonight. As if she was reining in tears. The fact that Freya had accepted a job at Farfield even though she hated Kitty and Julian. And then her searching look as she'd left the room just now. *You'll be glad to have Rhoda back...*

Eve lingered, waiting for Freya to go upstairs, but then followed.

The manager was ahead of her, walking towards the east wing. Eve checked over her shoulder, but Bonnie, Julian and Nate must have stayed downstairs.

'Freya.'

The woman turned.

'How long have you been in love with Nate?'

39

Eve would never normally have come straight out with such a personal question, but the dynamics at the castle mattered, and surprising Freya seemed like the best way of getting an honest answer.

Freya's eyes were huge as she turned towards Eve, and for a moment she looked angry, but then she dissolved into tears.

'Do you want to talk about it?' Eve said, walking up to Freya and putting a hand on her shoulder. 'Please, let's have a hot chocolate or something. You've been under so much strain.'

Freya looked uncertain.

'Off the record, of course. It certainly won't affect Farfield's review if I ever complete one. We have to be allowed to drop our professional masks at a time like this. We wouldn't be human if we didn't.'

At last, Freya nodded and gulped.

'I've got a kettle in my room. I can't go back downstairs. I don't want the others to see me like this.'

Freya led the way down the east corridor to an old-fashioned latched door and Eve followed her inside.

'This was one of the guest rooms when Craig and I lived

here,' Freya said as she put the kettle on. 'Our bedroom was on the other side. It's so weird to think how happy I was when we first moved in.'

It was a pleasant room with a portrait of a smiling woman in early 1800s dress over the fireplace, and chairs to either side. It would be cosy in winter. Gus was sniffing around the grate as though picking up on fires past. Currently, the room was nice and cool. Freya had left the window open, and the sweet night air filled the space.

'Would you like chocolate? Or a camomile or mint tea?'

'Mint please.' She wanted something refreshing to wake her up.

A minute later, she and Freya sat opposite each other, their drinks on a small table between them.

Freya had been leaning down to make a fuss of Gus, but now she looked up hesitantly. 'How did you know about me and Nate?'

Me and Nate. It wasn't just Freya who was in love with him, then. He'd fallen for her too. Perhaps that was the secret he'd been keeping. Kitty had said he was playing a dangerous game, and he wasn't the only one who might get hurt. Rhoda would be a possible casualty of course. And Freya, with all that she'd suffered, might be heading for yet more heartache. Despite Kitty and Freya's quarrel, Eve believed Kitty had worried for her friend.

She told Freya about the various things that had made her wonder, culminating in seeing her stroke the sleeve of Nate's jacket. And then she told her about the conversation Deidre Lennox had overheard between Kitty and Nate.

'I think Kitty was concerned for you.'

Tears came again. A lot of them. Her fists were clenched, knuckles white.

'We never made up before she died.'

It often happened that way. Eve hoped she'd done the right

thing in telling Freya. She'd thought it might be good to know that despite Kitty's actions, she'd still cared. Regretted what she'd done maybe. But now, she wasn't sure. Perhaps she'd interfered too much.

'Had you and Nate met before the sale of Farfield? Through Kitty perhaps?'

But Freya shook her head. 'No. I saw him first when he came to view this place. He knew it well already, of course; he was practically brought up here. I was prepared to hate him on sight; he was Kitty's brother and Julian's friend. And, of course, I loathed the idea of Kitty and Julian living here.' She drew a tissue from her pocket and blew her nose. 'When I heard how much Nate was offering, I was so miserable. I knew I'd have to take it; it would pay off all my debts and give me some savings to start over. It made me hate Nate all the more.'

Eve sipped her mint tea. 'What changed your mind?'

'It was the gradual realisation that he was still being nice to me, even after I'd agreed the sale. At first, I thought he was trying to charm me. After Craig, I was on the lookout for all the mean, low tricks in the book. But Nate's kindnesses were subtle. If he'd been in to measure up, and I'd offered him water, he'd refill the jug and put ice in it before he left. Tiny things like that. And then very slowly, as I unbent a little, we started to talk. I never told him what Kitty and Julian had done. It crossed my mind several times, but I always drew back. At last I realised it was because I didn't want to hurt Nate. And I didn't want to make him hate me. Or force him to take sides.'

Just as Nate's father had done.

'But although I didn't tell him about Julian's book, I did start to share what had happened with Craig. He's a good listener. And one day... one day I cried and he comforted me and before we knew it, we were in each other's arms.' She looked exhausted suddenly. 'But Nate's married. It's easy to forget. Rhoda travels so much, but she *is* his wife and she's coming back.' Freya hung her head. 'I've wronged Rhoda. Nate and I both have. But after Craig, meeting someone so kind and understanding... It was just hard to turn my back. And I didn't.'

She started to cry again. Eve felt for her – couldn't help herself. She was no fan of cheating husbands and their lovers, having experienced them herself, but Freya had had an appalling time. It was rotten that she should be caught up in all this, and very bad luck that Nate was already attached.

'I have no chance whatsoever against Rhoda.' Freya wiped her eyes and looked at Eve.

'But if Nate loves you, and their relationship was already shaky?'

'That will make no odds. It's Benet, you see.'

'Benet?'

'Benet's openly amazed that Rhoda would choose Nate. And opt to stay with him. And Nate's overriding goal in life is to prove Benet wrong.' She shook her head. 'If he and Rhoda split, Benet will say I told you so.'

'But Nate would be leaving his wife, not the other way about.'

Freya shook her head. 'It wouldn't matter. He'd say Nate wasn't equal to the relationship; not serious enough. And when he found out about me, he'd say I'm much more Nate's level. That it was natural that he should gravitate in my direction. It matters more to him than he'd ever acknowledge.' She sighed. 'At least I'm working with him. That's something. It's better than I could have hoped for.'

The situation explained so much. At last Eve understood why Freya had chosen to come and work in a house with unhappy memories alongside two people she despised. Freya's hands were over her face now. 'I had to lie to the police about what I was doing when Kitty died. The truth is, Nate and I had sneaked off to be together. We were so close to the icehouse, but I didn't hear a thing. Maybe whoever killed Kitty struck her before she could cry out.' She paused and blew her nose again. 'The first we knew of it was when Bonnie shouted. Nate ran out to see what was going on, and I sneaked through the trees so I could come out far away from him.' She shook her head. 'Even in an emergency, Nate didn't want us to appear together. He'd never leave Rhoda for me.'

40

As Eve lay in bed that night, she thought of everything Freya had said. Her heart ached for the woman, and for the general mess which life threw at people.

She made herself pull back and consider the latest news in relation to the case. Freya and Nate being together the night Kitty died didn't prove one of them hadn't killed her. They were both in the vicinity. Unless they could swear they'd been together kissing between eight forty-five and ten fifteen, they were still in the running. But Eve could see how heavily Freya had fallen for Nate. Her love made her more unlikely as a killer. She wouldn't want to hurt him, and she'd be desperate for the writers' retreat to work. It meant they could be together.

As for Nate, Eve guessed his relationship with Freya was the secret he'd been keeping and although he could have killed Kitty to silence her, it didn't seem plausible. Kitty hadn't been threatening to tell when Deidre Lennox overheard them. And through thick and thin, it seemed Kitty and her brother had been close. He had no other motive that Eve knew of.

He and Freya had always been well down the list; the latest revelations hadn't changed her mind.

Poor Luke. His death – if he was killed – triggered a new batch of questions. How had his killer known where to find him? Had they followed him to a convenient spot, where they could push him to his death?

Eve couldn't believe it. The alternative was that they'd made contact and arranged a meet-up. Who would he trust? Unbidden, the image of Ella Tyndall came to mind.

The following morning, Eve got up early, fed Gus and breakfasted alone. She'd made Freya promise not to cook a full English the night before – she needed some slack – but Eve found an array of cereals, jams and marmalades left out for her. A moment later, Freya appeared with toast, butter, coffee and orange juice.

She blushed as she set them down. 'Thanks for last night. I'm sorry I was such a misery. It was good to get it off my chest.'

She left again quickly.

Eve felt reinvigorated after the previous evening's chat. It was progress. Questions answered, relationships clarified. It made her feel she might solve the puzzle after all. Thoughts of Luke filled her with a sense of urgency. She still couldn't know for sure that he was innocent, but her gut instinct was firm. If only she'd worked faster, she might have saved him.

She ate quickly. She was about to go back upstairs to lie low when she glanced through the window and saw Bonnie, walking across the grass.

It was too good an opportunity to miss after yesterday's conversation with Roberta Fisher. She needed to know why the heck Bonnie and Julian had lied about the pendant.

She let herself out of the door at the end of the corridor and followed Bonnie round, catching her just before she went inside.

'Morning. Sorry to bother you. Did you ever find your missing necklace?'

Bonnie looked at her suspiciously. 'No, I didn't. But I told you, it wasn't dear to me. It doesn't matter.'

'Oh, all right then. Only I had to pop downstairs to fetch something the other night and I saw you searching some of the rooms. I thought you might be looking for it.'

Bonnie went red. 'No, not at all.' There was a significant pause. 'I'd mislaid my favourite pen.'

Ah, the old favourite pen excuse. *Yeah, right.*

'Did you ever see the pendant that looked like it? The one that belonged to Julian's grandmother?'

'Of course not. Why would I?' Her voice shook slightly. Eve imagined the adrenaline pumping round her body.

'Bonnie, are you quite sure it was Kitty who pulled the necklace off?'

There was no mistaking her look now. Panic and a flicker of fear before she could control herself.

'What a stupid question. It's not something I'd get wrong.'

Eve watched as Bonnie strode towards the door. She wondered about calling her back, challenging her further. But the more specific she was, the riskier the mission became. She'd already put Bonnie on high alert. The important thing was, she was certain Bonnie had lied, and felt sure it had been Luke who'd taken the pendant. Had he had it with him when he was killed? Did Bonnie or Julian have it back now? And why the heck was it so important? Meanwhile, the whereabouts of the laptop was still a mystery.

Eve thought of tackling Julian too, but she could already imagine the excuses he'd produce. She'd tell him she'd talked to Roberta, who'd denied the necklace's existence, and he'd say his grandmother had left it to him secretly, or passed it on before her death, not wanting to hurt Roberta's feelings. She might suggest he was searching for it or the laptop in Luke's room, but he'd throw that off too. Say he was worried and looking for clues. And that he couldn't have killed Luke to access his room. He wasn't even dead then.

And once again, the more she gave away her thinking, the more she put herself at risk.

So instead of finding Julian, Eve followed Bonnie into the castle and went upstairs. By Luke's door, she remembered the first time she'd heard someone inside, well before his disappearance and death. Perhaps Bonnie had searched initially, then Julian had had another go before the CSIs arrived.

Back in her room, Eve made up her mind to research the riding accident Daphne had mentioned. If she couldn't find the answer she'd ring Jo, but googling would avoid the need for a long conversation. She owed Jo an update, but other tasks were more pressing.

She sat at the table with Gus at her feet and got results quickly. There were no news reports from the time, but she found one about a tenth anniversary service to celebrate the life lost that day. Kitty's riding companion had been Stephen Appley, a local man, the son of a couple who ran a farm just inland from Farfield. Eve's heart contracted. He'd only just turned seventeen, still a boy. The article had a potted history of his short life. He'd been a keen sailor and loved the countryside. He'd attended the school where Ella Tyndall now taught.

Eve moved on to find Ella's details on the staff pages, working at speed, tentatively guessing what she might see. She was right. Ella had gone to the school too. She and Stephen had been close in age. Kitty a couple of years younger. Maybe they'd all socialised during the holidays when Kitty visited her grandparents. And Ella and Stephen had attended the village school; they'd probably been in the same class.

Eve saw the bouquet Ella had left in a new light now. Perhaps it hadn't been a tribute to Kitty, but to Stephen. Kitty's death could have brought it all back. Ella must have been fond of him. More than fond, if Eve was right about the flowers. She looked at Stephen's photograph. He'd been handsome, with blue eyes and a mop of wavy blond hair. Was there any chance she blamed Kitty for his death? Might she have killed her, all these years later, in revenge?

It was decades after the event. Why would she act now? But maybe Kitty, Julian and Nate trumping her bid for Farfield had brought her grief and anger back to the surface. Perhaps Kitty had said something the night she died and Ella had seen red. The old hurt coupled with the new one could have been enough to make her plan the murder. If Ella had loved Stephen, her motive was even more personal than being angry at Kitty for hurting her grandparents.

She needed to go and see Ella. Talk to her on neutral territory. She wanted to understand the friendship she'd formed with Luke too, and where that fitted in. She'd had one go at getting the facts, but that was before Luke's death. Emotion could bring the truth closer to the surface.

She wondered if Luke and Ella had interacted at the launch party. She hadn't noticed, but she'd taken lots of photos. She picked up her phone and scrolled through them.

She found shots of all the main players, but nothing showing Ella and Luke together.

She went through more, and came to one featuring Luke, Nate, Kitty and Julian. She was about to scroll on, when something stopped her. She pulled her phone nearer, examining the picture close-up.

Luke's bed-head hair was distinctive. She remembered noticing it the day he'd arrived. But seeing him next to Kitty, she realised it wasn't so unusual. He had a cow lick like her.

A faint tingling crept up her spine. Benet's hair was tufty like that too. But it wasn't that uncommon.

As she rationalised it, a fresh memory struck her. Kitty's hair had been chestnut brown when it was natural, just like

Luke's and Nate's. They shared the same high cheekbones too. She'd noticed the traits individually, but never seen the similarity before.

She shook herself. She was adding two and two and making five. But then other facts piled in. The interest Luke had shown not just in Kitty and Nate, but in Farfield and its history. The way he'd asked Ella all about the Marchants. His apparent attempt to talk to Benet when he'd come back to Suffolk. And his friend, Brad Salthouse. He'd thought Luke was obsessed with Nate *and* Julian, but he and Roberta had both said they came as a pair. What if it was Nate alone who Luke had been focused on? Eve recalled Brad's words about Luke's mother: 'It was just the two of them and they were close.' What had happened to his dad?

'Heck, Gus. I think I've been going around with my eyes shut.'

41

Eve found Ella inside her cottage, her eyes red-rimmed, a tissue clutched in her hand.

'You heard about Luke's death?'

She nodded.

It was all over the papers and websites. But of course, Ella could have known about it first-hand if she was responsible. Eve couldn't see her as the killer before, but if she was right about her and Stephen Appley it seemed possible. She could have killed Luke if he'd discovered she'd murdered Kitty.

'I wonder if we could talk. I heard recently about the riding accident, out in the fields where you left the bouquet. I want to understand about Kitty's relationship with the young man who died.'

Ella screwed the tissue up, tight in her fingers. Tears brimmed.

'Will you come and walk with me on the beach? I need to air Gus.' It wasn't just for safety. She wanted Ella off home turf. 'We can head away from the village. Get some peace and quiet. But I'd like to understand, for the obituary.' Eve doubted Ella would believe her motivation. 'I think I might have found out something about Luke too.'

Ella looked at her closely, but there was none of the fear and panic she'd seen in Bonnie's eyes. Just deep sorrow.

'Give me a moment.' She disappeared inside her cottage and reappeared two minutes later, looking more normal. Eve guessed she'd splashed her face with water. Strands of her hair were damp.

Eve started towards the coast using the main route through the village, not the lonely estuary path. Once they were on the heath that bordered the beach she let Gus off his leash and he scampered away, his healthy wet nose pointing north.

'How did you find out about Stephen?'

'Someone mentioned his death and the spot matched where I found your bouquet. The link between him, you and Kitty was too strong to be a coincidence.'

Ella nodded and closed her eyes for a moment, her chest rising and falling. 'He never normally rode without a hat. That was Kitty's doing. She was a daredevil back then. A rule breaker. Kicking against authority. Her dad encouraged it. Liked her being a renegade. Making his parents worry. It was her fault Stephen died. He'd be alive if it weren't for her.' Her fists were clenched, her voice strained, as though she wanted to scream and could barely hold it back. 'She was selfish. And then, after hurting her grandparents so badly, staying away as her grand-mother got weaker and weaker from her cancer, she suddenly turned up this year, wanting to live at Farfield again. Now. After all this time. Just when I was trying to buy it for the community. She took Stephen from me and then she took the castle.'

Whatever the ins and outs, rights and wrongs, Eve could see how badly Ella was hurting. Her grief was hard to watch.

'I'm so sorry, Ella. Losing Stephen, Sophie and Daniel must have been terrible. And Kitty coming back now was awful timing for you. But I think she'd changed. She was a child back then. Still finding herself. Trying to live up to Benet's expectations. She suffered over the years.'

They walked in silence for a moment.

As Gus leaped towards a seagull which had briefly landed up ahead, Eve turned to Ella again. 'You said Kitty took Stephen from you. Were you in love with him?'

Ella nodded, not looking at Eve. There was something there.

'Was it him you'd been crying over when I visited you last? I saw all the tissues.'

'Yes.' She breathed the word out. 'I could hold it together when I was with other people, but sitting alone at the cottage was too much. I had to let it out. It's not that I thought he was the love of my life. There've been others. It was just that he was so young. He had such promise and it was all wiped out in a moment. If only he and Kitty hadn't gone off riding together. And the worst of it is—'

She stopped abruptly, as though she'd changed her mind.

'Were they seeing each other on the sly?' Eve asked gently. There was clearly more to come.

But Ella shook her head violently. 'No, they weren't.'

She was wringing her hands. What was it she was keeping back? But before Eve could think of another way to push, Ella switched topic.

'What have you found out about Luke?'

'It's a guess, based on everything I know. Luke got in touch with you before he visited Farfield to ask about its history, right?'

Ella nodded, giving Eve a sidelong look with teary eyes.

'Which kind of makes sense. He was going to write an article about the place, just like me. But you wouldn't think he'd need in-depth information – more than you can read on the Farfield website, for instance.'

Ella was quiet.

'Did he ask you much about the family? About Sophie and Daniel Marchant? And about Benet, Nate and Kitty?'

At last, Ella nodded slowly.

'I thought he might have. He confided in you, didn't he? Isn't that why you had some kind of bond, beyond what you'd expect from recent acquaintances?'

At last, the teacher nodded again. 'How did you guess?'

'I was looking at a photo of Nate, Kitty and Luke. There are similarities. And then other bits of information started to add up.'

Ella nodded, her eyes sad. 'Once Luke told me he, Kitty and Nate shared a father I saw the likeness too.'

'Did he tell you after the history tour?'

Ella inclined her head again. 'I forced his hand, I think. His questions about the family were starting to seem intrusive. I was sharp with him and then it all came out. I suppose he must have been dying to share his feelings with someone.

'He said his mother had told him that his father was called Benedict, and his family were rich. She said she'd met him on a camping holiday in Suffolk and sneaked onto the grounds of the big house his parents owned. He'd shown her an icehouse in their garden, and they'd slept there overnight. She never told Benet about the pregnancy. He was already married.'

From those small details Luke must have worked out the rest. Started digging when his mother was killed, perhaps. He'd found Farfield. Traced Benet. Got close to Nate. Spent time in the icehouse where his parents had made love.

And perhaps Nate's reaction to Luke's seemingly cloying behaviour was understandable too. Luke *had* befriended him with an ulterior motive, albeit a harmless one. It was the kind of thing people sensed.

'Luke never told Nate?'

Ella shook her head. 'He said he got to know him with that

intention, but the more he found out, the less keen he was to come clean. He said Nate and Julian looked down their noses at him.' She shook her head. 'He overheard them. Julian said they'd have to come to the next social in disguise and that it was like having a needy limpet glued to their sides. And then he joked about how Nate probably liked it. How he seemed to encourage Luke by being too nice. But then again, he went on, he didn't have to cope with literary groupies like Julian did, so it would be a novelty for him. Nate said that was rubbish and he'd rather spend the evening with a rotting corpse than with Luke. And then they both started on a list of things they felt would make better company than him. It sounded awful.'

Nate was probably needled by Julian. If they'd both been drinking Eve could see how it had got out of hand, but it must have hurt Luke terribly.

'Something happened here that cemented his feelings,' Ella went on. 'He said they were spying on him. He was devastated about Kitty. He'd found her far kinder. I didn't tell him what I thought, but I'd told him about Benet refusing to help his parents when they ran out of money. It was before I knew who he was, and it was part of the history of Farfield.'

That might explain why he'd hesitated to speak with Benet when he'd come back to Suffolk. Maybe he'd got cold feet at the last minute when he remembered what he was capable of.

Eve thought of him following his half-sister and father to that café in London. Hanging around. Wondering whether to announce himself. Did Benet really have no idea who he was? The way he'd mentioned him, so casually, made Eve think he was in ignorance. It was tragic.

She was wracking her brains, trying to see if Luke's relationship to the Marchants might have provided a motive to kill both him and Kitty. Two half-siblings dead. Or was it more random than that? Not a coincidence exactly, but unfortunate cause and effect? Assuming Luke was telling the truth, he'd have wanted to befriend Kitty, work up to telling her who he was, so he'd followed her closely. Perhaps he'd seen something that gave away the killer's identity.

But where did the necklace fit in? And the laptop?

'It's hard to explain,' Ella broke into her thoughts, her eyes on the middle distance, 'but discovering Luke's relationship to the family made me feel I'd found an extra connection too. Nate and Kitty were like cousins to me when we were kids, and Sophie and Daniel treated me as an extra grandchild. I suppose I felt Luke was a kindred spirit – someone connected to the family but cut out. We talked very easily.'

'You knew he was alive after he disappeared? You were one of the few people who claimed to believe he'd been attacked. Because he'd run, and you wanted to protect him?'

Ella nodded. 'He came to my house, the day he went off, but I was out.'

She was sticking to that, then. Of course, he'd only been seen in Ella's garden. People assumed he'd visited, but no one said they'd seen him go inside.

'He left me a note, telling me what he planned. I don't think he was thinking straight. Kitty's death had had such an effect on him, and he was scared. He thought the police would think he had a motive if they found out he was Nate and Kitty's half-brother: that Kitty had rejected him and he'd seen red, perhaps. He told me he was their top suspect. Joint with me, I think. And that PA of Julian's, though I'd swear the police never paid her as much attention.'

'So Luke was scared of the police?'

She nodded. 'He didn't trust them. But he wasn't just worried he'd be arrested. He thought their focus on him would allow the real killer to get away. At first, he hoped they'd broaden their search when they couldn't pin the killing on him, but by Tuesday he was losing faith. He said in his note that if they believed he'd been attacked, they might change tack and find the person who'd taken Kitty's life.'

So that was his plan. But the police had been onto him from the start. Palmer had been correct to be suspicious, of course. *Even a stopped clock tells the right time twice a day.*

And then, seeing the news, knowing the police weren't convinced, he'd come back to Suffolk. Wondered whether to confide in Benet perhaps, but been unsure.

And within hours of the household at Farfield hearing he was alive, he was dead.

'I didn't get his note until after midnight.' Ella took a juddery breath. 'I'd been out with friends. It was far too late to stop him, but I was frightened. The thought of him going off in that little boat they have at Farfield, and him a Londoner. As far as I know he had no experience on the water. Something made me go out early to look in case there was any sign of him, but I drew a blank, of course.

'I think he was killed.' Ella had turned to face Eve. 'I don't believe he'd take his own life. He seemed frightened but determined. Angry, not depressed.' Her eyes were full of tears again. 'The note he left me was so sad.'

She took it from her pocket. It was creased and smudged, as if she'd looked at it repeatedly.

Eve skimmed down the page.

As well as explaining his plan and the reasons behind it, he told Ella not to worry if she heard about blood on the boat. He also asked her not to tell the police.

He'd ended:

I hope I'll be back, but if something happens to me, my favourite flowers are aquilegias. Please pick some for me and don't be sad. Look for the truth instead.

'It's as if he thought I'd be the only person who'd mourn

him.' Ella shook her head. 'And certainly the only one who'd believe in his innocence. He knew he was in danger, but he was determined. The trouble was, I don't think he was certain who to fear.' She turned pitiful eyes on Eve. 'I wish he wasn't dead. And I wish Kitty wasn't either.'

'You feel that way, even though you hated her?'

'I hate myself more.' The words were so quiet, Eve could only just hear them above the crashing waves.

'What do you mean?'

'Stephen and I had a row, the day he died. He asked me to ride with him, and I was so excited. I'd been mad for him for at least a year. Too shy to say anything, though we were close friends. I thought my moment had come – he was asking me on a date. Just the two of us.

'Then he explained Kitty would be there too and I was upset. Embarrassed. I was sure I'd given myself away. I told him I didn't want to come. I was mean to him, so he went off with Kitty.

'Later, Kitty hinted he'd wanted to ask me out; he was working up the courage. She told me how sad he'd been. He wasn't sure what he'd done to upset me. She said he'd galloped off at a rate of knots.' Tears were streaming down Ella's cheeks now. 'And he wore no hat. Kitty was reckless but he never was. Maybe he was reckless because of me.'

Her body was wracked with sobs. Eve was glad they'd walked away from the village. She hugged Ella.

'Life is so cruel. It turns on a dime sometimes. People part after harsh words every day. They usually get a second chance. You couldn't possibly know.'

But Ella continued to cry, her head on Eve's shoulder.

42

Eve left Ella at her front door. She'd agreed to tell the police what she knew, though she was still worried they'd decide Luke's family history meant he had a motive for Kitty. Eve knew it was a danger, but then so was holding back. It could be relevant, and though Palmer was useless, the rest of the team weren't.

For her own part, she wanted to talk to Nate. Get to him first with the news, so she could watch his expression – see if the idea of Luke as a half-brother came as a shock. She couldn't see why Nate would kill over their relationship. It wasn't as though there was a big family inheritance to fight over on the Marchant side. And though Benet was rolling in it, he wasn't the sort to sub his kids. But it was worth ruling it out as a motive.

'I don't like doing it,' she said to Gus, as they approached the castle. 'It's the very last way he should hear the news, especially under these circumstances.' But it was no good; she needed to explore all avenues. With every suspect still in the frame, she was desperate for leads.

On entering the castle, she went to the office and found Freya.

'I was hoping I might speak to Nate.'

She bit her lip. 'He's gone out with Rhoda. She arrived an hour ago.'

Eve wondered how the reunion was going, and what Freya would do next.

'I can let him know you're asking for him when he—'

But at that moment, Nate appeared in the doorway with his wife. Eve recognised her from her TV reports, with her grey eyes and delicate eyebrows.

But whereas Eve had always seen her looking in control, even when there were bombs falling in the sky behind her, now she appeared shattered. Not just exhausted but stunned. She took one look at Eve and Freya and walked straight up the stairs.

Freya looked uncertainly after her, then at Nate.

'Eve was hoping for a word.'

Eve was torn now. Nate looked pale too. He seemed in an almost trance-like state, his features immobile. 'Maybe it's not a good time?'

But he turned to her mechanically. 'No. No, it's all right. Let's go to the sitting room.'

Nate closed the door behind them, and they sat opposite each other on the white sofas. Eve remembered how tranquil she'd thought the room was when she'd first seen it. It had been under a week ago, but it felt a world away.

Nate sat staring into space, not inviting her to talk or asking what she wanted.

Eve decided to plough ahead. 'I'm sorry, but I've heard a rumour. It might not be true.' She waited until she finally had Nate's attention, his eyes on hers. 'Apparently, Luke Shipley thought he was your and Kitty's half-brother.'

She watched as disbelief flooded his face, followed by confusion, then a gradual dawning. The way Luke had behaved was starting to make sense now, she guessed. She was convinced Nate hadn't known.

'Where did you hear that?'

'He'd confided in someone in the village. Before she died, his mother told him his father was called Benedict and that his parents were rich. She mentioned they'd once sneaked onto the grounds of their house in Suffolk and slept in an icehouse.'

Nate stared at her, his brow furrowed.

'Luke used the information to trace you.'

'Why didn't he say anything?' He spoke slowly.

Eve hated saying it. 'I think he felt you and Julian hadn't warmed to him. I believe he was testing the waters with Kitty, and he probably wanted to approach Benet too. I guess he wanted to make friends first, create a bond, then admit the truth.'

Nate put his head in his hands. 'This is terrible. I wasn't kind enough to him.'

She could imagine what was going through his mind. His unguarded tirade against him with Julian. 'It's possible he was wrong. Got the wrong family. Or his mother was telling fairy tales.'

'You don't believe that.'

Eve sat there helplessly, feeling awful.

'I should have been better.' Nate swore: his pain and anger directed inwards. 'Julian said Luke made a huge effort to chat to us at the party where we met. Joked about his neediness. And I laughed with him. Joined in fully. I actually thought it was a bit creepy. But I had no idea.' He ran his hands through his hair and tugged at it. 'Does my father know? Did Kitty?'

'Not as far as I'm aware.' Eve wondered if Benet would have treated Luke any better than he had Nate and Kitty. Probably not. 'It all needs verifying.'

'I'll have to tell Dad.' He shook his head. 'It'll probably be water off a duck's back.'

The loss of a second child within a week, albeit one who was a stranger. But when Eve tried to imagine him getting emotional, she couldn't.

'Nate, I'm sorry to tell you this, but the person in the village says Luke thought you and Julian were spying on him. Does that make any sense?'

Once again she watched him closely. The way his brow furrowed.

'No. I mean, he seemed overly interested in Kitty, so I kept an eye on him. But I didn't follow him around or try to listen in to their conversations. I asked Kitty about it, warned her. I thought he might be keen on her.' He rubbed his forehead distractedly. 'She said she'd noticed but she told me not to worry. She'd handle it.'

Maybe Julian had gone further. He might have been unfaithful but that didn't mean he wasn't capable of jealousy. Eve could imagine him being a dog in the manger.

At that moment, Eve heard the crunching of gravel outside the window. Quick steps. She looked up and saw Rhoda walking towards a white Mondeo, bag in hand.

Eve looked awkwardly at Nate, whose attention had also been caught.

'Rhoda and I have broken up.' He said the words slowly, as if he could hardly believe it. 'It was my decision. To be absolutely frank, I've fallen in love with Freya. Telling Rhoda was the only honest thing to do.' He took a deep breath and put his shoulders back. 'I feel better now it's done. I hope I can overwrite Freya's bad memories with some happy ones here.'

In amongst all the tragedy, Eve's spirits lifted. She'd found it easy to believe Freya when she'd said Nate would never leave his wife, because of Benet. But Nate had broken free. The end of a marriage was sad, but if love was gone, it had to be the right thing to do. She couldn't wait for Nate to tell Freya the news.

43

Eve still hadn't eaten lunch, but she was filled with the urge to call Robin. She'd wanted to update him the moment she'd finished talking to Ella, but reaching Nate first had seemed important. Now, her mind was full of the case, but also of thoughts of relationships. How difficult they could be, but how precious. And time was limited, that day at least. Robin was due to travel back to London for the talk he was giving.

Eve went to her room, found the sweet spot for connectivity, and made the call.

'*I was about to ring you,*' Robin said. '*Let's meet.*'

Half an hour later, Eve and Robin were sitting under the trees that bordered the beach by Watcher's Wood. It was quieter than meeting in Saxford and breathtakingly beautiful with its dappled shade, the shingle-strewn sand stretching ahead of them to the sea.

Robin had stopped off at the bakers in Wessingham and bought crusty white rolls filled with Emmenthal and plum tomatoes. He'd brought the lemonade she especially liked from Moira's store too.

'You're a lifesaver. Have I ever said I love you?'

He grinned as he spread out a rug for them to sit on. 'Once or twice.'

A moment later, they were tucking in and Eve was feeling more human. 'You're all set for tonight?'

He nodded. 'They've got five hundred people signed up to attend. I'd be nervous if I wasn't distracted by what's happening here.'

She met his gaze. 'What news from Greg? No sign of an art deco pendant about Luke's person, I suppose?'

'I'm afraid not. And nothing found in his flat either. If he took Julian's laptop or the necklace then it looks like either the killer's got them or he hid them elsewhere. But Greg did have significant news. Someone rang Shipley using an unregistered phone, forty-five minutes before he died. The police will find out where the mobile was purchased, but I'll bet the buyer paid cash. Luke's was the only number called.'

'Heck.'

'Palmer's clinging to the theory that he took his own life, but there's an obvious question mark now. Who called him and why? He's at least having to consider that someone got him to the church and pushed him.'

'And it had to be someone he trusted.'

'Any ideas?'

Eve closed her eyes for a moment and felt the cool breeze on her face. 'I'd say Ella, but our talk today makes me doubt she's responsible.' She filled him in. 'Deep down she knows Stephen Appley's death was just terribly bad luck. She blames herself as much as Kitty. But let's say I'm wrong, and Luke was a threat to her because he knew she was guilty. Fine. But then why would he climb a tall tower with her and be so unguarded as to let her push him off?'

'And why would he write that note, telling her what he was up to?'

'Has Palmer put forward an alternative theory to Luke being guilty?'

'No. And when he gets the news about Luke's connection to Kitty and Nate I expect he'll argue that he must have felt left out, resentful. He'll probably suggest he told Kitty the truth and she tried to distance herself or didn't believe him. Whereupon he decided to kill her.'

Eve nodded. 'I expect you're right, but it doesn't wash. It's like I thought with Freya: I could just about imagine it if Kitty was especially cruel and he saw red, attacking her with the first weapon that came to hand.'

'But not if it involved opening the grille in advance, getting Kitty there and smuggling in a champagne bottle?'

'Exactly. Besides, he'd already been rejected by Nate, as a friend at least. If he was going to get murderously angry, why not pick on his half-brother too?

'True. Maybe we should focus on the call made from the unregistered phone and what happened next. Do you think Luke would trust any of the key players enough to meet?'

Eve considered. 'He'd rowed with Bonnie, so she seems unlikely. And he'd overheard Julian and Nate bad-mouthing him. Freya, possibly, Ella definitely. And his father perhaps. Luke wanted to approach him, by the look of things, but it seems he never did. But I can't imagine why Benet would want to kill Luke. I presume he was nowhere near Suffolk when Kitty died?'

Robin cast Eve a sidelong look. 'At a basement party in Islington, apparently. He was seen by the host at the start of the evening.'

'So unless he sneaked out, drove up to Suffolk and killed his own daughter without any motive that we're aware of, he's out of it.'

'Exactly. Luke put himself in a vulnerable position, going all the way up the church tower like that.' He shook his head. 'I drove past it on my way to the bakers. It's higher than most. Palmer reasons he'd never have taken the risk unless he was alone, so it must have been suicide.'

'It's one more puzzle to solve, because I'm sure as heck it wasn't.'

Robin nodded. 'Me too.'

Eve went back to Farfield, Robin and the case vying for her headspace. She wished she could be a fly on the wall at the talk he was giving. She was so proud of him. He'd taken a hard and lonely path when he'd reported corrupt fellow officers. His whole life had been turned upside down. Now he was back in the game and everything he'd done could be publicly recognised. But thoughts of him moving back to London played in her head again. His life was comprised of many parts now. It had opened up in a way he couldn't have dared hope when they'd first met. She'd miss him so much if he went. The casual chats, picnics by the beach. Cosy impromptu evenings at his place and hers.

She pushed the thoughts away as she drew up on the gravel outside the castle. On her way to her room, she and Gus bumped into Freya, who was looking pink.

'Nate said he'd told you what happened with Rhoda.'

Eve nodded as Freya crouched to tickle Gus's tummy. He was quick to spot someone in a good mood.

'I'm so pleased for you.' She deserved a break.

'I feel rotten inside. I shouldn't be so happy.'

'He and Rhoda might have broken up anyway.'

Freya looked doubtful, but nodded. 'Nate's suggested I come and meet his father. He's already broken the news about Luke. I'm a bit nervous, to tell you the truth.' She shook her head. 'Nate's spoiling for a fight; I can see it in his eyes. He knows Benet will think he's mad for breaking it off with Rhoda.'

'It's what Nate thinks that counts.' Privately, Eve wondered if she'd been wrong to assume Nate had broken free. Maybe this was an act of defiance.

'I hope you're right.'

Eve did too.

44

Eve led Gus back upstairs to her room.

'I'm going round in circles,' she said to him as she closed the door. 'I understand the lie of the land a lot better than I did, but there are still fundamental questions I can't answer.' She flumped down into the chair at her table and opened her laptop as Gus went to his water bowl. Her week at the retreat was up tomorrow. She'd have to leave without knowing who'd killed Kitty. It was desperately depressing.

She took a deep breath. This was no time to lose focus.

What were the key oddities and queries? Surely they had to lead somewhere.

She went through every detail she'd recorded and made a list:

- *Why did Julian invent an elaborate story about the pendant Bonnie wore at the launch party? Was Bonnie aware it was a lie?*

Eve guessed the answer to that second part was yes. She'd

looked shifty each time Eve asked about it, and if Eve was right, she'd been involved in the effort to get it back.

- *Why did the pendant upset Kitty?*
- *Two items went missing that night. There's circumstantial evidence that it was Luke who took the pendant and Bonnie's reactions seem to back that up. Did he also take the laptop? Why are they important? And how are they related?*
- *Both Bonnie and Julian were looking for something and Julian searched Luke's bedroom. Were they searching for the pendant, the laptop, or both?*
- *Why did Bonnie blank both Freya and Kitty on Sunday evening?*
- *There are possible signs something small was hidden in the icehouse. Could Luke have put the pendant there then re-hidden it or taken it with him? Might it now be in the hands of his killer? If it's still missing, where might Luke have hidden it?*
- *If Luke took the laptop too, where did he put that?*
- *Benet says Kitty caught Julian listening to a conversation with a friend of hers, and Luke accused Julian and Nate of spying on him. Is that significant?*
- *Why did Kitty tell Julian about the scene she witnessed between Freya and Craig Hardwicke in such detail? Why mention the hatch with the dead tree in the background if she was sharing something in the heat of the moment?*

Because Eve still couldn't imagine Kitty passing on the details callously, anticipating they'd end up in print.

She sat there, staring at the list, then forwarded it to Robin with a covering note:

In case you're bored on the train xxx

What did the laptop and the pendant have in common? The pendant might not be a family heirloom, but it could still be worth a lot of money. More than a laptop, Eve guessed. The information the computer contained seemed more likely to be relevant. Eve googled art deco pendants, but the ones she found were going for a few hundred pounds. Perhaps it wasn't monetary value that made it so significant.

Robin texted a moment later to point out that Bonnie had seen Luke walk towards the creek. She'd probably have noticed if he had a laptop bag or a rucksack with him. But of course, he added, she might not have admitted it, if she was helping Julian track the computer down.

He said he was about to leave the train for a meeting in advance of his talk but promised to message again if anything struck him. He told her to take care.

Time had worn on, with Eve lost in thought. Freya had knocked to see if she'd like supper a while back, but Eve hadn't been hungry after the late lunch. Freya had said she'd leave her a portion to reheat and Eve went downstairs to fetch it, returning to Gus, who looked up at her questioningly.

'No need to get excited. I'm still stuck.'

She reread everything as she ate, then googled each of the key players in turn, desperate for something that would move her forward.

The more she looked at the questions, the more she kept coming back to the laptop, the pendant and the way Julian had tried to hide its history. Yet what might connect the two? You couldn't get anything less electronic than vintage jewellery. Not that it had to be vintage. It could be a fake...

And with that thought, an idea came to her. When is a necklace not a necklace? When might it have more in common with a laptop than you might think?

A series of memories flooded her mind.

The fact that Bonnie hadn't turned round when Freya called her, the night Kitty died. The bizarrely detailed scene-setting in Julian's book. The way Bonnie had kept fiddling with the pendant. Making sure it was sitting nicely, pretty-side outwards. The fact that it didn't go with her earrings, or what she was wearing. That made sense, if it wasn't for decoration. Julian's reputation for spying on people. Luke's claim that he'd spied on him. His anger at Bonnie, who'd worn the necklace, and the fact that he'd yanked it off. And then the exchange Eve had overheard: *What the—?* Luke's voice, close to a roar. *I don't believe it. Is this your idea of a joke? I knew it! I knew there was something.* And Bonnie's response: *But you didn't though, did you? You had no idea. Not until now.* The way she'd crowed.

Even the highs and lows of Julian's writing career. He'd produced that first novel aged nineteen, to huge acclaim, relying on his own life experience, according to Roberta. The pressure had been on to do it again, but his second book bombed, just as Luke said. By the third, he'd hit his stride once more. Had he found a way to give his work that same fresh authenticity he'd delivered in the early days?

She googled endless photos. Julian at award ceremonies. Julian giving talks. Julian signing autographs. And there, at last, was a photo taken just over a decade earlier. He was standing next to a glamorous woman with jet-black hair. She was wearing an art deco necklace. Silver filigree on onyx. An identical match for the one Bonnie had worn.

Could Eve possibly be right? She googled and the answer came back loud and clear. Yes, she could.

No wonder Bonnie and Julian had wanted to find the necklace before anyone else did. And the laptop too.

Eve thought about going to Palmer with her theory, but he'd think she'd lost the plot. She had no proof and she'd never have come up with such a solution without the detailed notes she'd taken. Even Greg would have his doubts, she was sure.

She needed evidence. The pendant itself, or the laptop. Why hadn't Luke gone to the police with it? But Eve wasn't sure of the legalities. And maybe Luke hadn't been certain who the ringleader was. Or perhaps he was ashamed. Didn't want to give Julian or Bonnie the satisfaction. Of course, Bonnie was telling everyone it was Kitty who'd snatched the necklace. Luke having it might have made him look even more guilty. As though he'd taken it from Kitty. But if he had the laptop...

Her mind ran on as she stood up. Gus whined. Maybe Luke had never had the laptop.

But she bet he'd had the pendant. Where the heck had he hidden it? If he'd sneaked back to his London flat he hadn't left it there. The police would have found it. On impulse she called his colleague, Brad Salthouse. Luke could have mailed it to him. But Brad sounded nonplussed.

She went back to her notes and reread them twice. At last, she paused at the note Luke had written to Ella.

I hope I'll be back, but if something happens to me, my favourite flowers are aquilegias. Please pick some for me and don't be sad. Look for the truth instead.

And Ella's words. *It's as if he thought I'd be the only person who'd mourn him.*

Why hadn't she thought of it before? Wasn't the flower a peculiar detail for Luke to include? Maudlin and sentimental when he was focused on the practical business of escaping.

Look for the truth... Suddenly, that sounded like more than a throwaway line.

Aquilegia. Granny's bonnets. Was there any chance the message was a subtle clue? It would fit with her idea of Luke having some kind of insurance policy. Did Ella have granny's bonnets in her garden? Eve wondered if she'd followed Luke's instructions and picked some.

She rang Ella's mobile and tried to explain as best she could.

Ella took her much more seriously than Eve had feared. 'I do have aquilegias. They're in the back garden, but I haven't picked any yet. I felt low, so I decided to drive into Blyworth and see a film.' She took a long, unsteady breath. 'I'm having a coffee and then I'll drive back. You can let yourself in if you'd like. There's a key safe and the bunch includes one to the side gate.' She gave Eve the number.

A moment later Eve rang Viv and explained what was going on. She knew Robin would tell her not to go alone.

'I'm in!' Viv said, when Eve was halfway through her explanation.

'You don't even know the deal yet.'

'Pah! You're details obsessed. Meet me at my place, quick as you can. I was already about to give up on the programme I'm watching. Mind-bendingly dull.'

45

Eve finished her explanation to Viv in an undertone as they walked through the village under the lamps around the green. She'd left Gus at Farfield. It was late, he was sleepy, and he might make a noise if he came with them. The evening had turned cool and she zipped up her puffy jacket as they walked.

'Blimey,' Viv said, when Eve fell quiet, 'that's quite a theory. But I can see it fits. Though why was Luke so cryptic in his note to Ella? He could have just said I've buried the necklace under your aquilegias. If I was her, I don't think I'd have got it.'

And of course she hadn't. Not so far, anyway, though when she crouched by the flowerbed she might have spotted freshly dug earth. 'Perhaps he was worried his note would end up in the hands of the police or even reported more widely. If Palmer found the necklace, he might conclude Luke was guilty, and if Bonnie or Julian found it they could hide the evidence. But if Ella worked it out, she wouldn't rest until she understood what had gone on and who was responsible. She trusted him.'

'Poor Luke – if you're right he must have felt thoroughly trapped. Palmer would definitely take Bonnie's word over his. He's a sucker for a good-looking well-to-do woman.'

Gross but true.

They were at the top of Ferry Lane now and Eve glanced over her shoulder but it was late and all was quiet. A moment later, she was unlocking the key safe and putting the key into Ella's back gate, holding her breath.

She locked the gate behind them for good measure, though the conifer hedge at the bottom of the garden made her nervous. It didn't look like much of a defence against intruders.

'Which are the aquilegias?' Viv was waving her phone torch around.

Eve pointed to the patch of purple flowers.

'Oh, granny's bonnet. Why didn't you say so?'

Eve crouched down by the plants. The soil was visibly loose. Her heart was racing. She made an effort to take deep breaths and concentrate on digging. They'd brought a trowel from Viv's place.

Eve had asked Viv to keep watch as she worked, though each time she looked up, Viv was peering at her progress, not at the hedge.

Then suddenly, they heard rustling beyond the conifers.

Eve stopped in her tracks and went to push the branches aside. Nothing. It must have been an animal, not a human. She breathed again and went back to her work.

At last, Eve unearthed something that didn't belong in a garden: a plastic bag, with a solid object inside.

A moment later she was holding the art deco necklace and the cord which had hung round Bonnie's neck, only it wasn't a cord, just made to look like one. In reality, it was a cable. Eve shone her torch on the necklace. In the section where it attached to the cable was a tiny aperture.

'Looks like you were right,' Viv breathed. 'A camera.'

At the back, there was a microphone too. But no miniature video recorder.

'You think it was transmitting to Julian's laptop?'

Eve nodded slowly. 'Over Wi-Fi. I bet the recording's on there. And I don't think Luke took the computer after all. I wonder...'

'What?'

'I don't suppose Luke knew the extent of Julian's wrongdoing. To him, Bonnie's antics probably seemed like a cruel practical joke. But in reality, it was far more than that. Julian had been using a camera for years to spy on private interactions. It helped him make his work vivid and believable. Thanks to Daphne, we know Julian dashed to his study as soon as he heard Kitty was dead. He knew the police would come and search the castle high and low. He didn't want to be found out. If it went public that he'd used a spying device his reputation would be in ruins. I guess he'd face a prison sentence too.'

'You think he removed the laptop himself?'

'And hid it somewhere, yes. But he didn't have the necklace. He needed that to cover his tracks.'

'I don't understand. How does all this relate to Kitty?'

Eve put the pendant in her pocket and pushed the earth back in place under the flowers.

'I guess Julian persuaded her to wear the necklace when she visited Freya. Then he took her footage and used it. She must have had a portable recorder hidden on her that time. They couldn't have used Wi-Fi. Julian could never have dreamed she'd capture such a dramatic encounter.' It was sickening to imagine his delight. 'I still can't believe Kitty was cruel enough to go along with his plans, but maybe part of Freya's grievance with her was fair. She'd approached her initially because her grandparents lived at Farfield. It wasn't casual curiosity that led her to get in touch. She wanted to get back inside. Needed to lay the ghost. I could imagine Julian suggesting she wear the camera to get hold of some memories to keep forever without offending Freya. They were about to leave for France. Kitty knew she wouldn't be able to visit easily. Then maybe Julian viewed the footage and used it – possibly without telling her. She might only have found out when she read the book.'

They let themselves out of Ella's garden and put the key back in the safe.

'She must have forgiven Julian at that point,' Viv said. 'You can't deny that. How did she square it with herself? I couldn't have.'

Eve sighed. 'Nor me. I don't know how he got round her.'

Viv gave her a sidelong glance. 'Maybe she wasn't as nice as you thought.'

'Maybe.' But Eve still felt there was more to tell. With Kitty dead, though, there was a danger she'd never find out.

They were walking back through the village now. 'Either way, it explains why Bonnie wouldn't turn when Freya called her. Julian must have warned her she might recognise the necklace, though it seems a bit over-cautious after all this time. And he'd have said the same about Kitty. She was a different proposition altogether. She'd worn the necklace herself. She'd know Julian was up to his old tricks if she saw it, and that Bonnie was his new accomplice. Only Bonnie was tempted to let her see, because she was jealous. Julian had clearly been hinting he'd leave Kitty but he was taking his time about it. So Bonnie upped the ante by subtly letting Kitty know she'd been usurped. Only I imagine it had a bigger effect than she'd anticipated.'

'You think Kitty threatened to go public about Julian's fondness for hidden cameras?'

Eve nodded. 'I'd imagine she was already guilt-ridden about what had happened with Freya and probably miserable about Julian and Bonnie too. She'd have been primed to hit back.'

'What will you do?'

'Go and get Gus, then take the pendant to the police station first thing tomorrow. Julian has a first-class motive and Bonnie might be his accessory.'

'You think Palmer will see sense?'

'I hope I can persuade him. Maybe I can get Greg Boles onside.'

'I'll come with you. To fetch Gus, I mean.'

Eve hesitated. 'Thanks, but I think it might be more dangerous if you do. If Julian and Bonnie see I've got company they'll wonder why. I'll claim I'm taking Gus out for a walk before bed, then just drive off.' It might still look odd. Gus would probably protest if he'd been asleep.

'You could drop me off further up the drive. Or I could come after you in Monty's van, just to make sure you're okay.'

Monty's van was horribly self-advertising. It clanked. And it had bunting painted on the side. At the same time, she knew what Robin would say.

If she hadn't left Gus at the castle, or if she'd been confident she could convince the police to come immediately... But there wasn't enough evidence for them to arrest Julian, and Palmer wouldn't want to. Calling the police now would give Julian more time to prepare. She needed his laptop. Maybe she could go back the following day with Robin to search for it.

'All right. Maybe you could bring the van if you're sure you don't mind. But could you stay well down the lane? There's a passing point where you can pull up.'

'Absolutely.' Viv saluted,

'Check you've got coverage, and if I don't reappear in half an hour then please ring the police.'

Viv blinked at her in the moonlight, looking serious for once.

Eve felt anxious all the way back to Farfield. There was no reason for Bonnie or Julian to guess she'd found the pendant, but Bonnie knew she was suspicious about it. She'd never forgive herself if she put Viv in danger. And the thought of Gus, vulnerable in the bedroom, made her stomach churn.

46

It was as Eve neared Farfield that doubts started to invade her mind.

Tiny questions that refused to add up.

If Kitty had threatened to go public during her stand-off with Bonnie, why was Bonnie still wearing the necklace when she'd cornered Luke? Eve imagined Julian had only dared her to do it as a sort of prank. He thought little of Luke and Luke had been rude to him since he'd arrived. What better way to pay him back than to get Bonnie to make a pass at him, wait for him to fall for it, then let him know he'd been caught on camera? Eve could imagine Bonnie taunting him at Julian's suggestion. It seemed about his level. But Eve doubted Julian or Bonnie would have gone ahead if Kitty had threatened to out them. Why create another witness?

And if Kitty *had* made that threat why hadn't Julian hidden his laptop immediately? Eve would have, if she were him. Without hard evidence, it was Kitty's word against his, as Eve was now painfully aware.

Unless Kitty hadn't confronted Bonnie or Julian when she'd

realised what was going on. Perhaps she'd confided in someone else instead.

Who might she tell? Someone she was close to. Just as Eve made the next leap, a text came in on her phone.

Eve, sorry to bother you. It's Freya. (Not sure if you have my number.) I'm a bit worried about Nate. He's acting oddly. He's just gone off across the fields. He said he had to get away, but I'm not sure why or if he's really left. I saw torchlight in the deer park and he's left a weird note on his desk. I've called the police. I went to your room to knock but I guess you're still out. I thought you left Gus here but he didn't bark. Is he with you?

Eve dashed out of her car and stared across the deer park. Had Nate taken Gus? Images of him trustingly following Kitty's brother flashed through her head. Why would he take him? To ensure Eve followed? Because she'd be too scared to call the police in case Nate attacked him at the sound of sirens?

If so, it had to mean Nate knew she was onto the truth. How had he found out? She thought of the rustle in the hedge at Ella's place and looked at her phone. Maybe she could call Viv and get her to ask the police to approach quietly. But when she tried to get through she couldn't connect. The fleeting coverage had been enough to receive Freya's text, but not to make a call.

Think, think.

Eve went to text Viv herself, wondering if she was being crazy, imagining sirens might make Nate do something violent to Gus. But it seemed he was out of control.

She couldn't think straight. Didn't know what to do.

She looked at the park and saw torchlight. And up ahead, a shadow. Small. Dark.

Why hadn't she seen the truth? Nate had just as much to lose as Julian. It was this weird thing with his dad. His desperation to win – a reaction to Benet's constant disapproval, Eve guessed. If word got out that Julian had been secretly recording people, Farfield would go under. No one would come and stay anywhere run by Julian or his best buddy Nate. Nate might be innocent, but Eve doubted clients would trust to that. And Julian's name would be mud. His high opinion of Nate's work would count for nothing. Reviewers who'd been coming round would distance themselves. What's more, Benet had made it clear he didn't like Julian. He thought Nate had lousy taste in friends. He'd be proved right.

Eve had been following Nate subconsciously as she processed what was happening. He was beyond the deer park now, into the trees.

She glanced at her phone again, but her coverage still wavered. Even the text she'd tried to send to Viv wasn't going. And all the while, Gus was getting further away. She was lucky that Nate hadn't turned and seen her. She willed Gus to sense her presence and run. At least Freya had called the police. If only they kept their sirens off…

And then, as she stood there, a fresh thought hit her out of nowhere. Freya's text.

It's Freya. (*Not sure if you have my number.*)

Eve didn't, so the message wasn't unnatural.

It made her think of the person who'd contacted Luke on the unregistered phone and a wave of realisation washed over her. Luke and Nate had been friends for some time. His colleague, Brad Salthouse, had expressed annoyance about the way Luke tended to socialise with Nate in preference to him, even when Nate asked him at the last minute. That all made sense, of course, now Eve knew the truth. But it meant that Luke was bound to have Nate's phone number. He'd come up on screen as Nate when he called Luke's mobile.

If Nate had called Luke using an unfamiliar phone, Luke would have been suspicious the moment he'd answered. Especially if he'd already decided Nate wasn't the caring considerate brother he'd hoped for. There was no way he'd have agreed to meet, let alone go up a church tower with him.

Eve felt a lurching feeling inside her as a new scenario formed in her mind.

It's Freya. (*Not sure if you have my number.*)

Luke probably hadn't had it either, and Freya would have known that. 'Unknown number' wouldn't have rung alarm bells when her voice came on the line. And to Luke, she'd have seemed like an innocent bystander. He'd probably had no idea she'd quarrelled with Kitty. She could have told him she suspected Julian. That would fit with his theory. Then, when they met at the church she could have dashed in, saying she thought she'd been followed. That they must hide. Right now. Maybe she'd suggested the tower and he'd been caught up in her fake panic. Run up with her. She might have asked him to look down – see if he could see anyone from the top...

Eve stood behind a tree, desperately clicking send again on the text that refused to go. There must be coverage somewhere out there. If it was Freya up ahead, she'd managed to text Eve. Viv would call the police soon anyway. Eve wished she'd suggested ten minutes as her cut-off time, not thirty.

She imagined Kitty telling Freya about the necklace. Confessing how she'd worn it when Craig had treated Freya so appallingly. Pouring out the guilt she felt. And her anguish at seeing Bonnie being used by Julian, just as she had been. Kitty had sounded desperate to clear the air, earlier in the evening. She'd probably promised that Julian would finally get his come-uppance.

But from Freya's point of view, Kitty was as much to blame as her husband. She knew what he'd done, yet she'd let him get away with it. Only turned on him when he'd involved Kitty's rival. It could seem like self-interest. That would be enough to make Freya livid.

And then there was what she had to lose. Her happy ever after with Nate. A job that would keep her close to him, because she never believed he'd leave Rhoda. Not because he loved her too much, but because he was too bound up with Benet's opinion. If Kitty had gone public about Julian, the business would have collapsed. Nate would have gone back to London and his normal life. Or so Freya thought. She'd waited so long for happiness and now here was Kitty, who'd already betrayed her once, ready to smash her dreams to smithereens.

Eve felt sick. If she was right, Freya had got her dashing through the woods, away from help. And the police weren't on their way. They wouldn't come until Viv called them.

As she had the thought something swished past her shoulder. Fast, hard. So close she felt the rush of the wind it created.

An arrow was embedded in the tree next to her.

47

Eve tried to speak but her mouth was so dry no words came.

'That wasn't an accident, it was a warning.' Freya was pulling another arrow from her quiver as she spoke, fitting it to the bowstring. 'I'm a good shot. I found Nate and Kitty's old archery kit in one of the sheds here. I used to practise when Craig was out. Imagine him standing where the target was. I got to hate him so much.'

'I'm not surprised.' Eve wasn't. But she was terrified. 'Where's Gus?' She could hear the shake in her voice.

'Back at the castle.'

'But I saw him.'

'Fear and imagination are powerful things. You probably saw a rabbit or something. Chuck me the pendant.'

Eve swallowed. 'I haven't got it.' Why the heck hadn't she left it with Viv? She'd been so keen to fetch Gus and get clear that she hadn't thought.

'Oh, I think you have. I'm afraid I was listening at your door this evening. I knew you were onto something, the way you tucked yourself away like that. I heard your call to Ella. All about Luke's note and where you wanted to look.'

Eve swallowed. Freya hadn't mentioned her call to Viv. Maybe she'd stopped listening by that point. Eve could tell her they'd gone together. That Viv knew the truth too. But it was too big a risk; she'd be her next target.

'Chuck it here,' Freya said. 'If you don't I'll have to shoot you where you stand. I wouldn't have far to drag you to the boat.'

'The boat?'

'Ella and I chatted when she bid on Farfield. She told me she used to sail. I'd already pinched her old tender in case you got to the truth. Broke into her garden, took it from her shed and hid it out here. It's inflatable. Easy to transport. Ella's the most likely suspect after Luke. The police will think she's guilty.'

'But you like Ella. You wished you could have sold her the castle.'

'That's what I told everyone. And against Julian and Kitty she seemed marginally preferable. But you didn't see her eyes when she heard what Craig had done. She was excited. She didn't say so, of course, but I could see it, buried just beneath the surface. She guessed how desperate I'd be to sell. She approached me while I was still in shock and told me she'd be interested. Can you imagine how that made me feel? The horror of what I'd been through was unimportant compared with her grand plans.' She was gasping. Sobbing.

It sounded horribly unfeeling – Eve could see that – but Ella hadn't seen things clearly either. Her desire for Farfield was bound up with people she'd loved and lost. She wanted to feel close to them. To honour them.

'I can't forgive her,' Freya said.

Eve had to find a way to get through to her. 'But what about Luke? What had he ever done to you?'

Freya gulped again. Eve could just see the bow and arrow quaking slightly in her unsteady hands. 'I didn't want to kill him. I told myself we could talk. Work something out. But as soon as I saw him at the church, I knew I was trapped. Stuck in the situation Kitty had made for me. She told me about the pendant. Said Bonnie was wearing it that night; she was pleading for me to listen, telling me she'd make things right. Tell the world. Now. Now, when it was too late to stop Julian from using my story. As if that made it okay. I was rushing around, serving drinks. I told her I couldn't talk then. I asked her to meet me at the icehouse for a proper heart-to-heart. I could see the consequences of her reporting Julian straight away. And that she was determined to make him suffer now she could see he'd replaced her with Bonnie. It was all self-interest. But I didn't kill her out of anger. When I swore to you, I didn't lie. I killed her because of the damage she was about to do.

'But afterwards, I still wasn't safe. I needed to make sure news of the hidden camera didn't get out another way. I was scared. I knew Bonnie had lost the pendant. She kept looking. Then Julian searched Luke's room and I guessed Luke had it. Knew he must know all about Julian's games. He was planning to tell someone, sooner or later. Why hide the pendant otherwise? And when he went public, the writers' retreat would be over. Nate would go back to London and wait for Rhoda's rare visits. I'd probably never see him again. I never thought he'd leave her. Not in the face of his dad. Not for me.' For a split second the bow and arrow lowered – but only by an inch. Freya yanked them up again. 'Kitty left me with no choice. When I raced up the church stairs, I didn't have to pretend to be frightened, I really was. Terrified of what I was about to do. And of being found out.'

'And now it's my turn.' Eve's mouth was bone dry. She could hardly speak. 'You think Kitty's making you kill me too?'

Freya paused, but only for a moment. 'I'm protecting Nate's future. He's desperate to make the retreat work. Kitty had no thought for that! And he's left his wife for me. I can't let him find out the truth.' She was crying again. 'I'll put you in Ella's boat with a slow leak and row you out then swim back. I've got dry clothes to change into.'

Eve was desperate to make her think again. 'It's a risk. The others will notice you're out.'

Freya shook her head. 'Bonnie's gone off to London for the night. She said it's all been too stressful. Julian's propping up a bar somewhere. He stormed out when she told him she's been offered another job. As for Nate, he's having dinner with his father. I ducked out of it in the end. Said I was too nervous this time. He booked a room at the Pear Tree so he could have a drink. He said he'd probably need one. It's sad that he's still so affected by Benet, but that will change with time. I can't let you ruin things for him, Eve. Throw me the pendant. If you do, I can tie you up and let you drown instead of shooting you. It'll be a nicer way to go.'

Eve couldn't believe Freya was saying this. Was prepared to kill again.

'I know you've had an appalling time, Freya, but these are your actions now. Claiming Kitty—'

Freya cut across her, her voice quaking. 'Kitty was a traitor who only cared about herself. Last chance.' She raised the bow and drew back the arrow, aiming at Eve.

Eve threw the pendant. She didn't know what else to do. Viv should have called the police by now, even if she'd had to drive to get coverage. But what if there was a delay? How long would it take? Would Viv convince them? Eve listened but there was nothing.

'Walk towards the boat,' Freya said. 'Tie your feet together with the rope that's inside. Then turn your back on me, hands behind your back.'

Eve thought about telling her that help was on its way. That Viv was looking out for her and would have raised the alarm, but all the while she was terrified that something had gone wrong. That Viv's phone was out of battery or the police had been called to a major incident elsewhere. What if Freya found Viv after she'd killed Eve and attacked her too?

Eve moved towards the boat and all the while Freya kept her arrow trained on her. The pain of being shot didn't bear thinking about.

Eve got closer to Freya as she moved towards the creek.

'Stay back. Keep moving!'

It was at that moment that Eve wondered. Freya's words. *Stay back.* Physics had never been her strong point, but instinct told her they hadn't been casual.

Eve took a deep breath. Thinking. A possible plan forming. Based on guesses that were a matter of life and death.

Dare she risk it? She had no idea if she'd be fast enough to stop Freya and if she wasn't, she'd be dead in minutes. Unsavable, quite possibly, once the arrow pierced her, even if the emergency services arrived.

Instinct took over. Calculations made in microseconds. If Freya got her into the boat, immobile, she'd make sure she drowned before help got near.

Eve was barely conscious of her actions as she leaped towards Freya, her heart in her mouth. She wanted the arrow up against her with no room to fly. She was terrified of the damage it might still do if Freya released it. She had nothing but a thick jacket to protect her. But much of the force would be lost.

The sight of Freya's shocked face in the moonlight seemed to freeze in time. Eve felt like she did in nightmares, when instant action was needed but her limbs weren't obeying her brain.

Then suddenly, she was functioning again.

Freya had been too shocked to react to Eve's move. Eve grasped the arrow by its shaft, tugging it with all her might.

Only now did Freya release the string. It was as though she

couldn't cancel the automatic action she'd been prepared to perform.

Eve had the arrow and she was undamaged.

They stood face to face and then with no warning, Freya pulled the bow away, slipped it over Eve's head and twisted it behind her, pulling the string taut with her hands like a garotte.

Eve almost dropped the arrow in her automatic desperation to free herself. She fought the impulse even as her grip loosened.

Instead she jabbed the arrow behind her. She was fighting for her life.

Freya yelled and the string slackened, though the bow was still around Eve's shoulders. A moment later, Freya grabbed an arrow from her quiver, darting at Eve. Using it as a hand-held weapon.

Eve kept jabbing back, ducking and weaving.

At last she saw figures running through the trees.

Freya's eyes were wild, like an animal's. Eve knew she'd carry on fighting to the last.

In the distance, she could see someone holding Viv back as DS Greg Boles, DC Olivia Dawkins and a bunch of uniformed officers rushed forwards, moving from tree to tree.

As Freya hurled herself on Eve, Greg landed just behind and dragged her off.

48

The police crawled all over Farfield after Eve told them what Freya had admitted to. They'd recovered the pendant from her.

Robin had dashed back from London on hearing what had happened. He'd been keeping Eve updated and was currently leaning against her kitchen worktop, watching her sitting at the table as if she might disappear if he turned his back. Eve was secretly enjoying the attention.

She listened as he talked to Greg on his mobile.

After he hung up, he came to sit with her. 'They've found Fisher's laptop. You were right. It seems he'd taken it and hidden it himself. It was bagged up tight under the lilypads in the pond in the formal garden. The video of Luke's been recovered, with Bonnie making up to him, then pulling back and laughing when he took the bait.'

'Poor Luke.'

Robin nodded. 'And that's not all. Fisher had a couple of cameras and microphones up at the castle too. He must have removed them before the police came, but the recordings are there on his computer.'

It was almost too much to take in.

'I wonder how Luke guessed about the pendant,' Robin said after a pause.

'Bonnie kept fiddling with it. It's one of the reasons I looked at it so closely and remembered the design. I realise now she was perpetually checking it. Making sure it was pretty-side outwards. If she was acting oddly too, and he noticed the cord round her neck looked strange, or spotted the tiny camera or microphone...'

'That makes sense. So he yanked it off, but he didn't tell anyone. He was probably embarrassed. He might not have known Bonnie was collaborating with Julian, but he suspected. He held on to the pendant while he tried to work out what was going on.'

'I think so, and then when I told Bonnie I didn't believe she'd lost it, she made up that story about Kitty taking it. She needed to come up with a reason for someone ripping it off because I'd seen the welt on her neck. In the end, she must have decided it was worth admitting she'd quarrelled with a murder victim to divert attention from Luke and the real reason. She and Julian must have been terrified he'd talk. He had the most to lose, but it would have been disastrous for her too. It would make her unemployable. They wanted the pendant back, so it would be his word against theirs.'

Robin nodded. 'That's right, and by chance or design, claiming Kitty pulled the pendant off helped them, don't you think?'

'Yes.' It was as Eve had thought. 'Word got around. The police knew and at that point, if Luke had admitted he'd got it, it would have looked like he'd taken it from Kitty. I guess he was too scared to report it then; he was already a key suspect for her murder.

'But Julian and Bonnie weren't off the hook, and neither was Freya. Luke kept investigating privately and did his disappearing act, hoping the police would refocus their efforts and find the real killer. But he left the pendant in Ella's garden. He must have hoped to go back for it himself. I guess he was never sure whether it related to Kitty's death or not, but he wondered. The cryptic note was an insurance policy. He wanted someone to investigate if he couldn't.'

'Sounds about right. He can't have suspected Freya. Greg says she admits she called him on a burner phone. She told him she'd found out something worrying about Julian. That she'd heard Luke was alive and she needed his help. He fell for it. She rushed into the church saying she thought she'd been followed and pointing to the tower as a place to hide. When they reached the top, she pushed him over the parapet.'

Eve shivered.

'Greg says she stares into space as she talks, as if he's not there.' His gaze met hers. 'The CSIs have found a journal belonging to Kitty. It was hidden in a shoebox in Freya's room. I presume she must have taken it soon after she killed her.'

Eve held her breath, hoping it would answer the questions she still had.

'It's clear she felt horribly guilty about what happened with Freya. According to her notes, Julian suggested wearing the camera so she could gather some proper memories of Farfield, as you suggested. Kitty sneaked into her old room, and Nate's, and the ones belonging to her father and grandparents. Then she went downstairs and captured the horrible scenes between Freya, Craig and Craig's lover. In her diary, she says she was upset when she got home and left the pendant and the recording device on the table. She never bothered taking the recording off. It wasn't the memory of Farfield that she wanted.'

'But Julian watched it.'

He nodded. 'Unbeknownst to Kitty, according to her diary. She only realised he'd used the material when his next book came out. She was stunned, and Julian was full of contrition. He claimed he'd watched the video out of curiosity, to see her family home. He blamed his age. Said the scene had made an impression but months passed and he'd no idea he'd retold it so closely. He begged Kitty not to rush off and apologise. He said it was a genuine accident, and that he'd be finished if it came out. He argued that probably no one – including Freya – would ever realise. He was self-deprecating. Said how few people read his books. Why hurt Freya when she could remain in blissful ignorance?'

He was utterly despicable. 'So Kitty gave in. She still loved him at that point. Is there any indication that she knew Julian had done it before?'

'None.'

'So that realisation probably came when she saw Bonnie wearing the necklace. It would have confirmed the affair, but my bet is she was just as devastated to find Julian had acted deliberately and it wasn't a one-off.'

'You might be right.'

'She must have guessed Freya had read the book as soon as they met again. She was clearly livid about something, and as Kitty's friend she was more likely to be curious about Julian's work.'

'I wonder if Freya read Kitty's journal.'

'My guess is not. She talked about her as though she was as evil as Julian. I'd imagine she intended to destroy the journal in case it mentioned his spying.' It was interesting that she hadn't done it immediately, but on reflection, Eve could see it. She'd hated Kitty. It would have left her loath to read her words but looking for answers too. She was probably torn. Eve bet she'd thought about it each night before she'd slept. If she could sleep.

'Has Julian admitted to what he did?' she said at last. 'Has Bonnie?'

'Not yet, but it will all come out. Fisher will be utterly discredited. He'll face prosecution.'

It was a pleasing thought when happy endings were few

and far between. Nate was devastated, of course. Eve had managed to pick up Gus shortly after Freya tried to kill her, but she'd had to wait until the following day to fetch her things. She'd found Nate there with Rhoda. It was clear there was no going back for them. The break-up was down to more than just Freya. But she was still there for him as a friend. It made Eve feel emotional. Benet was nowhere to be seen. There was no point in expecting miracles. But Nate had been talking about him as Eve approached. Maybe he'd start to realise the poisonous effect his father was having on his life.

Hope had come in the form of a meeting between Nate and Ella. They'd each wanted to offload, to talk about Luke and Kitty and share regrets. They both had a lot of baggage, but they understood each other.

They'd begun work on Nate's plans to make Farfield more inclusive and Eve thought Nate was starting to believe he could run the place without Julian. He'd find a way forward and maybe Ella could work through her guilt and sadness about Stephen Appley too.

Eve felt a deep knot of regret at the life Freya could have had if circumstances had been different. She'd been caught up in a horrific story that began with Craig Hardwicke's violent, manipulative character and Julian Fisher's desperate selfishness. It had ended with her crossing a dreadful line, brutally murdering two innocent people.

Robin sat opposite Eve and took her hand. 'I wish I hadn't been in London when all this happened. The journey back felt like forever.'

He looked serious.

'It's natural that you're spending a lot of your time there now.' She had a feeling he was building up to something. An announcement about the future. She didn't want to make it hard for him. 'London was your home.'

He nodded.

There was a pause.

'But it's not now. I missed you so much. I wanted to see you when you visited Benet and the twins, but I didn't want to crowd you.' He paused. 'For me, home is where you are.'

Eve felt a lump in her throat.

'We both have independent lives,' Robin said. 'I don't want to rob you of yours. But I'd like to come back each night to the same place you do.'

Gus pottered up to the table and looked at Robin questioningly.

He patted him but his eyes were on Eve. 'What do you think? Would it work if we moved in together? Here or my place or wherever you like? I don't want to be apart.'

Tears were pricking her eyes. She realised she needed to say something. 'I'd like that.'

Catherine (Kitty) Marchant, wellness coach, author and presenter

Kitty Marchant was born into the wealthy Marchant family. At the time, her grandparents occupied Farfield Castle, a grand fortified manor house in Suffolk dating back to medieval times. Kitty and her brother Nate spent many happy days at Farfield with Daniel and Sophie Marchant. The household was inclusive: open to passing locals and a haven for anyone in need of a temporary home. Kitty had idyllic memories of it.

But tragedy hovered on the horizon and storm clouds were brewing. Kitty's mother died of a drug overdose when Kitty was

just sixteen. Her father Benet's relationship with his parents was already
strained. Following this terrible loss,
it imploded. It must have been a time when
each of them was at their most raw. Benet
was desperate to bring his children up in
a commune amongst friends who reminded
him of his wife. His parents were equally
frantic to bring the family to Farfield;
their desire to protect Benet and the
children was probably overwhelming.

There was a stand-off. Benet made
Kitty and her brother choose between him
and his parents. Kitty, who'd elected to
attend the local London school her
father preferred, chose to stay with
Benet. Nate stuck with the boarding
school his grandparents were funding and
made his base with them. But that was no
longer at the castle. His grandparents
lost all their money to a chancer who
took advantage of their good nature.
Benet decided not to help them, and they
and Nate moved to a tiny cottage.

The family rift had a profound effect
on Kitty. She remained close to her
brother but never patched up her relationship with her grandparents. She was
heavily influenced by her father, but it
left her with a profound sense of
personal guilt. She saw Farfield as part
of a perfect past she could never
regain. In a cruel twist of fate, it was

that feeling which led her back to Suffolk, where she met her death.

Despite the family rift, Sophie and Daniel Marchant influenced Kitty with their generosity towards the local community. Kitty launched boxing classes for young people when she was little more than a child herself. She never lost her desire to help those in trouble and leaves a legacy to set up a new drugs charity in memory of her mother. But as with her grandparents, her generosity went with a tendency to be overly trusting. Some of the people closest to her took terrible advantage of the fact.

But Kitty's brother Nate was a steadfast friend. Benet might have rejected his parents and Farfield, but Nate bought the castle back. With Kitty's input, he'd begun to make plans to open it to the locals again, like his grandparents before him. Details of Kitty's charity and the plans for Farfield, including bursaries for writers, appear at the end of this article.

Robin and Gus seemed to have spotted the look in Eve's eye as she paused in her typing.

'Finished for now?' Robin said.

Eve nodded and took the hand Robin held out, looking into his kind eyes. Feeling overwhelmed for a moment.

'Let's go down to the beach,' he said. 'Blow the cobwebs away. Talk about the future.'

'That sounds like the best plan I've heard all day.'

Gus was already dashing towards the door.

As Robin picked up his keys, his mobile went. The moment he answered Eve could see he was on high alert. As he stopped breathing, she did too.

'I see.' His chest rose and fell again. 'Thank you. Thank you for letting me know.'

Eve looked at him.

'The jury's given their verdict. All the accused found guilty on all charges.'

There were tears in both their eyes, and she hugged him for all she was worth.

A LETTER FROM CLARE

Thank you so much for reading *Mystery at Farfield Castle*. I do hope you had fun trying to solve the case! If you'd like to keep up to date with all my latest releases, you can sign up at the following link. Your email address will never be shared, and you can unsubscribe at any time. You'll also receive an exclusive short story, *Mystery at Monty's Teashop*. I hope you enjoy it!

www.bookouture.com/clare-chase

The idea for this book started with the setting. I had a vision of Farfield as a beautiful fortified manor house where time seemed to stand still, and wanted to contrast that with the reality of ever-shifting sands. It being a crime novel, I dreamed up relationships that had fallen apart, estrangements and recriminations!

If you have time, I'd love it if you were able to write a review of *Mystery at Farfield Castle*. Feedback is really valuable, and it also makes a huge difference in helping new readers discover my books for the first time. Alternatively, if you'd like to contact me personally, you can reach me via my website, Facebook page, Twitter or Instagram. It's always great to hear from readers.

Again, thank you so much for deciding to spend some time reading *Mystery at Farfield Castle*. I'm looking forward to sharing my next book with you very soon.

With all best wishes,

Clare x

www.clarechase.com

 facebook.com/ClareChaseAuthor

 twitter.com/ClareChase_

 instagram.com/clarechaseauthor

ACKNOWLEDGEMENTS

Much love and thanks to Charlie, George and Ros for the feedback and cheerleading!

And as ever, massive gratitude to my brilliant editor Ruth Tross for her incisive input and wonderful ideas. I'm also indebted to Noelle Holten for her superhuman promo work and to Alex Holmes, Fraser Crichton and Liz Hatherell for their expertise. Sending thanks too to Tash Webber for her excellent cover designs, as well as to Peta Nightingale, Kim Nash and everyone involved in editing, book production and sales at Bookouture. It's a huge privilege to be published and promoted by such a skilled and friendly team.

Love and thanks also to Mum and Dad, Phil and Jenny, David and Pat, Warty, Andrea, Jen, the Westfield gang, Margaret, Shelly, Mark, my Andrewes relations and a whole bunch of family and friends.

Thanks also to the wonderful Bookouture authors and other writers for their friendship and support. And a huge, heartfelt thank you to the generous book bloggers and reviewers who pass on their thoughts about my work. It makes a vast difference.

And finally, but importantly, thanks to you, the reader, for buying or borrowing this book!

Printed in Great Britain
by Amazon